Beatrice Hitchman was born in London in 1980. She read English and French at Edinburgh University and then took an MA in Comparative Literature. After a year living in Paris, she moved back to the UK and worked in television as a documentary video editor; she has also written and directed short films. In 2009, she completed the Bath Spa MA in Creative Writing, and won the Greene & Heaton Prize for *Petite Mort*, which is her first novel.

Praise for *Petite Mort*

'There's a touch of Angela Carter about Beatrice Hitchman's beguiling debut *Petite Mort* – a sly, erotic thriller concerned with doubleness and duplicity that's both a primer in the early history of French cinema and a reflexive study in female self-fashioning – or should that be "self-editing"? ... Complex and cerebral, *Petite Mort* is softened by beautifully drawn characters, lightly drizzled period detail and an abiding suspicion that love and cinema might be part of the same illusion' John O'Connell, *Guardian*

'Movie junkies will love this surprising and original novel ... the story winds itself in knots, then unravels deftly, providing a satisfactory judgment day for the sexy yet heartless central characters in a wholly unexpected ending' Imogen Lycett Green, *Daily Mail*

'An impressive and enjoyable debut: nimble, deft and wrapped luxuriously in the velveteen glamour of the movies' David Evans, *FT*

'Sumptuously set, elegantly written, evocative and quietly subversive' Stella Duffy

'Like the silver screen world Hitchman portrays, her writing shimmers, drawing you in with glamour and trickery. A fascinating, beguiling and wily debut' Katie Ward, author of *Girl Reading*

'Compelling … Hitchman's confident debut is a story about relationships and the risks we take to get what we want. Universal themes, beautifully explored' Eden Carter Wood, *Diva*

'Gorgeously written … with a fantastic twist at the very end … fascinating' Rachel Glover, *Image*

'Fans of silent films and historical fiction will delight in this chocolate box of a novel which mixes love, lust and scandal with the stardust of 1900s Paris' *The Simple Things*

'Sumptuous … part *Moulin Rouge*, part Alfred Hitchcock' *Grazia*

PETITE MORT

Beatrice Hitchman

A complete catalogue record for this book can be obtained
from the British Library on request

The right of Beatrice Hitchman to be identified as the author of this work has been
asserted by her in accordance with the Copyright, Designs and Patents Act 1988

First published in this edition in 2013 by Serpent's Tail
First published in 2013 by Serpent's Tail,
an imprint of Profile Books Ltd
3A Exmouth House
Pine Street
London EC1R 0JH
website: www.serpentstail.com

ISBN 978 1 84668 907 9
eISBN 978 1 84765 868 5

Designed and typeset by sue@lambledesign.demon.co.uk

Printed and bound in the UK by CPI Group (UK) Ltd, Croydon CR0 4YY

10 9 8 7 6 5 4 3 2 1

Thanks to: Antony Topping and Rebecca Gray for their brilliance, generosity and tact; to Anna-Marie Fitzgerald, Ruthie Petrie, Serpent's Tail, Greene & Heaton; Tricia Wastvedt, Clare Wallace, Bath Spa comrades and tutors; Clare George and the SW Writers.

To Richard Abel, Ginette Vincendeau, Rebecca Feasey, Kathrina Glitre, Luke McKernan, Paul Sargent, Catherine Elliott for their help — inventions, inaccuracies or flights of fancy are mine alone. The line *Who Doesn't Come Through the Door to Get Home* is an excerpt from 'Song' by Cynthia Zarin.

To Danny Palluel, Jo Hennessey, Churnjeet Mahn, Vin Bondah, Jen and Lucy, Tim and Ed, Pete and Lee, Anna Rutherford, Lou Trimby, Alison Coombe and LEBC, John and Lesley Hodson, the Sear-Webbs; Frank Hitchman, Bruce Ritchie, Richard and Jay Hitchman, Ellie Hitchman; my much-missed grandmother, Betty Allfree. And most of all, to Trish Hodson with love.

for T.

Le Monde, 2. juin 1967

MYSTERE!

PARIS, Tuesday – Film technicians examining a recently redis-covered silent film print, *Petite Mort*, have found that a segment of the film is missing.

A fifty-year-old revenant

Though it was shot in 1914, the film had never before been viewed.

An inferno at the Pathé factory destroyed the film's source material before it could be distributed.

The film was not re-shot because of the involvement of the star, Adèle Roux, in a murder trial later that year – and *Petite Mort* passed into cinematic legend.

Last month, a housewife from Vincennes brought a film reel in to the Cinémathèque for assessment. She had found it during a clear-out of her basement.

The whereabouts of the missing sequence, however, remains a mystery.

Juliette BLANC
News Team
Paris

THE ASP

1909

LIGHT IN A LIGHT-BOX, light in your beloved's eyes, is not as light as the morning sun filtering through leaves. Light in the south moves differently; everything takes its time.

Today, it moves like treacle and so do we. I and my only sister, Camille − a bright-eyed, sly duplicate of myself − are lounging on the riverbank.

For once, we're allies. 'We don't have to go back,' I say to her, trailing my fingers in the shallow water, 'he can't make us. She should do her work properly. We can't do everything.' We pause, picturing our mother straightening her back after sweeping the kitchen. Out of spite, I don't tell Camille what I've come to suspect: that our mother's ballooning knuckles make even the smallest movements painful.

'Where will we go?' Camille asks, turning the idea over to catch the light.

'Oh, I don't know,' I answer, settling back and shutting my eyes, 'we'll find jobs as maids in some large house. We've had the practice.'

Not for the first time, I fight down the feeling that she is buttering me up: Camille should not be, at eleven, as sharp or as secretive as she is. She isn't remotely interested in my cast-off clothes, or in dolls, or reading, or in religion; nobody seems to know what Camille is interested in. I so wanted a younger sister to admire me and to confide in, and still she simply gives the impression of biding her time.

They aren't there, and then they are: ten boys from the

village, a gang, round-shouldered and low-browed, skirting the fringes of being men. They rise in clumps from the scrub around the stream. The largest is Eluard, the stableman's son, a boy who promises to be handsome, who knows how to charm, but whom we avoid, because everyone knows there is something wrong with Eluard. He doesn't go to the village school any more, although the little girl lived. Her family couldn't afford to move more than a few hundred yards up the hill away from Eluard's family home.

'What do you want?' I ask, Camille standing behind me, her breath ragged. Eluard doesn't even bother to study his nails. 'A little kiss,' he whispers, and makes a grab at my wrist, which slips through his grasp. The other boys step closer. Their faces look as though they've been melted down and clumsily pressed back together, as though someone had tried to mould them into what-is-presentable. As I step back to get away from them, the curve of a tree-trunk bumps my spine. The nearest house is a mile away.

Eluard smiles, as though it doesn't matter that his first attempt has failed. He knows he has us cornered, and it will only please him more that there are two of us, one to be played with and one to watch the show. He stands, rocking back and forth on his heels, hands in pockets in an exaggerated display of nonchalance. As he tilts back and forth, *rock, rock*, I think about pushing him over and running. In my mind's eye, I see myself streak up the hill, making a furrow in the corn, my mother opening the door to safety; I imagine Camille, left behind as the boys close in.

Eluard lays his palm under his mouth, puckers his lips and releases them. The sound hisses to us, an arrow finding its mark. 'What if I don't want to?' I say, feeling Camille start to climb the tree behind us. Eluard shrugs and the boys move a step closer in, laughing at her attempts to get away. Camille's boot scrapes a peeling off the bark by my ear. Eluard merely stands watching her, and when I can hear she is out of reach I steal a glance up. She sits atop the tree, a strange bird, black skirt buffeted by a wind that has come from nowhere. Eluard snatches at me again and this time his grip is firm, so I bite till I feel my teeth scrape bone and he yells and I jump for the lowest branch and pull myself up.

The lower branches snap as they try to swarm up the tree after me; not one of them is light enough, and each tumbles to the ground. 'Help me up,' I say, and Camille looks blankly at me. Then her hand wraps around mine and we sit together on the highest branch. Eluard prowls at the foot of the shelter, crying over the pointed wounds on his wrist.

'We can wait,' he says, and he points to the lowering sun, mouth still wrapped round his wrist. One by one they all sit down cross-legged around the tree, and all faces turn to his as he produces a stick and starts to whittle it, whistling. The sculpture is half-finished, a totem like a mandrake root, pin-head perched on voluminous breasts. Eluard flicks shavings off the wood swiftly and indiscriminately. Camille stares at the knife. 'I promise nothing will happen to you,' I say to her quietly, 'someone will come.' She shakes her head.

The story is an old one, and it goes like this: in the Middle Ages, our local city was under siege from the Saracens, and the people had all but starved to death. So the aldermen fattened up their one remaining animal and sent it out as a gift to the invading forces. Deducing from this gesture that the inhabitants of the city were healthy and well-stocked with food, the Saracens gave up the fight, and as they retreated, the bells of the city rang out in gratitude – *carcas sona*. But perched atop the sapling, ridiculous and terrified, Camille and I have nothing to offer the boys but ourselves.

After a while, the light changes, speeds up; the wind whips up clouds and a gentle rain begins to patter down. The boys grumble and kick stones, but they don't dare to disobey their ringleader, and Camille hunches trembling into my shoulders as the rain finds a way down the back of our necks. Eluard is standing now, kicking the base of the tree savagely, his boot slipping on the wet bark. 'When I get down,' I whisper, 'run for the house. It's me they want.' As I say this Camille studies me oddly, as though offended – *how can you be so sure* – but in the short silence that follows, she nods.

'I'm coming down,' I shout, starting to lower myself down the central branch. Away across the valley the thin wail of the evening bells begins, calling the handful of faithful, the old and the sick, to worship; Eluard smiles, just as the lanky figure of Père Simon, our priest, breaks cover from the nearby scrub and pauses, his thin legs stepping high in the long grass. 'Adèle,' he calls, voice full of concern, 'whatever are you doing up that tree?'

I slither down the trunk before the world can change its mind. Camille grips my hand as we stand at the foot of the tree, while Père Simon looks at each of the boys in turn, his face blank. 'I think this is a good enough spot for my washing,' he says, and sits down on a rock by the edge of the river. He settles, arms folded, watching Eluard. Camille and I start up the path towards the house. When I turn, further up the hill, Père Simon is still cross-armed on the rock, and the boys are sidling off in sullen dribs and drabs.

'He didn't have any washing, eh, Adèle,' Camille repeats over and over, tugging my hand all the way home.

1911

THE IRONY OF THE *CARCAS SONA* STORY is that church bells never meant anything to us. Around Carcassonne, we remembered another faith: cultish, medieval, heretical, and in our village, the bells were melted for scrap the year after my rescue from the treetops. We all wondered what Père Simon, who always seemed so studious and calm, could have done so wrong that he was banished by the bishops to our desolate region. Shortly afterwards, we – or rather, I – found out.

'It's here,' says my eldest brother, bursting over the threshold, pigeon-chested. My father turns back to his soup, and we shift impatiently, waiting for his verdict. Eventually he nods, and we scud, Camille and I, out of the door and clatter down the hill towards the church. In the twilight, I can just make out my brothers' silhouettes threading their way, slow and steady, down from the upper fields.

By the time we arrive, the entire village is already huddled together on the broken-down pews. At the back, I recognise Eluard and his surly, faithful followers; and at the front stands Père Simon, folding and re-folding his hands in amazement at the size of the congregation before him. The church is open to the elements, but a white sheet hangs down from the rafters, held by twin pegs and rippling in the evening breeze. Behind Eluard's gang there is a mechanical contraption propped up on a table. A man I don't recognise stands with one hand on a large wheel attached to the machine, watching Père Simon. A cigarette droops from one corner of his mouth, smoke trails heavenwards and, as I watch, Père Simon points at him with one trembling hand, the man begins to turn the wheel, and images begin to pour out of the white sheet.

Next to me, Camille breathes an almost silent *oh*. My superstitious aunt shrieks; in the front row a fully grown man kicks out his legs and snorts like a frightened horse. A woman has appeared on the sheet, sitting on a garden bench, one hand across her brow. OH! says white writing on a black background, WHO WILL RESCUE ME FROM MY PLIGHT? The woman turns to face us. She is so real, more real than anyone I know. I put my hand out in front of my face and compare it to her: she wins. Now another figure has appeared on the sheet: a man with eyebrows like upside-down Vs. He moves stealthily towards her: she cringes away from him. HELP! says the writing, I FEAR FOR MY VIRTUE! By now half the village are on their feet. The men shake their fists as the vicious baron advances, uttering words I was told I should never have to hear. And then, in a puff of smoke, grimacing wildly, the baron snaps his fingers and vanishes. The audience looks around the church, astonished. Père Simon stands up and pleads for calm; his palms try to flatten out the uproar, but Eluard is on his feet, trying to wrestle the machine out of the operator's hands. It takes several men to drag them apart.

When the film comes back on, the woman in white is wearing a veil, standing next to a handsome moustached man. AND SO THEY WERE MARRIED says the writing. The woman turns to look at her new husband, as from one corner of the frame the vicious baron capers and grips the bars of his cage. Her look says everything: I don't need the rest of the story to tell me how happy they will be. After the sheet goes blank, the others get up and mill about, re-enacting the story in hoarse leaps and shouts. I continue watching, desperately hoping the woman's face will reappear.

The neighbours beg the machine-operator to tell us another

story, but he snorts and shows us the damage Eluard has already inflicted on his projecting device. 'Twelve sous,' is all he says, holding out a calloused palm.

The following afternoon I shrug off my chores and trot down the hill to Père Simon's house. Up close, it doesn't seem as clean: paint peels and flutters from the door as it creaks open. And close to, Père Simon's skin looks white and fragile, like parchment. I had always thought of him as a young man, but now I wonder how old he really is.

'You've come about last night,' he says, following me into the one main room. My mother has taught me that a lady always sits, so I take the only chair and press my knees together. Père Simon remains standing, fingers laced behind his back.

As I speak, I feel ashamed of myself and of what he must see: a girl with her hair in disarray, eyes large and pleading in a thin face. I ask him what the name of the woman is, where she lives. I ask him who was responsible for last night's story, whether there will ever be any more like it.

He stoops and folds his hands round mine.

'The woman's name is Terpsichore,' he says. 'She has her own particular magic, Adèle, a quality all her own: one of the greats. At her first premiere, in Paris, of *La Dame aux Roses*, the audience was moved to tears.'

I ask him how he knows that. He pauses. 'Because I was one of them.'

Père Simon watches me for a moment, then moves to the fireplace. He moves jerkily, just like the woman in the film, half-eager, half-held back, leading me to it: what I didn't see before, which is that the wall above the mantel is covered, to the ceiling, in photographs of people. They are laid half over each other in a jumble, hundreds of them.

I have only ever seen one photograph before: a daguerreo-type of my grandparents, who had left us the money that my father drank, and the farm we lived on. My father's father sat; my father's mother stood, her hand on his shoulder. Neither of them was smiling. But these: these were a thing apart – each one was a young man or a woman with a dazzling grin and gleaming hair, staring out directly at me as if it was me making them laugh.

I cross the room to look more closely.

Père Simon says softly: 'Promotional postcards. The studios, who make the films, hand them out in advance of the films' release.'

She is right in the centre of the display: unlike the others, she isn't smiling, just staring back at me, her huge eyes rimed with kohl, the rest of her body stretched out on a chaise longue. There is a scribble in the corner – I can just make out the words, *Best wishes* – and before I can stop myself I have reached out and snatched the card from the wall.

I imagine the spells I would need to transform myself into her. In my mind's eye I see myself in a dress that shimmers like fish-scales, my face heart-shaped, all my gestures graceful, surrounded by people who love me.

Père Simon is standing with me. He sees how shocked I am, and gives a bitter little laugh and a shrug. How must it have felt for him: the young priest, stepping out from his seminary one evening, wandering the Paris streets, perhaps visiting a cinema of attractions on a whim, and leaving an hour later with his carefully constructed world a world away.

And that was how I got religion: my parents watched in amazement as I walked dutifully down the hill to visit the priest every single Wednesday. Père Simon bought a second chair, and under his careful tutelage, I studied the dramatic monologues of the great playwrights until I was word-perfect. We nursed my ambition as Cleopatra nursed the asp, letting it grow over the years.

Adèle Roux fixes me over the rim of her coffee cup: all bird bones, black sleeves flapping around the wrists. Fine silver hair in a bun at the nape of her neck and one concession to couture, a miniature hat, perched at an angle and secured with vicious-looking pins. Perhaps it's the cup, obscuring everything below the nose; perhaps it's the way the waiter passes behind us, whistling, or reflecting light over us with his silver tray: but suddenly I can see it. And, seeing it, can't see how anyone can have missed it.

Watching me, she smiles. 'You are thinking,' she says, 'that the cheekbones are the one thing which never changes.'

'I did wonder if you'd ever been recognised.'

'Never.'

'It was such a famous trial—'

'Famous in 1914. People forget.'

'But you've been living in Paris all this time…'

Her smile widens: becomes wicked. 'You've read *The Art of Living Invisibly*?'

'No.'

'No? The ancient Chinese text by the philosopher, Sun Tzu? It's a later book. Perhaps you are familiar with his more famous companion work, *The Art of War*?'

'No.'

She raises her eyebrows; then waves it away. 'A surprising number of lessons we can apply to 20th-century Paris. You'll have heard how, struck by the way a panda-bear fades into the forest of bamboo, Sun Tzu invented camouflage. But to my mind, the most important advice he gives to those seeking anonymity is the simplest: *be eccentric, but not too eccentric.*'

She nods as I think about it. 'Take my hat. A relic. People look at it and think: *poor thing. Clinging to her youth.* They give me one swift glance and move on.'

I nod. Look down at my tape-recorder, because she really has embarrassed me this time.

She beams at me. 'One other thing: Sun Tzu recommends particularly − I quote directly from the text − *in the quest for invisible living, do not offend your concierge. You'll come home and find her going through your underwear.*'

'They had concierges in ancient China?'

'Oh, yes,' she says. 'They're a universal plague.'

She holds my gaze for a moment longer. I feel myself go suddenly red.

Her eyes sparkle. 'Admit it. The panda was a good touch.'

I don't know where to look.

She says: 'But how could I resist you? Such faith in the world.'

At 2 p.m. today, I was at my desk at *Le Monde* when the telephone rang.

'A woman for you,' said the switchboard operator − bored, Friday afternoonish. 'Calling about your article. Says she has some new information.'

I was still scribbling on my yellow pad; a four o'clock deadline loomed.

'Put her through.'

A hiss on the line; a crackle, and then the crisp voice, sounding as if it was coming from miles away: 'Is this Juliette Blanc? The author of the article in last week's paper, about the recent rediscovery of *Petite Mort*?'

'That's me.'

A breathy pause: high whining, ghost-voices brushing past.

'This is Mme Roux, whom you mentioned in your piece.'

The phone clamped to my ear, some instinct forewarned me: *don't gush. Don't say: I thought you'd be dead. Say what's on your mind.*

I said: 'This is a surprise.'

A chuckle. Then she said: 'Mlle Blanc, I wish to engage a person of vigour and conviction to write my memoirs. All about the film, and everything before and after. If this sounds like an assignment for you, please meet me at the Café Conti at five o'clock tonight. Café Conti, Place St André-des-Arts, 6ème. We will treat this first meeting as an informal interview of sorts. To see if we *get on*.'

She pronounced *get on* like an illness. I reached for a pen and paper, scribbled the address, and was about to ask any one of a hundred questions, when I realised the line had already gone dead.

25. janvier 1913

CAMILLE'S BREATHING stays steady. She is lying on her front: early light is creeping over her outstretched hand.

The mattress of my twin bed creaks as I pull out the little wallet from beneath it. *Enough to get you started*, Père Simon had said, dropping it into my satchel. *You'll want to address yourself to Studios Gaumont in the 19th arrondissement. Ask for M. Feuillade.*

When I tiptoe to the door and look back, there is a gleam underneath Camille's eyelids.

'You're running away,' she says.

Then she just looks at me: long and solemn like when she was small.

PARIS!

2. février 1913

TO THE NORTH, the tip of Notre Dame's spire rises, cut out against a dirty gold sky. The plume of Agathe's cigarette smoke lifts next to it, a signal; it drifts away from the windowsill and curls out over rue Boissonnade, hanging in the space between our attic apartment and the roofs across the street. A premature sun is winking and struggling over the rooftops opposite, and in one of these gleams the smoke is lit orange for a moment, then vanishes.

Beside me, Agathe lets out a hiss of a sigh. She squints as she removes the cigarette stub from her mouth. She doesn't offer me a final pull, but presses the stub delicately out on the window ledge – the broken sill leans, slack as a jaw and pock-marked from this morning ritual. And then, as it does every morning, the camaraderie of the shared cigarette vanishes, and hostilities resume. The sill jumps as Agathe lifts her meaty forearms from it, jolting my elbows; she turns and lumbers back into the salon.

A nasal sound comes from the kitchen: it is Mathilde, our landlady, singing as she prepares breakfast for us. Agathe readjusts her dressing gown as she reaches the one plush chair in the tiny salon; she sits and snaps open *Le Temps*. I take my seat at the table, Mathilde's song reaches a climax, and our meal arrives: thin porridge, borne aloft by Mathilde, like a waiter at a fashionable restaurant. '*Et voilà!!*' she trills. The newspaper crumples as Agathe lays it aside; she lumbers over to the table; *chink* goes the bowl, set down on the table-top, and Agathe's spoon is already ploughing a furrow through the food, ladling an enormous portion onto her own plate. As usual, she starts to eat straightaway.

Mathilde smiles apologetically at me, and whispers *bon appétit*. I dip my spoon into the porridge and try a few bites. Only once she is satisfied that I've started eating will Mathilde begin her own meal, stringy wrist lifting and lowering mechanically. Her gaze flickers between Agathe and me as she watches for the first sign of trouble.

Agathe's hatred for me sprang out fully formed on my very first day at 14 rue Boissonnade. The three of us sat in the salon, starchy with formality; I squinted into a patch of afternoon light, my valise propped next to my ankles, as Mathilde's hands writhed over each other in her lap.

'We are constrained by circumstance, Mademoiselle Roux,' she said, 'to invite another lodger into our little family.'

Agathe sat looking out of the window, ignoring us, her face wreathed in smoke. It was six o'clock in the evening; her scarlet silk peignoir was stretched tight across her stomach, her face painted into doll-like lines.

With a little jolt I realised what she was.

Mathilde leapt to her feet: 'Let me show you your new room!'

Though it was low-ceilinged, dusty, and filled with drab things, I exclaimed over its quaint charm. After years of sharing with Camille, I truly was a little excited at the prospect of my own territory; and I had little choice – my small fund would not stretch to anything better.

In the salon, I bent out of the window to admire the view; I did not notice how thin and grey the curtains fluttered in the evening breeze. I admired the room's one ornament, a fine miniature on the mantelpiece. 'My dear mother,' Mathilde sighed, pressing a hand to her breastbone, 'from whom I inherited the apartment.' Agathe snorted, and I wondered whether we were thinking the same thing: that Mathilde had also inherited the beaky nose and querulous expression.

'And what are you here to do?' Agathe asked, turning to look at me for the first time.

'I am going to look for an acting role, in the moving pictures,' I told her proudly.

Agathe's cigarette end glowed orange in the shadows.

'And how are you proposing to do that?' she asked.

The afternoon after my arrival at rue Boissonnade, I smoothed my best dress down in front of the rust-spotted mirror, stepped out into the waiting city and took the Metro to the 19th arrondissement.

At first I thought I had the wrong address: the north end of rue des Alouettes was a street like any other, with apartment blocks rising high on either side, cafés, even a greengrocer's. But as I walked along the buildings gradually gave way to tall grey walls, constructed in the modern style with cement brickwork. If I stood on tiptoe it was just possible to see the roof of a glass structure, like an enormous greenhouse – that must be the studio Père Simon had told me about – and next to it a factory chimney, puffing smoke into the crisp morning air.

If it was not what I had expected, then I supposed that every river had its source; I walked confidently along the edge of the wall until an opening presented itself – a wrought-iron gate flanked by what seemed to be one-storey cottages.

In my mind's eye, there had been bustle and buzz. This place seemed deserted. Moving closer, I noticed a sign fixed to the door of the left-hand cottage that read CONCIERGERIE. I marched up to the door and rapped on it.

A slip of a man in a stained shirt and pince-nez opened it. Through the half-open door I saw a cluster of desks with men and women sitting at them; a woman pecked at an odd sort of machine with her fingertips, and the men lolled about, smoking and chatting.

I told him I had come to see M. Feuillade.

The man put his hand out, palm up. 'Is he expecting you?'

I shook my head – perhaps I hadn't been clear – and told him I had come to ask M. Feuillade for a part in whatever film they were making.

The man pinched the blood from the bridge of his nose. 'Perhaps you can explain this to me, Mademoiselle: how is it men and women train for years at the Conservatoire to become actors, and yet everyone who's seen a two-reel at the funfair thinks she's the next Bernhardt?'

In the room behind him, one of the men had lowered his newspaper and was staring at me over the top of it.

'I've practised,' I said quickly, 'memorised the roles of Célimène and Phèdre and I am working on Lady Macbeth de M. Shakespeare—'

'Bravo,' he said, and made to shut the door. It closed, and closed some more; his beady eyes still wide and staring at me as the gap tightened – I put the toe of my boot between the door and the frame.

I said: 'You don't know what I can do.'

His face was startled; he chewed his lip. Suddenly the air fell out of him. 'Mademoiselle, this isn't the line of work for you.' The mocking light had gone from his eyes; they were sad.

I pulled my toe back; drew myself up. 'I want to see someone in charge,' I said. 'I want Feuillade.'

'You're talking to him.' He slammed the door before I could do my trick with the toe again.

I waited for a moment; leant my knuckles against the door, rapped on it, a continuous hammering like a woodpecker's.

'Do you know where I can find the right people to help me?' I shouted. Inside the room, there was just the sound of the woman typing, drowning me out.

~

Who could I ask for help? Père Simon? I couldn't bear it. His poor, eager face, reading my letter of bad news.

To buy thinking-time, I walked along the quai de la Tournelle. It was early evening: barges were gliding downriver towards the dark struts of the cathedral, their captains perched on their roofs, still as the boats themselves. I crossed the bridge and wandered towards the Boulevard St Michel. The book-sellers were closing the green doors of their boxes; I caught a flash as I passed of a series of postcards of Max Linder's grinning face, along with other stars. As I lingered, the bookseller caught my eye. 'Beautiful shot of Max?' he asked, and when I shook my head, he plucked a newspaper from his rack and rattled it at me, 'Max Linder, Mademoiselle! His new film is reviewed today in *Le Temps*! Two for one, let's make that pretty face smile…'

I shook my head and walked smartly past: but at the next corner kiosk, I bought a copy of *Le Temps*, then ink, envelopes and stamps from the stationer on the Boulevard Montparnasse; hurried to my room, ignoring Mathilde's piping voice offering a little restorative, and began to turn the pages. The articles about film were hidden at the back underneath the theatre reviews.

So that, in the early days, was my routine. Every morning I went out to buy *Le Temps*, and every afternoon, I directed a volley of enquiring letters to cinema stars, care of the relevant studio, congratulating them on their recent success and enquiring about roles in their next film; I planted a kiss on the back of each envelope and pushed it into the postbox on the corner of rue Boissonnade. At night, I lay awake, listening to the bored cries from Agathe's bedroom and the heavy tread of gentlemen's boots.

Two weeks passed and not a single reply. My anxiety grew: please let me not have to confront another studio face-to-face. The postman's pitter-patter steps passed our apartment every morning; jealously, I heard him ring the buzzer of Madame Moreau's apartment across the corridor.

The third week came and went. Over tea, I told Mathilde that I would pay her double-rent the following week. Though I tried to sound nonchalant, my cheeks coloured, giving me away.

Mathilde tilted her head to one side and looked at me brightly. Then she dropped her embroidery in her lap, put her hand onto my shoulder and squeezed it. Her grip was firm – quite unlike her usual quavering hands. I shrank back; surely she was measuring the flesh on my bones.

The day came when my fifth week's rent was due, and still there had been no response to my missives. At four o'clock in the afternoon, I leapt out of bed, convinced I had heard the postman's step on the stairs. I ran into the hall just in time to see that I had made a mistake: what I had heard was the door just shutting, and beyond it I caught a glimpse of Agathe's bulk, her empty string bag whisking round the corner. Her heavy steps plodded down the stairwell. She must have got up early to go shopping.

I stood in the hall for a moment, willing a letter to appear. As I turned, disconsolate, I noticed that Agathe's bedroom door had been left ajar.

A mere push with the tips of my fingers and it creaked wide open.

The room smelled of stale cigarette smoke. Cracks of light filtered through the shutters and laddered the chenille cover on a double bed. This was so vast it almost filled the room, leaving only enough space for me to stand at its foot. Beside my feet was an ancient blanket-box. I placed my fingers experimentally on the bed cover and pushed the springs, which protested. Then nothing: just the silence and the smoky smell. There was an ashtray on the bedside table, spilling over with old cigarette ends and fine grey dust.

I stroked the ceramic of the ashtray, but it was the bed that drew my attention back. I patted the pillow, then slid my hand underneath it and felt stiff fabric; drew out an enormous brassiere. Old sweat caked the material around the armpits; flaring my nostrils, I dropped it and slid my hand down underneath the pillow again.

Letters – a bundle of them, tied up with a faded red ribbon; but carefully, bound together twice over. I sank to my haunches and listened; hearing nobody, I slipped the knot and bent over the topmost sheet of paper.

It was just a few lines. The handwriting was ill-formed and masculine: all scratch marks and ink blobs. *Darling*, it began, *do not be downhearted. When you've made your name, and you have finished treading the boards of the Comédie Française, the wedding bells will sound in Domrémy again. Remember the little house behind the orchard?*

The date was from five years ago.

I thought how her slippers cut into her puffy ankles as she walked around the apartment.

A movement in the doorway: Mathilde stood watching me. She took in the letters, me.

'You mustn't think of it as a failure,' she said. 'We don't all have the talents we'd like.'

She stood there, the silence stretching around her—

She opened her mouth: her lips hovered around a smile. 'It isn't such a bad life, dear. Food on the table, good friends all around. We are all friends at rue Boissonnade, aren't we?'

The slap of an envelope onto the parquet in the hall.

Mathilde blinked, turned to look and was herself again. 'Oh,' she bleated, 'we so rarely get any post—'

This morning, over breakfast, there is no way to tell whether Mathilde has told Agathe about my searching through her room yesterday or not. Agathe is concentrating on her share of the baguette, which she breaks into tiny pieces and eats. There are particles of leftover sleep around her eyes.

'Here,' I say, 'take mine.'

She accepts it without even looking at me.

In my pocket is the letter that must take me away from all of this. This morning I could fly away, stepping off the windowsill and lifting, stretching my arms out to love the whole of Paris.

Something of this must show in my face, because Agathe leans in over the table. 'Will you be going out to look for work this morning,' she asks, 'or do you have a scrapbook to fill?'

'Actually, I have an appointment,' I say, trying to keep my voice light.

Mathilde drops her spoon and leans over towards me, her lips stretching into a smile, and takes my wrist. 'I have a feeling,' she confides, 'I have a feeling, Adèle, that this is going to be a very special day.'

Her touch makes my own fingers curl; I tug away, slip one hand into my pocket and feel the letter crackle reassuringly.

'Well, good day,' I say, rising from the table. As I walk towards the front door, I feel Mathilde's gaze on my back, taking in my smart dress, the sway of my hips.

I pelt down the stairs three at a time. Monsieur Z lies in his usual tangled heap at the bottom of the stairwell, filthy rags concealing clinking, empty bottles. He raises his head and shouts his familiar greeting – 'Trollop! Whore!' – as I vault over him – and then, as usual, he cringes, a vision of terrified penitence. His cries fade siren-like behind me as I rush into the street: *sorry, sorry, sorry.*

4. avril 1913

THE COLOURS FLICKED ON: sunshine flared through the grubby windows, and the train surfaced at Vincennes, hissing as it came to a halt. I stepped down onto the platform and was immediately caught in a group of other passengers. All were women, and all dressed the same: dark skirts, dark hat, dark gloves. 'Come on, Louise, it's five to nine, you can walk, can't you?' tutted one, as another bent to tie her shoelaces. Chastened, Louise straightened up and the group hurried on.

Guessing who they were, I followed in their slipstream. After the station exit, they marched straight ahead with an uncanny single purpose, geese strutting across a lawn, down the broad avenue; and as we swept past an omnibus stop, more women stepped off and swelled the group, all wearing the same uniform of dark clothes. They exchanged a few demure greetings and then the flock moved forward again: the sound of a hundred heels rapping smartly on the pavement.

Suddenly the women swung to the left, and there was the Pathé factory.

My first impression was of unfriendliness. It looked like the barracks I had once passed by at home: a collection of buildings running continuously the length of a block, but with no windows at ground-floor level, at least not on the outside; they only began on the second floor and stretched upwards to the height of a city block. It was as though nobody could be allowed to peer in, only to peer out. The buildings were faced with white stone of a startling cleanliness: a palace ruled by some fastidious, self-regarding creature.

Then there was the smell, already seeping into me: shoe polish and fireworks. I pressed my handkerchief to my watering eyes. None of the others seemed to notice it: bored, they moved on. An entrance to the mystical kingdom came into view up ahead: a gleaming pair of tall, spike-topped gates stood, swung open, with a crowd before it waiting to shuffle through: 'Hélène! Late again!' called one of the women suddenly to a girl standing near the back of the crowd. The girl grinned back, then rolled her eyes as the crush of bodies began to push her forward.

None of the women made any comment as I was carried along with them into a wide courtyard. A shadow fell across our faces – directly in front of me were three towering industrial chimneys, belching steam upwards, and on the central stack was a giant clock, fat and white above the crowd. As I watched, the huge second hand tocked heavily to one minute to nine and a siren started somewhere very close by; I jumped, the hairs lifting on my arm, but the workers around me only murmured their irritation and began to hurry. With a creaking sound, the gates swung shut behind us, pushing us into a crush as the workers bunched together.

The siren wailed to a halt – a baby that had cried itself out.

As we came close to the chimneys, the stream of workers diverted – they called their goodbyes to each other and marched smartly to left and right, disappearing along the avenues between the factory buildings, until nothing was left but the ringing sound of boots in the distance.

Then it was quiet, and I was alone, and stood .clutching my invitation. In every direction were buildings whose shining windows gave nothing away.

'Mademoiselle? Can I help you?'

A young man trotted towards me across the courtyard. A wide, anxious face peered at me from beneath a fringe of carroty hair; the buttons on his guardsman's uniform were carefully polished.

I showed him my note. He peered at it. 'The *Fée Verte* audition? You want the *Société Cinématographique* studio. That glass one there.'

I thanked him with my warmest smile, just to watch the colour flood up from his neck and drown his face in pink.

'I'm Paul,' he said, to nobody, as I walked away.

I had expected glamour – a taste of my future – in my surroundings, but the audition waiting room looked unloved: dusty, with seats arranged around the walls, and just one small window giving onto the courtyard. The only sound came from the rustling of notes and play texts; five other women sat around the room, their heads bent in nervous last-minute study.

My hand went to my hair, and I sat down next to the window, and opened my play text at Lady Macbeth's famous soliloquy.

The door to the audition room opened, and a man's head appeared in the gap. Everyone's head snapped up. 'Lemesurier, Bérénice!' the man said. A woman on the other side of the room got to her feet, smoothing her skirts nervously, and followed him through.

It grew stuffy in the little room. I turned my face to the window behind me and let the breeze dance across it. The sun was high in the sky, which was a faint, creamy blue. In the distance I thought I heard, carried to me on the wind, the sounds of the city: catcalls, the hum of traffic.

I recited my audition speech under my breath to myself one more time.

Five minutes later the door to the audition room opened, and Bérénice Lemesurier walked across the antechamber without hesitating. At the exit she paused and turned to face the room.

'Good luck, everyone,' she said, and left.

The morning progressed. One by one the women went silently in, came out just as quietly, and left. At last there was just me and one other; a thick-waisted woman in her thirties with a bright, expectant look on her face. She was obviously too old, and her features too coarse, to hope to succeed; but even so, when the door opened and her name was called, and she turned to smile bravely at me, I wished she wouldn't go.

A siren wailed, very close this time. There came a patter of feet on flagstones, and a gaggle of dark-uniformed women crossed the courtyard outside, laughing to each other. Behind them came three young men, jumping and whooping. *Of course she will marry you!* cried one man to another; *of course!* and one of the girls turned round and beamed at him. The sun lowered itself another notch, and the door burst open, and the woman hurried out, head down, not looking at me; a man's voice called my name.

Three men sat behind a table at the far end of the room. The windows were small and high on the walls and gave little light.

The men looked at me with interest. One narrowed his eyes and drew on his cigarette, then puffed the smoke from the side of his mouth thoughtfully; the second, a large man in an embroidered waistcoat, looked up from doodling on the notepad in front of him.

It was the third man who caught my attention. He sat very still, with his hands loose on the table in front of him. His hair was dark and curly, worn too long, I thought, for a man in his thirties; his chin was a point as sharp as a weapon.

'Mademoiselle Roux, Adèle,' the cigarette man said, drawing out the *e* in my name. He frowned at a piece of paper on the table. 'You wrote a letter, is that right? To M. Durand here?'

He indicated the curly-haired man, who inclined his head

and smiled as though a private joke had been made.

'*I am of no little beauty,*' the cigarette-man read out loud, '*and have memorised the principal roles of the theatrical oeuvre.*'

He sat back and folded his arms. My hair stuck damp to my forehead.

'Shall I start?' I asked, finally.

The fat man put his fist to his throat and cleared it, a loud, amused *harrumph*: 'Please do, Mademoiselle.'

Halfway through my speech, the audition room had faded into a castle shuddering in high winds, its walls spongy with moss. Crows tottered on the battlements; ambitious servants whispered behind cupped hands. The curly-haired man was the one I had chosen to fix upon as my nerveless husband; he watched me back, but with an expression that I couldn't read.

I shuddered to a close.

The curly-haired man had sat back away from the light so that his face was invisible. The thin man stubbed his cigarette indifferently into a saucer. The fat man's face was stretched in a yawn. 'No,' he said. The material of his waistcoat strained as he sat forward to the table. 'No, André,' he said to the curly-haired man, 'it won't do. What was all this business with the hands?'

He moved his arms in a grotesque windmill, and swivelled to stare at me crossly. 'Don't tell me you can see her playing the Absinthe Fairy.'

None of the other men spoke.

'Our old faces do us perfectly well,' he said, drawing a line in ink on his notes – which could only be my name, being crossed off a list – 'no need for any new ones.'

I made a twitching movement towards the door, and nobody tried to stop me.

The sky was speckled with early stars; when I reached the exit I laid my forehead on the stones of Pathé's gatepost and thought of Mathilde's thin smile.

It was only vaguely that I heard the sound of purposeful steps coming towards me, and my eye caught the flicker of a coat-tail; then the curly-headed man was leaning against the wall next to me.

His eyes were very fine: amused, smoky-grey, with pupils which extended far into the iris.

He smiled widely. 'I am André Durand and, as I think we have established, you wrote me a letter.'

I tossed my head. Had he come to humiliate me further?

'You may know we have just set up a department of seamstresses for our larger productions. We need a costumière for the *Fée Verte* film.'

There was a twang in his accent – *kos-toom-iaire* – a tiny imperfection that gave him away: not French.

'Steady work with prospects,' he said. His gaze travelled brazenly up over my best dress as far as my throat. 'Anyone can see you are interested in couture.' (*Koo-toor.*)

My one chance had slipped through my fingers, and now this man was offering me a job handling cloth. Was it mockery?

But André gave me the gentlest of reassuring nods.

5. avril 1913

ALL THAT NIGHT I thought about him; about the point of his chin and the way his voice sandpapered over its vowels.

The very next morning, I appeared at the Pathé gates, a quivering vision in my best shawl, certain that André would be waiting for me, craning my neck to look for him as I was bumped along by the waiting crowd; listening in rising irritation to the creak of the gates and the complaining siren. He would appear out of nowhere, take my elbow and smile an apology: *Yesterday was a travesty. Chances like you don't come up very often*; then usher me into my own dressing room, the pressure of his fingertips warm on my forearm.

But when the crowd cleared, instead of André a lumpen young woman stood in the courtyard, her hands folded officiously over her apron. Where her flesh met her blue uniform it stuck in great damp patches; her waist was thickish, her feet flat. When she saw me she attempted a smile: a crooked thing, more than half dislike.

'I'm Elodie, the head costumière. M. Durand sent me to show you where we work.'

I returned the smile in the spirit it had been given. She turned on her heel and crossed the courtyard, turning left into an alleyway between buildings.

In a minute or so, we came to a long, low block at the end of the alley. A number was painted in white on the side facing us.

'Building Number One,' Elodie said, 'where Charles Pathé

has his offices,' but I was unable to comment, for a cloud of flies had materialised in front of us: I spat several into my handkerchief. Elodie laughed. 'The chemicals from the filmstrip building bring them. You'll get used to it.'

Eyes streaming, too proud to complain, I pressed my handkerchief to my nose, and was glad when we walked up the steps and in through the front entrance of Building I; corridors flashed past; soon we were in the bowels of the building. I craned my neck round every corner, hoping to hear a confident laugh, or catch a glimpse of André's immaculate torso and curly hair.

'In here,' Elodie said, pushing open a heavy door.

The room's single humming light bulb showed me an Aladdin's Cave of garments: racks of clothes, rubbing shoulders gorgeously, stretching away into felty darkness.

Nearest the door was a set of tables with sewing machines upon them, and a set of women to go with it.

'Solange,' Elodie said, pointing at a pale woman in her fifties, who blinked at me from behind enormous spectacles. 'Georgette,' – barely fourteen years old, with wrists like twigs; 'Annick,' a woman with pale ginger hair that sparked under the electric lights. All the women were sewing costumes made of green velvet.

Elodie indicated a sewing machine on a vacant table near the entrance. 'We'll get you a uniform sorted out tomorrow. It's costumes for that absinthe film today. A hundred forest fairies, we need. Patterns are on the cards in front of you.'

I stared at the machine.

'You do know how to work one of these?' she said.

Two hours later my foot ached from operating the pedal; my fingers were rubbed raw and pricked full of tiny holes, and my first fairy uniform lay mangled in front of me. The other women appeared to notice nothing; their faces were bent over their work. The hammering of the needles rang in my ears.

My nails sank viciously into the velveteen flesh of the fairy costume. Why had he buried me alive in here if he wanted nothing from me?

Pathé as a studio, of course, was never empty, the great production line worked twenty-four hours a day, would have worked more if it was possible; but in our small department we always went home on time.

At five o'clock on my first day my quota of costumes was nowhere near ready; I announced that I would stay until I had finished. The other women nodded indifferently and, one by one, vanished. Only Elodie paused in the doorway, looking at me suspiciously; thinking, I suppose, that I was plotting to usurp her role as chief costumière. During our midday break she had told us about her son, Charles-Edouard, to whom she longed to rush home each night; now she was caught between her affection for him and her own ambition. She had shown us a photograph of the child: a jowly baby and a younger Elodie, posed ridiculously in front of a painted seaside backdrop. I had eyed her scornfully, but was forced to admit that, once upon a time, she might have been attractive. Attractive enough, at any rate – I found out later that Charles-Edouard's father was a minor aristocrat whose occasional cheques were never quite enough.

At last, with a worried smile, Elodie picked up her purse and straightened her hat on her head, and left. The door closed on her and I was alone; I stopped pressing the pedal, stretched and got to my feet, jubilant. I had never really intended to do any more work. On my own I could explore the studio further; perhaps seek out where André's offices were, the better to bump into him as if by accident on some subsequent day.

In fact, I never left the costume department. Is there anything more gorgeous than a place of work without workers? Loneliness hung on the air; from the corridors outside I heard nothing. I went first to the racks of old costumes behind our desks, and buried my face in their mothy scent. *It doesn't matter*, I told the clothes, *I still love you*; their arms waved helplessly in reply.

Let's be clear: it was not the word 'love' which summoned him; but there he was anyway, lounging in the doorway.

'Evidently you are enjoying your first day.'

I dropped the dress which I had been holding up to my cheek in an asinine fashion.

'You are an unusual person, Mlle Roux.'

'Why is that?' I asked.

'Beautiful people do not usually feel the pain of inanimate objects.'

It was all I needed him to say. I surprised myself with my boldness in stepping up to him, and raising my chin so that it almost met his, asking for a kiss. He looked at me – eyes grey as the Pas de Calais – and we stood for a while. I placed hot palms on his chest; he laughed again, and then he did kiss me.

The kiss said, *look at you, a snake with your prey*. It said, *do you suppose this will secure you an acting role?*

And mine said, *yes*.

I went home. Agathe, sensing a change, turned in her chair and looked at me for ten seconds or so. She rolled me a cigarette and we smoked it together. Far off, the pinnacle of the Bastille was pointing at the moon; that evening, the weight of her arm next to mine was not an intrusion but a comfort.

One other thing: I leant back after the act, gasping as women are supposed to gasp, and asked that hackneyed question: 'Where did you come from?'

And to my very great surprise, he told me. Not all in one go – and not everything – only a fool would suppose André Durand ever bared his soul to anyone – but a little each night, piece by piece. Just enough to keep me wanting more.

André, i.

Grosse Tete, Louisiana, July 1886, population 245: a few tin huts, eternally catching their balance on the crust of mud separating settlement from bayou. Beyond the Grosse Tete Convenience Store and the Grosse Tete Laughing Woman bar, a signpost extends its white finger –

NEW ORLEANS 85 MILES

– but that is 85 miles away; here, every log is a potential crocodile. The heat cracks wood and peels paint from doors.

The town has just one permanent fixture. The Orphanage stands at the Grosse Tete's edge, its windows gazing northwards: two storeys of incongruously imported marble, dotted with mica which dances in the ever-present sunshine. It is run by nuns, stern and secretive, virtuously hiding their faces from strangers; the building has been there for as long as the town's oldest inhabitant can remember.

Today is the first Sunday of the month, around midday, and shutters are slamming closed all around the village. Everyone knows it is Adoption Sunday: a monthly event when wealthy gentlemen seeking a new child visit the Orphanage, to take tea with the nuns and make their selection. There are few inhabitants who haven't at some time or other, when passing the Orphanage, seen a child's fingers spidered against an upstairs window – and in Grosse Tete, where superstitions outnumber residents, it is considered bad luck to witness the children being taken away.

Strange, thinks Auguste Durand, *to find the place so deserted.*

37

He peers from the curtained windows of his carriage, which rattles down Grosse Tete Main Street. His only audience are cats, sunning themselves, who leap to their feet in offence as the wheels spin gravel over them. *It is as though all the inhabitants have been spirited into the swamp overnight,* Auguste thinks – and it seems to him a plausible explanation. Don't they say that is what happened to Thibodaux, thirty years ago? That the town vanished, leaving only the spars of foundations sticking up out of the bayou?

A part of Auguste's fifty-four-year-old brain knows this cannot be true: Auguste has been a sugar-cane man, a plantation owner, all his life and his younger self would laugh at such fancifulness. But Auguste is not young. So, as he smoothes down his sober dark suit, and grips the Orphanage door knocker in his signet-ringed finger, his hand trembles: what if nobody answers, and his journey has been in vain? What will he tell his wife, waiting expectantly at home?

The nun who opens the door to Auguste sees a short man with faded blue eyes. From his clothes she would say he is a rich landowner, but his white beard is unkempt. She senses something: a halo of incipient madness. But a client is still a client, however eccentric, so she shakes hands in welcome.

Auguste doffs his hat and whispers his name to her. Once his relief has passed, he finds he is cowed by the schoolishness of the place – as though it is he who is on display, hoping to be picked, not the orphans.

The inside of the building is a shaded atrium; colonnades, festooned with thick ornamental swamp-creeper, run around the walls. The sun arches down into the central courtyard; Auguste blinks, dazzled; and realises that, directly in front of him, what he had taken for more columns are ten children, standing in a line, arranged from tallest to shortest.

The nun's smile tautens. 'M. Durand,' she says, 'if you would like to step this way—'

The children stand with their hands behind their backs, eyes fixed on a spot somewhere higher than his head: a mixture of boys and girls and – a little shock to Auguste's sense of propriety – races. They all wear the same grey serge uniform; faces are scrubbed clean, and the girls' hair is plaited where possible. The smallest is a toddler still, with a halo of nappy fuzz standing out from his head, and his finger hooked through the hand of the boy next to him. The oldest and tallest, a girl whose thin white hands seem to be all bone, looks to be about seventeen.

What will become of you, Auguste thinks, staring into her face, *when you get too old to live here any more?*

The nun clears her throat. In his scrutiny he has walked right up to the tall girl: she is leaning back away from him, nostrils flared, a sapling in wind.

Auguste steps back, embarrassed. These children are all too old; they already have pasts and histories to themselves. He looks around the room in despair and notices something, someone, else: a boy of about eight, standing watching from beside one of the columns. He is looking directly at Auguste.

The boy's eyes remind Auguste of the sea, which Auguste visited once as a child. The beach was disappointingly grey, and so was the water, not the blue of picture-book illustrations. Undaunted, Child-Auguste had run to the line where the water met the land; but dipping his fingers in the surf, the froth bubbled away to nothing.

The nun has noted Auguste's interest. Ideally he would take away one of the older children who has less time left to find a family, but she understands an inevitability when she sees it; she moves across and places a hand on the boy's shoulder – but gingerly.

'This is André,' she says. 'A fine strong boy, who loves his building blocks. He would be an asset, M. Durand – am I right in thinking you are in sugar?'

'Yes,' Auguste says, distracted.

'And as you and Madame Durand have not yet been blessed—'

The nun lets her voice trail off, intimating visions of the heirless future, the plantation burning, lighting up the night – Auguste pictures the stillborn boy, its full head of black hair, and shakes himself down. He ought to ask a question. He looks at the child's bewitching stare.

'Who were the boy's parents?'

The nun spreads her arms in a shrug. But Auguste's thoughts have already flitted into a great uprush of joy: he is going to be a father. Just as quickly his eagerness becomes paranoia: is the nun thinking him unsuitable? Will she snatch defeat from the jaws of victory?

'Yes,' Auguste barks, 'I'll take him.' With one arthritic hand he gestures to the boy to follow. André trots after the old man as he scuttles out to the waiting carriage. A curl of smoke drifts lazily upwards from the chimney of the Laughing Woman. Though Auguste turns, triumphant, to display the child to the waiting world, there is nobody to see them go.

The sun is an unforgiving white disc; a fine house comes into view as the carriage rattles on down the dusty trunk road, like something out of a painting: white and formal against the blue of the sky. The carriage sweeps through the valley below the house – a forest of rustling stalks, head-high. In between the stalks, heads lift. Plantation workers – the sons and daughters of sons and daughters of slaves – have paused in the cutting of sugar cane to see the carriage, with its precious cargo, sweep by.

The carriage rocks uphill, arriving at a verandah that extends to the front of the house. Auguste leaps out as the wheels stop rolling; his feet make the verandah's floorboards creak. André follows him, taking in the view with his arms laced behind his back, as the nuns taught him, indicating his politeness.

'Caroline,' Auguste calls, repeatedly and in mounting excitement.

A young woman steps from the dark oblong of the door. Caroline is all porcelain and gold and in her early twenties.

'This is André,' Auguste says, his voice quivering: it is his great moment.

She looks at André, looks at his poor serge suit. André's pose shifts and becomes genuine: he wants to please her, never having seen anyone like her.

But though she stares at him, he understands that she does not really see him.

She kisses Auguste's dry cheek and turns to go back inside.

Over the next few weeks, visitors come to pay their respects to the child. They perch on the horsehair settee and look at André, and he feels special, he feels somebody, in his new suit with the high white collar. He learns to rank them in importance based on how anxious Auguste becomes when greeting them. Caroline isn't upset at all, not by anyone: she sits, laughing at their jokes, when he can see she doesn't really mean it; when he turns to look at her, she quickly looks away, and coldly, as though he has been too bold.

One day a man with a handlebar moustache comes. He takes tea in the salon like the others, and the moustache twitches when he drinks and André longs to put his hands up to it and feel the bristle against the palm of his hand. This is Maître de la Houssaye, Auguste says, he is a lawyer come to help Papa with a dispute amongst the workers: would André like to come to the office and see?

André nods, one eye always on Caroline. He wants her to be the one to give permission.

'Kiss your mother goodbye, then, we'll be a while.'

The room hushes; André knows that this is a kind of test; and also that he isn't the only one being tested. He slips off his small chair and hurries across to Caroline. She bends down, awkwardly, and loops her arms round his neck. He understands from her stiffness that she is not used to this, that perhaps she doesn't hold people. It feels entirely strange.

'Come on, boy,' calls his father from the doorway. 'We haven't got all day.'

7. juillet 1913

SOMETIMES ANDRÉ WOULD pop his head round the door of the costume department during the day. With a very straight face he would say, 'Everything ticking over, ladies?' And I would bend my head to the sewing machine and beat my foot on the pedal, and his gaze swept over me and back. He would nod and retreat: the picture of the caring boss.

'Such a charming man,' my colleagues would sigh, touching their hands to their hair; and I would feel the secret warm me up.

The only person who remained immune to André's charms was Elodie; when he came in she bent her head more closely to her work and hunched her shoulders as though trying to disappear. I could see no reason for her dislike; but in the end, I did not have long to wait before the answer was revealed, some weeks after my first encounter with André. At the eleven o'clock pause Elodie handed round cups of coffee and we rested our aching wrists. Along with re-modellings for the *Fée Verte* picture, due to be filmed in a few days' time, we were making revolutionary outfits for the filming of Hugo's *Misérables*. A hundred extras were to storm an improvised barricade in the Pathé courtyard that afternoon; blue, white and red strips of fabric were scattered around the room.

André stepped into the room with his usual deference. 'Ah, the Uprising,' he said seriously, reaching for an abandoned tricorn hat. 'I must tell the other overseers to watch their step.' I thought he had never looked so handsome than when he positioned the hat on his curls.

My colleagues tittered like schoolgirls and he doffed the hat to us – I coloured as with its final flourish he met my eyes. Then he dropped the hat onto my desk, and stepped back out into the corridor again. As he closed the door, when nobody else was looking, he winked at me.

There was a contemplative silence, then: 'He looks tired,' said Annick, winding a strip of electric-ginger hair around her finger.

'Well, that's no surprise,' Elodie said, 'considering who he's married to.'

The other girls tittered, and I joined in, so as not to stand out. I had guessed from the start that André was spoken for. An air of well-fedness, of being adored – he did not have the lean look of a bachelor. But what other ties he might have had had little bearing on what I was asking from him. Night after night, I asked him to try me in a role.

The evening before, he had laid on his back next to me, drowsing; I had rolled into the crook of his arm to look up at him.

'Do I get the part?' I asked playfully.

He turned onto his elbow to look at me. 'You're certainly moving up the shortlist,' he said. I kissed him again, in triumph. He had almost said it: it was only a matter of waiting for the right opportunity.

So as Elodie chattered on, I was able to tap my foot on the pedal and listen calmly – I was naturally intrigued to find out the name of my rival. 'Of course he looks tired,' she continued. 'She keeps him busy enough, with all her carryings-on.'

'Poor hen-pecked man,' said Solange.

I tossed my hair back for my own benefit. André's wife was suddenly taking on a form that differed from my idea. Tantrums: that didn't fit, because he was such a connoisseur of women. Didn't he tell me, every evening, *you are a beautiful little thing*? *My mannequin – my doll*? She must be rich by birth, a patroness whom he'd married for her title. Liver-spotted hands chinking with rings

Georgette said: 'They say she sleeps on a mattress made of peacock feathers.'

Annick said: 'I heard she employs a poison taster, and the last two died.'

Elodie stared at her work and said: 'They say she's a hermaphrodite.'

This met a blushing silence.

Georgette ran her needle along a line of cloth and sighed: 'But the talent goes with the temperament, doesn't it? And she can move an audience to tears.'

My stomach plummeted, my needle stabbed my finger; I pulled it away, sucking the blood off the tip. I felt the others staring: Elodie's quick, bitter glance and Annick, her mouth hanging slightly open, flushing to clash with her hair. Only Georgette failed to notice. She prattled happily on: 'At her *Dame aux Roses*, the crowd went quite wild! They say Sarah Bernhardt wept with jealousy!' She giggled; and then, interpreting the sudden quiet, her face froze and she looked at Annick, Solange, Elodie: me.

'What's her name?' I asked her.

'Terpsichore,' she said.

Juliette and Adèle
1967

I say: 'So that was how you discovered they were married?'

'Yes. Through their pity.'

'Pity?'

Adèle narrows her eyes. 'Of course! The girls were trying to help me. They had kept quiet about his wife, out of tact, for months. But when they decided it had gone too far – when they could see me pale before them, becoming absent-minded, losing myself to an impossible conundrum – then they told me who she was.'

'They planned it?'

'No. But it was an attempted rescue, just the same. I ran outside and stood against the wall of the factory building, where nobody could see me.'

She takes a demure sip from her coffee cup. 'Kindness is so often mixed with other things. It can be hard to see it when it comes.'

André, ii.

André was fifteen years old when his gift was discovered.

It was harvest season, an October day; he was idling in the salon, long legs lolling as he sketched on thin paper at the table, when Caroline, threading a needle through embroidery, raised her head, the perfect skin between her brows puckering into a frown. Through the salon window the small dot that had caught her attention was getting closer: Auguste's head and flyaway white hair, running towards them along the rows of cane. Following his progress, other heads were bobbing up from the cane on either side: indentured workers, sensing trouble.

Caroline laid down her embroidery and waited.

A minute later Auguste burst into the room. 'All wrong,' he said, 'no good,' and put his hat down on a horsehair chair. On his face was the kind of look that once, she might have wanted to comfort. 'What is?' she asked.

'The engine in the mill. Stopped.' He tried to smile and ended up grimacing instead. 'Can't fathom it. Just stopped.'

The steam engine they used for grinding cane was twenty years old, and a friend to Auguste. He still remembered setting the donkeys free from the old horse-powered mill; opening the new mill, his first wife cutting the ribbon, already frail but smiling at the childishness of the task. But it was also the *sine qua non* of his business. Merchants in New Orleans were tapping their watches even now, waiting for him to deliver cargo. What nobody knew but Auguste: how perilously the whole enterprise tottered on the edge of disaster. His friends had all made the switch into other crops when the slaves were set free, and laughed at Auguste for keeping going. He had shaken his head and smiled at them, not understanding how anyone being set free could be a cause of loss.

'What do the engineers say?' Caroline asked.

Auguste reddened. 'How should I know? I don't understand a damn word.'

He put a hand to his eyes; took it away, and sat slowly and gingerly on the arm of a chair. 'I don't know,' he said again. 'I don't know.'

'It will be all right,' Caroline said, and when he looked at her, child-like, she nodded once, encouragingly, and waited for him to get to his feet again, and put on his hat and walk to the verandah door. 'Best go and see,' he said, and ducked his head sheepishly under the lintel.

It wasn't fixed. Auguste reappeared once more, an hour later, to curse and slump on the arm of the horsehair chair; soothed by Caroline, he departed for the mill again. The light began to fail: an orange Louisiana sunset, twinklings in the cabins of the workers, and Caroline finally closed the door.

'Tidy away now,' she told André, 'we'll have supper, just us,' and she clicked her fingers for the maid.

The soft chink of cutlery, neither of them looking at the other; and it was not until the dessert course that Auguste walked into the dining room, his face so thunderous as to preclude any conversation.

'Don't ask me,' he said shortly, and then immediately began to tell them, talking as if to himself. 'It's not the crankshaft, and it's not that a cog is missing,' he said. 'What the devil do I pay them for?'

André said, stabbing at his dessert, 'If it's heated beyond endurance it will fissure. Perhaps that's it.'

Auguste's fascinated face; Caroline's frown. André got up

from his seat and walked back into the salon. After a moment Auguste and Caroline followed, to find him standing over his sketches. André indicated a spot on a delicate drawing of the interior of a steam engine and said: 'Here is your weakest point.'

That night, Auguste undressed thoughtfully.

'He needs proper tuition,' he told his wife.

Caroline put her book aside. 'I can give him lessons,' she said, 'more advanced than what he gets from the governess. Until we can find someone more suitable.'

Auguste nodded; nodded faster. It had always been a source of great pride to Auguste, the son of a farmer: his wife's urbanity, the unusual lightness of her mind. She could teach him things a tutor couldn't, all the accoutrements of a gentleman. Wasn't that what Auguste wanted for his son, at the end of it all? Hadn't they seen, this afternoon, the proof that André could be not just a good person, but a great one?

So it was decided: they would convert the fifth bedroom into a schoolroom. Auguste clambered into bed; out of the dark bloomed the thoughts he kept for bedtime. The thoughts had started the first time he had seen André, but he dared not confide them to Caroline; they required careful handling in case they be disbelieved. Auguste might be the only one to see it for the time being, but it was clear that André's grey eyes were growing to look more like Auguste's blue ones every day. The boy's lengthy stride was becoming shorter, to match the famous Durand bandy knees. Auguste tried not to breathe too fast, so as not to wake Caroline. It would be a wonderful surprise for her, when the time came. The boy he had brought home had turned out to be theirs, after all. It would help her be a mother to him: there had been, from the start, a sort of coolness towards the boy. He would wait until the evidence could no longer be ignored. He would wait until he could see signs of suspicion on Caroline's face: and then he would break the great news to her.

Outside the bedroom window the cicada song became a buzz. He let his drowsiness gather momentum. It made perfect sense to Auguste that the child had found its way back. There was no reason why all those lost years should stay lost for ever.

Two days later, Auguste left for Thibodaux-Nouveau before it got light. Caroline went downstairs with him and clasped his shoulders as she kissed him goodbye. The carriage stood waiting, the horses whinnying their discomfort at the cold air. Auguste was more distracted than usual, his eyes darting to left and right but never finding her face.

'Give my regards to Maître de la Houssaye,' she said to him, pressing her cold lips to his cheek.

'Certainly,' Auguste said, then hurried to rectify his mistake. 'You wanted the blue silk, didn't you? Or would you prefer muslin? I have it written down here somewhere.'

Caroline smiled. 'I don't mind. It doesn't matter, does it?'

Auguste fumbled with the reins; guiltily he geed up the horses and was away.

But Caroline did mind. Over the past six months she had seen the depredations of senility on her husband: she'd seen the way Auguste watched André – a fascination that bordered on the awestruck; she had listened to Auguste's excited breathing at night, and heard his elaborate, circumlocutive mutterings when he thought he was alone. His trip to town today was not to buy cloth for her Christmas dresses but to see the lawyer and change his will in his son's favour. Now that André was grown, and apparently a prodigy, why delay?

When her husband died – and Caroline thought he must die soon, because how could his softening brain withstand everyday pressure for much longer? – she would not inherit.

Caroline had not been forced into marriage, but she had been pushed. She would have nothing to show for all the long dry years – André would acquire everything: the roof over her head, the clothes on her body.

But was he not also a commodity of sorts, something to be acquired in turn?

Auguste was not expected back from town till late. At two o'clock in the afternoon she summoned André to the schoolroom.

While she waited for him she arranged herself underneath her own portrait, which had been commissioned by Auguste shortly after their marriage. She was painted alone, wearing her white high-necked costume, the cane-fields swaying behind her. Her knees were pressed together and turned slightly to the right, sensuously outlined beneath the flowing white fabric in the painter's one concession to the feelings she gave rise to. Her eyes met the painter's; her hands rested on a sketchbook which lay open at a drawing of the whole scene in miniature, complete with green cane and tiny white figure.

Caroline looked up and saw André; smiled and patted the chair beside her with a white-gloved palm.

He stayed where he was, uncertain; but also something else.

As she crossed the room to him, she registered his tallness, and wondered who the boy's father had been, to have given him such long legs. She reached him, put her arms around his neck and leant the whole of her weight against him.

7. juillet 1913

THAT EVENING, I didn't stay late for André. I left early with the others, and Paris was drowning: rain fell in sluices, pooling in the courtyards and battering our umbrellas as we giggled and hopped our way out towards the street. The Metro steamed with the closeness of our bodies pressed together. Further down the carriage, a man smiled shyly at Annick; she smiled sweetly back and then, turning to us, she crossed her eyes and stuck her tongue out; we burst out laughing and the man looked down at his feet.

Annick and Georgette were the last to get out, arm looped in arm. The train moved off: for the final ten minutes of the journey I stood alone, looking at the pitch-black of the tunnel walls. *Let him wonder.*

The train surfaced and I left the station and crossed the Boulevard Montparnasse with its array of winking red lights, and turned into rue Boissonnade. The surface of the cobbles shone with water; the rain had stopped, washing everything clean.

From the salon came an unmistakable clicking sound. Mathilde was sitting in her shawl, hunched over the flicker of her hands. When she saw me, she paused in her knitting and brought her lorgnette up to her eye.

'There you are,' she said, 'working hard as usual.'

She paused, as though picking words. I rushed to forestall it: 'I get paid at the end of the month,' I said. 'I can give you all of it, I promise.'

'No, dear, it isn't that,' said Mathilde.

She paused again, as though trying to find how to say a delicate truth. Then she said: 'A young lady came asking for you, who says she is your sister. I told her there must be some mistake because your family were all dead. But she insisted.'

Camille is sitting on my bed, facing the window. On the coverlet next to her is an envelope which I recognise as one of my own. It belongs to the letter I sent to Père Simon; the return address is scribbled on the flap. Inwardly I flinch, as I recall the closing phrase: ...*almost certain that I shall be engaged as the lead in M. Durand's* Fée Verte. *And we both know, my dear friend, to whom the first invitation for the premiere shall be sent!*

Camille doesn't turn straightaway.

'I like your dress,' I say.

She twists to look at me. With a jolt I see that the months since I last saw her have transformed her: the childish scarecrow has been replaced by poise. She plays with the hem of her calico – *this old thing?*

'Pa gave it to me as a leaving present,' she says. Already she is lying to me; our father would never have allowed her to come of her own free will. She looks up at me, a trick I know well because I use it myself, the slow lifting of the gaze, making me feel the force of her eyes.

'You can stay for a week,' I say, at the same time as Camille says 'I thought I could stay here for a while.'

The impasse stretches out into a silence that feels like falling. I let myself drift – how can I do otherwise: it comes to me suddenly that wherever I go, it will never be far enough. Seeing my face, Camille peels down the sleeve of her dress, revealing a series of vicious welts across her shoulder.

Putting my forefinger over them I can feel how the skin is raised to the touch: the stripe of a willow cane like the one my father used. And there are others, none of them very old, forming a complex knot of scars intertwined.

Did I already know this, at the back of my mind? That when I left home our father would look for someone else to beat?

'I can find work as soon as they've healed,' she mumbles into my shoulder. I have pulled her into an embrace so tight that neither of us can speak.

Camille half-woke at three o'clock in the morning.

'It's so loud here,' she complained groggily. I listened, and heard only ordinary sounds – the clink of Monsieur Z's bottles in the stairwell, the carolling from the all-night restaurants on Boulevard Montparnasse.

I brushed the hair off her forehead to soothe her, and within a few moments she was asleep.

The noise from below faded; there was just the rustle of an old newspaper crackling on the pavement, and then the room was silent. But still I couldn't sleep.

The street cleaners sluicing water over cobbles woke me at half past five and I lay watching the pale light filter in through the shutters until it was time to get up.

Camille turned over just when I thought I had reached the door without waking her. She propped herself on one elbow, and my heart sank as I recognised the expression on her face: matchless cunning that was not cunning enough to hide itself. It was as though the previous evening's reunion had dropped away.

'Are you off to work with Durand?' she asked.

I was immediately on guard. 'How did you know?' I asked, trying to keep the strain from my voice.

'Your letter, silly.' She yawned. 'Père Simon was so impressed. *A senior producer*, he said, *I always knew it*, he said, *always*, like this.' She made her voice fluting, and clasped her hands piously to her chest, eyelids batting, expecting me to join in the joke.

Then her eyes narrowed.

'You're wearing your smart dress,' she said. 'There's a boyfriend. You didn't write about that.' Her eyes glittered with joy of the discovery.

What tic of the mouth could I employ to convince her of my truthfulness, when my mouth was the same as hers?

'It's just an ordinary dress,' I said.

She studied me for a few seconds, then her mouth twisted into a smile. 'When you see Durand, you can tell him about me,' she said. 'Tell him I'll come and work with him too. Tell him I've got a *skill*.'

She nodded proudly to her valise, still standing by the bed. For the first time I noticed it was new – square and black, more like an artist's paint-box than a suitcase.

'What *skill*?' I asked.

Camille bit her lower lip between her front teeth, and shook her head at me. 'Tell you tonight,' she said. She flopped back down onto the bed and closed her eyes.

Of course I did not take her seriously. What skill could she possibly have to rival my own?

On my way out of the apartment it occurred to me that I did not even consider telling Camille the truth.

It would have been a relief. *There is someone*, I could have told her, drawing innocent patterns on the bedspread with one finger. She might have folded me up in her skinny arms; it might have wakened the impulse I had longed to see in her; that she might want to take care of me a little, too. But even now I can remember the precise way her lip curled as she laughed at me; the prideful way she pointed out her valise.

I do not know why they say that the present draws a veil over the past, when it is only later that one sees things as they really were. Now I understand that I could not have done otherwise, because the jaws of the trap had sprung shut when we were children. I told myself, as I set out for work, that my secrets were mine to keep.

That day, my mind was so full of Camille that I barely paid attention at work. The others read my mood: Elodie watched me from behind the safety of the sewing machine. 'Something on your mind?' she asked, and I shook my head.

At five I hurried away; when I got home I found Camille sitting on my bed, perusing my scrapbook of newspaper cuttings.

'They're mine,' I said, and she glanced up, lost in the stories, brow furrowed – a child. 'But of course you may borrow them,' I added, and felt idiotic. I would never learn; she would always unseat me.

She stared at me for a moment, glanced at the clock on the wall and then hopped off the bed. 'I'm going to take tea with Agathe now,' she said.

'You'll have to be quick,' was all I could think of to say to this, 'don't let her eat all the biscuits.'

Camille ignored me and skipped away down the corridor.

I called after her: 'Have you seen Mme Moreau about that cleaning position?'

Camille looked at me blankly. I knew what she was seeing: a fussy ten-year-old, trying to make her tidy her half of the room. She shook her head and pushed the door of Agathe's room open. When I turned back to my bed I noticed that she had taken the scrapbook with her.

André, iii.

She taught him to hold himself back until she was ready; taught him to be quiet and stealthy. More than once they paused, Caroline's hand plastered over André's terrified mouth, as Auguste called out merrily that he was home. André would scrabble for his shirt: she would draw him round, place her hands on him and soothe him: they had a few more minutes, at least. He was such a great joy to look at: his long limbs, his cheekbones, the skin like milk.

An afternoon, six weeks after the first time: early November. The autumn had cooled the earth outside, but Caroline lay on the bare floorboards of the schoolroom floor, her white dress beside her, in a pile with André's blue trousers; and on the other side, arms and legs spread-eagled as though he had fallen from a great height, was André.

Caroline played with the curls on his forehead. Everything was peaceful. The house slumbered around them, basking in the sun. She felt him squirm, and sit up. They smiled at each other as they began to dress.

A curious thing happened: André turned away from her as he knotted his cravat, and when he had finished, he turned back and his cheeks were scarlet – startling Caroline, who thought he must have succumbed to a sudden illness. Then she saw it, and wondered why she had not seen it before: the boy had fallen in love with her in the way that is indeed a sickness. The display of passion frightened her: she sat down on her chair to think what to do.

André knelt before her. His fingers pressed into her waist as he said what she'd feared: 'We must go away somewhere together.'

But the house, the sugar-fields, the lace collar on my finest dress… she shook her head. 'Where would we go?' she said, with a touch of temper.

His face was mutinous.

Why, she asked, when they had everything they needed here.

He's my father, André said. *I don't want to be dishonest any more.*

She almost laughed. Honesty: the preserve of rich men.

'Let's talk about it later,' she said, and began to stroke with one hand the fork of his trousers. André pursed his lips and turned his face away.

The door slammed; later, she heard him stalking up and down in his room. She stood at the classroom window and bit her nails, one by one, down to the pink.

As they had never known when André's real birthday was, it had always been celebrated on the same day as Auguste's – the twenty-first of November – with a special meal. 'A pack of blessings,' Auguste liked to say each year, rubbing his hands, 'we shall be spoiled, shan't we? I plan to eat until I cannot move!'

When Caroline woke on André's birthday morning, she found Auguste with his back to her, standing out on the balcony which adjoined their room. His hands were spread on the railing; as she watched he took a theatrical breath in.

She padded over to him. It was indeed a glorious winter sunrise, hazy and gold as a bitten coin.

'Sixteen today. Can you believe it?'

It wasn't a question; as always, it was a statement to which Caroline was only expected to murmur her assent.

'All this,' said Auguste, and instead of finishing his sentence, he waved an arm over the rich brown sea of the plantation; small dots of cane-workers trussing and tying the husks of cane for winter.

Suddenly he was clutching her hand. 'You've been happy, haven't you? We've been happy, the two of us?'

His face was so strange: so earnest and terrified, she took fright.

'Of course we have.' She searched wildly for safe ground, and found it by showing him the plantation. 'Look what you've achieved.'

'Yes,' he said, 'I suppose so.' To her relief, he rallied. 'It's a great day today, isn't it?' He clapped his mottled hands together and walked to the door, where he paused and blew her a kiss.

Caroline dressed carefully and went downstairs to eat breakfast. André was out there working in the field: she could feel him, picture him listening to the overseer with all that respectful, youthful attention.

After she had eaten, she went to the reception room and read until it was time for the note to be sent. She wrote: *Your birthday present will be waiting for you at four o'clock in the library*, rang for a servant and told her to take it to André. The servant bobbed and hurried away. Crossing to the window, Caroline saw her running down the paths between the corn until there in the distance was André. Squinting, Caroline could just make him out receiving the note; then he looked up towards the house and raised one arm: *yes*. She could not see if he was smiling or not.

Caroline's heart pressed on her ribcage as she sat down at the little walnut bureau and wrote out the second note. *Auguste – forgot to tell you, have ordered birthday cake for A. A birthday tea, quarter past four in the library? Say you'll be there. Love as always, C.*

She looked at her handiwork. It was beautiful: glistening black ink on the white paper.

It was time to decide what to do. Another stroke and she would no longer be able to see the land.

She smoothed it out, sprinkled sand, folded it and beckoned to the servant.

Caroline sat, read, stood, sat again to table but couldn't eat; thought the servant's gaze on her was speculative as she waved away her plate; sat again, this time in the salon, folding her hands first one way then the other.

She could stop if she chose, at this point *now*, or this one; or this new second, the tock of the clock's longest hand slotting into the next, then the next. But she didn't move; she sat, hands in her lap, looking at nothing. And then, at five to four, she stood and went out of the reception room and down the corridor to the library.

A Southern belle to her core, Caroline's body gave her advance warning of barometric changes: she could feel the oncoming rain in little damp pinpricks up and down her forearm; as she took her seat in the library, dry-throated, rain began to scatter against the French windows which led out to the plantation.

A few moments later André appeared at the French doors, his face swimming in the wash of water on the glass; she unlatched the doors to let him in; and then left them carefully ajar. She scanned his face for evidence of a change for the better, and saw none: André looked like a boy dying for love. As he smoothed the rain out of his hair his movements were quick, jerky and doll-like, his pallor extreme.

Since that day in the classroom, they had barely spoken, still less been alone together; Caroline's heart fluttered. It was important to play the game perfectly. She bent her head, as if in apology, waiting for his next move.

André looked not at her but up at the books, a smooth skin of leather covering all the walls. He looked at the furniture; over at the door, swallowing; anywhere but at her.

She took his hand. 'I want us to go away,' she said, and he looked back at her, astonished. She smiled. 'We'll get somewhere far away and start again.'

He reached for her as she'd known he would. She let herself be pulled in but with one eye on the clock – it was getting late, almost ten past – so she held him away from her as he tried to lead her to the door. 'Here,' she said, pointing to Auguste's reading armchair. 'Please,' making her mouth open, her eyes glaze as she knew they did when she was possessed by feeling.

André picked her up and settled her on his hips, where she could feel he was hard; now it was all simple. They half-walked, half-fell towards the chair. He knelt in front of her and reached under her dress; she squirmed against his hand, tilted her head to check the time, and reached for the fastening on his trousers.

How silky he was, already pearling with excitement. He raised himself on his toes and pushed himself into her; she gasped – it hurt a little – and as André scrabbled for purchase on the parquet, knuckles bulging on the arms of the chair, the French doors opened inwards and Auguste stood in the room. In his right hand was a poorly wrapped package; André's birthday present.

Do it now.

Caroline filled her lungs with air and screamed to Auguste to help her, flailing at André with her hands; André turned and shouted out in shock, then pulled away from her and knelt, covering his shame.

Caroline made her eyes wide and pleading, she looked up at her husband. 'The shame of it! He forced me,' she whispered, 'as though possessed…'

Seeing Auguste's face turn purple, she thought: *He will send the boy away. He will cut him out of the will. I have done it.*

But: 'My love,' Auguste said to Caroline, and then he toppled. The servants ran into the room and took him by the shoulders and ankles; one of them ran screaming for horses, to fetch the doctor.

They found André's present afterwards, skidded under a chair. It was a book: a fine new edition of a new book. The inscription read: *To my son, who I always knew would come back*, and the spine said: Thomas Edison's *PRINCIPLES OF MOTION TELEGRAPHY.*

Juliette, i.

The Pathé archivist unrolls the promotional poster lovingly, smoothing the edges with her white cotton gloves.

'This was made in preparation for the release of the *Petite Mort*,' she says. 'It's all we have in terms of promotional material. Everything else was lost in the fire.'

The poster isn't as large as the modern ones I'm used to seeing – only a bit bigger than typewriter paper.

At the top of the page, in curvaceous black type, is the title – **LA PETITE MORT.** Underneath, down the right-hand side, is a drawing of a slender woman in a floor-length black dress. Her posture is elegant and composed apart from her face, held between her cupped hands as she stares directly at me. Her lips are pulled back from her teeth as she screams at something we can't see. In the background, there is a slit window and bare stone walls, and in the corner of the room, a full-length mirror.

The left-hand side has text on it. In the same bold font, it reads:

A TALE OF MYSTERY AND SUSPENSE!
FEATURING A NEVER-SEEN-BEFORE
DOPPELGÄNGER TRICK BY ANDRE DURAND!
PATHE FRERES

I signal to the archivist, who comes over to stand beside the desk.

'They told me the Doppelgänger trick is what's missing from the print that's turned up?'

'Yes, that's correct.'

'Do we know what the trick consisted of? Aren't there any papers?'

She shakes her head apologetically. 'All we know is the studio gossip. It was supposed to be a great coup, a hitherto unseen trick, and everyone was excited about the film's release. Only then, there was the fire.'

I look at the poster for a minute longer, as if there might be some hidden detail somewhere, but there is nothing: just the girl, and the mirror, and the castle room.

'Don't you have a script somewhere? Couldn't we get an idea from that?'

She touches the tips of her gloved fingers to each other in turn: 'No. I'm sorry. We looked all through the archive when the film print was found, but there was nothing.'

The girl's eyes in the poster are dark blots in a pale face.

9. juillet 1913

THE FOLLOWING DAY, something happened which eclipsed even Camille's arrival.

When I got to the costumery at ten past eight Elodie was already there, holding something up to the light for inspection.

'Is that the Absinthe Fairy's costume?' I asked.

It was venom-green: the seed pearls on the bodice were winking at me.

'That's it,' Elodie said, admiring it. 'Her assistant's coming to pick it up in a minute. They're filming today.'

Terpsichore was somewhere close by; perhaps in the very next building, putting on her make-up in front of a mirror, being fussed around by executives and flattered by the director.

I sat at my station and started my machine, trying not to steal glances at the costume. Five minutes later, we heard a clattering of boots in the corridor, and a girl about my own age appeared in the doorway.

She wasn't wearing a uniform: instead she had a smart dress on, which had been well-tailored, and her boots were polished to a bright black shine.

She stepped into the room as if she owned it; I felt the collective hackles rise. 'Is this it?' she asked, and when nobody answered, picked up the green dress and swept away, nose in the air.

~

As I remember it, that morning was full of gossip: enough to distract me totally from the problem of my sister. An ageing wolf had escaped from the zoological film section of the factory and was at large in the Bois de Vincennes; it was not proposed to retrieve him, on the basis that a lifetime of being fed treats had made his teeth too soft to bite. Another rumour: they were going to divert the course of the river to run through the Pathé lot in order to film the story of Moses. Moses was to be played by Charles Pathé's grandson, widely considered an ugly baby – but of course everyone was too afraid to object.

At half past eleven, we heard running feet again. The door opened and a runner stood there, excitement all over his face. 'You've got to see this.'

We all looked at Elodie, but she was already half out of her seat.

At the joining of the corridors we met a crowd of other workers – the secretaries and producers from the first floor – the whole of Block One was emptying in front of us.

We spilled out onto the building's top step and into the back of a crowd made up of the other workers. The sky was a mutinous grey, and fat drops of rain bounced up from the paving stones. Across the courtyard, workers were crammed into every crevice of the doorways of the other buildings.

'There,' murmured Elodie, pointing to the centre of the courtyard, where a few people stood huddled. A low-slung studio car was waiting there, and next to it was a group of men in the expensive suits of high-ranking employees, talking to André. The men had their arms crossed. The rain had damped André's curls to his forehead. It was clear from his gestures that he was losing the argument.

And standing next to André was a person who must be Terpsichore. She was wrapped in a fur coat, holding an umbrella tilted against the rain.

I whispered to Annick: 'What's happening?'

'They're saying she threw a glass vase at her assistant.'

'Why?'

'Apparently the costume didn't fit right.'

'Is she all right? The assistant?'

'She'll live, but it's not the first time. They're putting her on leave of absence,' Georgette whispered.

The tall figure turned towards us, bending to open the car door. She shut her umbrella with a shower of raindrops; the door clicked open and she bent to get in.

'She's beautiful, isn't she?' said Georgette.

Then the door closed, and all I could see was a shadowy profile, sitting quite still and unconcerned in the cab. André leant in to speak to the driver, their heads bent close together, then stood back from the car. The engine fired, and the car purred away down the narrow alleyway between the buildings.

André, iv.

Three o'clock in the afternoon, the day after Auguste's stroke. Rain drums on the roof, but the sick-room itself is quiet. Caroline sits beside Auguste's bed, brushing the creamy edges of the coverlet with her fingers.

The doctors have said that Auguste won't survive. His breathing is slow and gurgling, like a person drowning. Caroline remembers how apologetic he was on their wedding night and how scornful and impatient she must have seemed to him. She recalls the way Auguste patted her knee after her miscarriage; how he held her hand as she cried herself to sleep.

The door shuts quietly, and André is standing just inside the room.

She knows why he has come: because the carriage is outside waiting, because he is leaving. His face has changed: all the pallor and the passion is gone. Caroline has one weapon remaining, a final effort dispensed through gritted teeth.

If you'll only wait for the will.

Perhaps if André knows about the money he will be persuaded to stay; perhaps in time he'll understand why she had to trick him.

Last night's scenes come back to her. André, wild and hysterical: *You wanted him to find us together,* he said. *You wanted him to send me away.*

She had moved towards him, and the shock on his face vanished so quickly, replaced by arctic cold.

Now, standing in the sick-room doorway, André shakes his

head as though shaking off a fly. *I don't care about the money. I'm going now. I want to be someone to make him proud*

Caroline crosses to watch his departure from the sick-room window. Perhaps now he will remember her crooked smile in the schoolroom; perhaps now he will recall the night-sweats and fevers and her thumb on his jaw. But André steps through the puddles and into the waiting carriage without looking up at her. She stays watching at the window anyway, even when the carriage has vanished. The clock ticks softly on.

When she turns back to the bed she sees that Auguste's chest has stopped rising and falling.

She is fascinated by the change in him: in death his face is fixed and molten at the same time, like wax.

Then André dips out of view for a while. There were sightings in a brothel in New Orleans; reports of a young man in blue serge hiding out in a railroad car. Tramps along the Montana line, presented with a sketched likeness, shook their heads and could not swear to it.

It was easy to lose him because nobody really wanted to find him. Auguste's family lawyers made a cursory investigation and then recalled their agents. There had been rumours of an unfortunate entanglement at the plantation, the details of which were vague but damning; better, they thought, that André make his peace with himself in his own time.

On January 3rd 1897, André presented himself at the offices of Mr Thomas Edison in New York.

The office door was opened by Edison himself – now in middle age, with tufty grey hair and a lean, narrow-eyed cast to his face. He saw a gangly teenager with grey eyes and a careworn shirt in expensive material. André in turn took in the view through the half-open door: three foreign-looking gentlemen were sitting in the offices. One gentleman's hand rested protectively on a machine which André immediately recognised: a projector. With Edison distracted at the door, the gentleman leant across to his colleague and André heard him say, in French: *Let's not sell for less than a million.*

Edison saw André peering round the edge of the door. 'Are you the interpreter?' he grunted.

The French gentleman wore a fur stole and a monocle and spoke very quickly, in a Parisian accent; André, translating, struggled to keep up. The man accorded his salutations to Mr Edison; it was his pleasure to present the new Visiscope, his very latest invention, a revolutionary projecting machine that could show images to an ever-larger audience. He patted the projector's casing, extolled its many virtues – *Think of the profits, sir!* – and sat back with folded arms, waiting for Edison to make an offer.

André was bewitched. Auguste had taken him to a nickel-odeon once in Baton Rouge, and he had seen illustrations, but never the apparatus of such a thing before. When the inventor opened the casing to demonstrate the mechanism, André leant closer and looked at the loving, ingenious armatures, savouring the hiss of the machinery. When the Visiscope started, and shapes leapt to life on the blank wall of the office, Edison was transfixed; but André did not glance at the wall once. He looked only at the way the film unspooled, smooth as water, inside the projector.

Edison hemmed and hawed and twirled his moustaches. He hated to lose money on a deal, but feared still more that he would lose to one of his competitors. The inventor waited politely, with a smile like ice. Finally Edison sighed, crossed his arms behind his head and said to André: 'Damn patent's worth a million. Tell them I'll pay it.'

Though he did not understand English, the inventor leant forward, sensing victory.

'I wouldn't do that,' André said to Edison.

Edison coloured instantly. He was the inventor of the light bulb, of X-rays; it was years since anyone had contradicted him. 'What the devil do you mean?'

'The mechanism that holds the film in place could be improved. If we were to introduce a simple loop here, you would reduce the pressure on the film as it passes through. It would be safer. And sufficiently different to qualify for a new patent. We wouldn't have to buy theirs.'

Edison peered into the body of the projector and saw the boy was right.

The inventor's eyes darted from one face to the other.

Edison sat back, the Visiscope forgotten, and stared at André.

The year 1897 was a busy one at the New York State Patents Office. There were ten patent applications for new cinematic equipment. And, though they ranged enormously in technology – projectors and cameras and primitive sound-cylinders – eight of those patents bear the same blocky and youthful signature. Beneath the first signature was the confident flourish that the patent office knew so well – Thomas Edison – which signified joint ownership.

In the year that followed, the patents continued to flow thick and fast, all with the same scribble and confident employer's countersigning. It is only in 1899 that the rate of invention tails off: it peters out in a series of applications for licences. One for a 'folding mirror device' and another, a 'handle-operated smoke-producing machine'.

These were the traditional paraphernalia of the fairground attraction, with minor modifications. They were not countersigned by Edison, and not original enough to be considered seriously. They were rejected by the Patent Officer out of hand.

~

Electricity was Edison's business. He understood that a current will not always run smoothly: instead, it may leap erratically from point to point, arriving at its destination through the route that suits it best. And, though he never shared his view with anyone, Edison believed that people worked like electricity – coursing for the most part drone-like through life, but sometimes throwing up an anomaly. He, who had been expelled from school as mentally deficient, when all the time he was studying the flight patterns of the birds through the window, was his own proof.

Therefore – knowing that brilliance, physical or metaphysical, might flare in unexpected ways – Edison gave André a long leash. Along with the rest of his engineers, the boy was set up on a decent salary and given workshops on Edison's lot. By and large he was left to his own devices, to tinker in whatever way he chose. And for almost two years Edison's policy bore fruit.

Nevertheless, by the summer of 1899, André's erratic ideas could no longer be ignored. All spring, the guards had come running to Edison with reports of men in fur coats drawing up to André's offices late at night; peering through the window, the guards saw the room lit up by zoetropes in action, by mirrors laid out in odd formations on the floor. They saw André's pensive face as he poured hard liquor for the men, listening to them give away their fairground secrets one by one.

Was this some kind of fad? Edison told himself that he was angry because André was inviting dubious characters onto the site, and called André to his office.

The young man stood before his desk. Edison made him wait a full minute before looking up from the papers he was signing.

'What is this I hear about inviting trick-film merchants in?' he asked.

André had known it was only a matter of time.

'The mechanisms are ingenious—' he began, but Edison held up a palm.

'Charlatans and misfits: it must stop.' He didn't want reasoning; he wanted contrition. Why didn't the boy make it easy for himself?

André knew he could not convince Edison to see the world the way he did. Edison looked down at his papers, dismissing him. 'Don't be careless with your future,' he said, more sternly than he felt; his faith in his electric metaphor was undimmed. André might fizz and crackle, but he would eventually find his way home.

André packed the same night. He bore Edison no personal grudge, his decision was calculated on the basis purely of profit and loss. Nobody saw him slip out of the compound. He stayed the night in a hotel by the docks, and boarded a ship the following morning.

9. juillet 1913

ALL THAT MORNING, the studio talked of nothing else. The vase had been crystal, and had lodged in shining splinters in the assistant's face. The assistant had found a lawyer; the assistant had been paid off handsomely.

'It's the Absinthe Fairy producers I feel sorry for,' Georgette piped. 'Having to replace Terpsichore at the last moment.'

The others shook their heads. I stared at her, dazed by a new idea. Unsettled, Georgette gave her shoulders a mutinous little shake and said, 'Poor M. Durand. All his film in tatters, and his wife too.'

There was general assent, and gradually the subject died away. But I was listening only to myself. I was overdue this, wasn't I? With Terpsichore gone, who would replace her in the role, if not me? Somewhere in the building across the courtyard, André would be persuading the casting directors. *Let's give the Roux girl a chance*, he was saying. And one by one the others would be slowly nodding: *Let's*.

There was no sign of him in the early afternoon; three o'clock and four o'clock came and went. By the end of the day I was cross, taking it out on the others with needling little asides; Annick flushed once or twice and bit her lip; I had almost made her cry.

It was only at ten to five that a runner came to the door. 'Message for Mlle Roux,' he said, 'M. Durand wants to see you in his offices immediately.'

Elodie looked up, surprised.

I beamed as I rose, smoothing the cloth of my skirt.

'This way,' the runner said, and I followed him up to the second floor of the building, where the upper echelons of staff had their offices.

There was a corridor with just one door at the end of it. The runner knocked, and André's voice called out: 'Come in!'

I opened the door to a long, low-ceilinged room. At one end was a green baize desk. Two of the walls were lined with book-shelves, and stuck to the third was a mass of paper – sketches and geometric drawings.

Where was André? I heard a clock ticking – no, not a clock – and there, making its waddling way towards me, was a monstrosity. A clanking figure made of metal, the size of a child. Someone had painted a crude face on it: red for the lips, blue for the eyes, though the paint had run on the mouth before it had dried, and it was this that made me squeak.

André's laugh rang out, and he stepped forward. 'Do you like her?'

I watched the automaton come towards me. It was nothing to be afraid of – stage-magicians used them. But this one was unfinished: though its legs marched smartly, its arms were mismatched pieces of metal and hung by its side. It wheezed up to me, fell over onto its side and froze, fixing me with its blue eyes.

André peered down into its face. 'Back to the drawing board,' he said.

'Did you make it?' I asked. 'What for?'

'Work,' he answered, and for some reason, the room felt flat and irritable.

'I was sorry to hear about your wife,' I prompted.

He looked at me. 'Adèle, she's not dead. She just needs a rest.'

I decided to press my advantage, and crossed to him, placing my palms on his chest. 'You have something to tell me, don't you? That's why you sent for me.'

His hand slid under my breast.

'No,' I said, pushing him away, 'tell me what you want me for.'

He sighed. 'Very well,' he said. 'It is an offer of some importance, after all.' He was looking at me strangely, I thought, his lips twitching. 'You will make a wonderful new assistant for my wife,' he said.

In the corner, the automaton convulsed and then was still. 'Are you—?' I said. 'Are you joking?'

Smiling, he shook his head.

From the stairwell outside the apartment, I heard an entirely new sound. High, yet girlish: it sounded like Mathilde laughing.

Shuffling from the ground floor caught my attention. I peered down through the banisters, and saw Monsieur Z rustling on his newspapery bed; he looked up at me and grinned, revealing pink and toothless gums. 'Happy,' he cackled, and indicated upstairs with his chin.

I opened the front door and stepped inside. The hall was in darkness, but a wavering, flickering light – candles – came from the salon. I hesitated, listening – and heard low chatter: Camille's voice, as though telling an anecdote. And then again, Mathilde's giggling.

I peered round the corner so that I could see into the salon.

The first thing I saw was that the furniture had been rearranged. The dining table had been dragged to sit cross-wise in front of the fireplace, and the large mirror from over the fireplace placed on top of the table, so that the mirror's back was supported by the mantelpiece. Mathilde's family miniatures lay piled carelessly just inside the door. The room was lit by two candles, one on either side of the mirror; and on the dining table were scattered an array of pots of powder and kohl.

Mathilde was sitting up to the table, facing the mirror, expectant and child-like; Camille was to her right, leaning in to dab at Mathilde's eyes with a finger greased with Vaseline. Agathe stood behind Mathilde, watching the proceedings. Even she was smiling, enchanted at Mathilde's transformation.

When she saw my movement out of the corner of her eye, Mathilde swivelled to look at me. She was painted chalky white, with black swirling details on her cheeks, and one black tear-drop eye: a pierrot.

Camille stood back, smiling. Her glance flickered to the corner of the room, where I saw the squat black valise she had arrived with. *A skill,* she had said the night she arrived: *I've got a skill.*

'You weren't the only one who was clever,' Camille said. 'I've taught myself. I used to practise on the little ones after school.'

'You never told me,' I said.

Camille tossed her head, which meant, *you never asked.*

'Isn't it wonderful?' Mathilde said, 'Isn't it exciting – you can find her employment at Pathé! Surely some of the directors could make use of Camille?'

'The actors do their own,' I said coldly. 'Most of them,' I corrected. For what did I know about the individual habits of the stars?

Camille had waited patiently for Mathilde to stop speaking, and now bent gently to dust powder over her cheeks: I suddenly saw, as she moved into the candles' range, that she had made herself up. It was no more than a touch of rouge and the lightest shading around the eyes, but she looked *finished.*

'So I'm afraid there are no opportunities at present,' I said.

Mathilde turned to look at me, bewildered.

Camille said smoothly: 'But you could have a word, couldn't you, Adèle? I thought you and M. Durand were close.'

I fled to my room, curled up in bed, and held onto my own toes for comfort. The rain continued whispering at the window late into the night, and still the laughter came from the salon, and Camille did not come to bed.

I thought back to that afternoon. *What on earth were you thinking?* André had asked, grabbing my wrists after I had reached up to try to slap him. *An established actress will take over the Absinthe role. What did you expect?*

He had let me struggle, turning my head away from him.

'Think about it,' he had said, 'just think,' over my tears. 'Don't you know how often the assistant becomes the understudy?'

I had sniffed and hiccuped, caught out.

'Besides, you'd come and live with us. My wife finds it preferable to have someone there all the time. She and I each have our own quarters. You will be in the room just above mine.'

André smiled and gave my shoulders a little shake, till I began to smile in turn.

'Really?' I asked. 'Really?'

'You will have your pick of gowns. All the advantages of knowing the studio people. And me, of course. As much of me as you like.'

I thought of myself, whisking a costume away from my own assistant: *You have not sewn the hem correctly. Take it back, please.* Would I say please?

André looked at me with narrowed eyes.

'I don't want to be a costumière for ever,' I said, trying out the words.

In the early hours, Camille came to bed. She turned away from me, and soon I heard her breathing steady and slow. Her nightgown fell below her shoulder blade, exposing the new skin growing over her scars. They were healing on their own, without any help from me

André had said: 'I'll send my driver for you tomorrow evening. Of course you will have to be vetted by my wife. My car will take you to our house in the Bois de Boulogne. All you have to do is be there to meet it.'

André, v.

A rainy November evening in 1904: five years after André stepped off the boat from New York to Paris, and into his proper life.

As usual, he was in the Pathé building long after everyone else had left, reclining and doodling on his sketch pad. He had nothing to do apart from be perfectly himself: there was an invitation, of course, to a gallery opening later in the evening, but he was not obliged to attend. He loved above all things the long hours after dark, when the hum of the human factory workers had subsided. He had his best ideas at night, because it was then that he was left alone with the noises he loved: the clanking of the stage-machinery pistons, the hiss of water in the pipes above his head, on its way to douse down the film-strip laboratory floor.

Then, mixed with the mechanical sounds, André heard something that should not have been there: footsteps, approaching his door. He frowned: a little flare of temper, and dropped his sketch pad as the knock at the door came.

'Come in,' he barked. The door opened a crack, and one of the runners poked his head into the space. 'This came for you, M. Durand,' he piped, holding out a flat, oblong parcel in trembling fingers.

André snatched the parcel, tossed it onto the table, and tried to get back to his thoughts. He locked his fingers behind his head and closed his eyes. The pitter-patter of the runner's feet receded, and he sighed and inhaled the factory sounds.

But the parcel had made a dent in the weave: an oblong silence where there should have been noise. It lay staring up at him.

André swore. Who had sent him a film idea at this time of night? What could possibly be so urgent? But he would get no rest until he had, at least, looked at it.

One quick peek – and then it would go where ninety-nine per cent of the ideas he received went. Giving in, he tore the manilla envelope that was used for inter-departmental traffic, and found, as he had expected, a note from Charles Pathé:

This came from a friend. Of interest. Difficult trick. C.

André smiled. Declaring something *difficult* was a lure of Charles's, designed to pique André's interest: but it was a phrase without bite because they both knew that André never found camera tricks difficult. His films were the talk of Europe: his speciality was the illusion; films which made the audience cover their face with their hands; and he did it all with a shrug and a smile, finding it easy. Inevitably he would stride into Charles's office the following morning and toss the script onto his desk, along with the sketch book containing the solution. *Not so difficult then*, Charles Pathé would smile, and André would answer: *Apparently not.*

He turned the paper over:

LA PETITE MORT
A drama of a haunting

André's lip curled. Charles was losing his touch: when had there been a ghost which André could not conjure? Mercifully, the script was just a few pages long, and well formatted – not like some of the scribbles he got nowadays. He quickly found the scene which would require his attention:

The Doppelgänger, enraged, steps out of the mirror.

Intertitle:

HOW DARE YOU CONJURE ME WITHOUT MY PERMISSION?

The Doppelgänger wraps its hands round the girl's throat.

The sluicing of the pipes overhead faded out and was replaced by the tingle in his elbow that signified an idea.

André tossed the script aside, and reached for his pencil and sketchbook. Designs ran down his arms and fingers and onto the page. He drew a stage model of the standard set-up for Pepper's Ghost, the illusion which had so amazed London three seasons ago. The action ran as usual on the stage: but a sheet of glass was added during the interval, running invisibly stage left to right. Via a series of projections, the reflection of an actor in the wings was thrown onto the sheet of glass: and a ghost appeared to walk back and forth on stage.

In the silence of his room, André furrowed his brow. It was easy enough to duplicate a person in the same shot. One simply filmed the same scene in two passes, confining the action to one side of the shot only on each pass, and then laid the two sections of film over each other to get the full picture in the finished print. Or a better option might be to block off a part of the camera lens, and expose one side of the film – have the girl step towards the mirror – and then rewind the film, block off the other half of the lens, and shoot the other side – have the same girl play herself stepping out of the mirror.

But in this type of trick, the doubles usually stayed firmly on their respective sides of the set, and never touched each other. The contact of nebulous hands on living throat: that was more difficult.

Half an hour passed; the clock struck eight, and André tore the sheets from his pad and ripped them into strips. He flung the script into a drawer.

As he stared at his desk, unseeing, the invitation to the

gallery opening swam into focus. Suddenly he did not want to be alone in his office any more.

He locked the drawer with its shameful contents before he left, locked his office, smiled at the night porter on his way out, and hailed a cab which took him to Montmartre, and to a rainy pavement outside a gallery lit by electricity and champagne.

Juliette and Adèle
1967

I say: 'But he did work out a method by the winter of 1913.'

'Yes.'

'How was it done?'

Adèle shrugs. 'I don't know exactly.'

'Why not? You were there.'

She leans forward: 'Have you ever stood under cinema lights? After two minutes, you smell your own hair burning. I was alone, faint and dazzled, being told what gestures to make, one by one. I do remember there was a mirror, and that the director became very irate, and kept moving me around, saying I wasn't hitting my marks. But apart from that – a blank.'

'I can't believe it,' I say. 'There must be something.'

A hiss of steam from the coffee machine; someone comes into the café, and Adèle Roux is looking at me.

'I've got you wrong, haven't I?' she says. 'I thought you were a person who let things happen to them, but you're not. You have to find things out. You won't rest until you know.'

It's the best summary of myself I have yet heard.

She passes her hand in front of her mouth as if hiding a smile. 'But when we come to the part about the film,' she says, 'you will see why I wasn't concentrating.'

10. juillet 1913

THROUGH THE GLASS PARTITION, André's driver tells me about his daughters. 'Our eldest, we hope, may be a doctor one day.' His eyes crinkle. 'Why not? It's changing everywhere, isn't it?' Failing that, he says, a doctor's wife. 'She's turned out good-looking. A bit like you.' He winks: complimentary rather than lascivious, but I've turned my face away.

Outside the car, the city has gone away without anything to go on. It seems one moment a white-aproned waiter inclines over a lady in furs, frozen in the act of obsequiousness; the next, the avenue is white dust and lined with poplars – neat façades behind high walls – countryside, but pruned and arranged for the rich, speeding along too fast, pressing me into the sides of the car as we corner. I fold my hands over my valise and wish he'd watch the road.

'First time in an automobile?' the driver says.

'No,' I say, and then: 'When I was little there was a horse and trap; we hired it to take us on picnics. Only the pony was used to deliver milk the rest of the time, so it kept trying to stop in at every house on the way.'

He laughs out loud, confident hands on the wheel, and I feel a little better.

The house radiates wealth: gold stone, its shutters beaming wide, its windows blue in the summer evening. The mansard roof is slate and the lawn trimmed a perfect poison-green. In a spin of gravel, the car swings round a turning circle in the drive and stops outside wide steps leading up to the front door.

The driver hops off the cab and clicks the car door open for me. He touches his cap: 'Hubert, Mademoiselle,' he says. 'I look forward to being of more service to you in the future,' and smiling, he steps away.

Inside, led by the butler, Thomas, the house isn't what I expected: a smell of camphor and the old stone of the marble floor. The hall is dark apart from the yellow pool of a lamp, standing on a marble occasional table: as we move through, a wash of colour from a stained-glass window dapples my feet. Further back, a glimpse of a snail's shell staircase, drifting up into the floor above.

Thomas stands for a moment listening outside a door halfway down the corridor, his hand in readiness on the door knob; he raps with his other knuckle and without waiting for an answer, goes in.

She is sitting on a sofa under the large front window, head bent over a book; as we enter, she puts it down on her lap.

'Mlle Roux, Madame,' Thomas says.

She says: 'Oh – the new assistant!' as if she has never heard of such a thing; Thomas withdraws, closing the door behind him.

She looks down, produces a bookmark and inserts it, marking the page. Makes a business of it; smoothing the covers and closing it and putting it down again, this time beside her; and then we look at each other.

You always ask yourself: how much of what I remember is real, and how much of it is detail that I have embellished afterwards? In my mind's eye, she makes a quick movement, as if she is hesitating to speak, and we stay like that for I don't know how long – but when I try to square that trembling image with what I know of her now, I can't imagine her doing it.

I felt, in those couple of seconds, that I'd known her for a long time. I thought, as she finally started to smile, and her teeth appeared, I saw her recognise me too. Perhaps that was what she had been going to say, but stopped herself: *Don't I know you?*

'My husband tells me you have aspirations in the cinema.'

Now she has fixed her eyes on the window behind me, with a slight frown, as if momentarily distracted by someone passing by, and I'm glad of the interruption, because her voice is a disappointment. Unremarkable: the accent aristocratic but not Parisian. Not the rich chocolate I'd imagined.

'Yes,' I say, 'I am extremely keen to learn.'

'And can you read?'

'Fluently.'

'Good. And you know the duties involved in being my assistant? Clerical, as well as the social aspect? You'll answer my correspondence and help me keep my paperwork in order. And you don't mind about the money? You will have your own rooms, your own suite, and you can eat your meals with us if you like. I expect M. Durand explained.'

I nod, thinking that I'll have to be careful not to use his first name.

'Are you able to start immediately? We can send for your things. There isn't anyone at home waiting for you?'

'No.'

'Then I'll ask Thomas to show you to your room.'

The smile broadens until all her teeth appear, and above them, her eyes, wide and amused.

Three days later I returned to rue Boissonnade one last time, to collect my things.

I went in the last hours of the night so that nobody would see me. Wisps of mist hung in the street and wreathed themselves about the hall door; I crept past Monsieur Z and up the creaking staircase and turned my key in the lock of the apartment.

From Agathe's room came the sound of snores. I moved on, past the salon door, which was propped open. In the dead light the furniture looked august and almost expensive; Mathilde's family were frozen on the mantel, glinting in their silver frames.

The door to my old bedroom creaked under my hand.

The room was warm with sleep. Camille lay in my bed, huddled over on herself like a small animal, the blankets clutched between her legs. On the tiny desk, she had laid out the tools of her trade – the half-used pots of rouge, the eyelash curlers, the hand mirror.

As quietly as I could, I stole my best dress from the cupboard and then I fled into the street.

Two days later, the letter would have arrived.

It was a Sunday – Agathe's day off, and so she would have been up early – it would have been Agathe who found it and tore it open, never mind that it was addressed to Mathilde, greedy hands ripping the paper in case there was something personal inside. Levering herself into a chair, she would have read André's brief note explaining where I had gone and why. *Post as secretary. Hope this will cover unpaid rent. Expenses. Thank you for your kind understanding. Do not hesitate. Yours, &c.*

And then it would have dawned on her that money was in the envelope – she would have held it upside down and the notes would have fluttered out and lain on the parquet, twitching in the breeze from the open window. One hundred, two hundred, three hundred. Agathe's fingers flexing; her piggy-eyes glinting, for André, with his rich man's lack of understanding, had more than bought off my deposit and my three months' notice; the three hundred francs was a sum the like of which Agathe could not have earned in several months.

She would have made a rapid calculation, and folded the

notes quick as winking into her pocket, and the letter – the letter she would have burnt, letting the fragments sprinkle into the breeze, as she stood at the window where we always used to smoke together. She would have spread herself with a grunt into the place I used to occupy, and thought no more about it.

Mathilde would have continued hoping for a word from me to explain my sudden absence. 'Do you think we should alert the police?' she would have asked, and flinched at Agathe's snort. And then, what would she have said? *We run an honest little boarding-house, officer, visited only by a few discerning gentlemen…*

Nevertheless, she would have waited for a note or a letter. Late at night, thinking she heard a light step on the stairwell, she would have paused in her needlework and listened.

'You shouldn't be surprised,' Agathe would have said, flicking her cigarette end high over the rooftops and watching it fall in a firefly, ember-tipped arc, 'she was always flighty.'

Juliette and Adèle
1967

'So you just left without saying goodbye? Without leaving an address?'

'Imagine if she'd followed me to the house. It was my big opportunity.'

She looks out of the window, and I don't interrupt her: I'm getting used to these pauses.

Eventually she says: 'Did you say you were going to see the film tonight?'

'Yes.'

'Then you'll see what I was like as a girl. I was beautiful.'

She still has that absent expression. I wait.

She says: 'One day, five years ago, I went to see a plastic surgeon, a man with fine hands and an office behind the Palais-Royal. He took my face like so, pinching the skin here, and smoothing it here, and he never once looked me in the eyes. At the end of the examination he said: *Good news, Madame. We can nip here, tuck here. I can give you back what you've lost.*'

She draws herself up, indignant at the memory. 'What do you think I told him?' she says.

I think about it. Realise I know the answer.

'Nobody can give another person what they've lost?' I say.

She looks at me, faintly surprised. Then she levels her finger, like the barrel of a gun, right between my eyes. 'Very good, Mlle Blanc.'

Juliette, ii.

In the dark of the viewing room, a flickering light, and then the picture forms.

An intertitle:

LA PETITE MORT
OUR TALE BEGINS IN BOHEMIA, A LAND ROAMED
BY FELL BEASTS AND BANDITS...

The screen changes: a jagged landscape, triangular mountains and floating cardboard clouds, and in the background, a tiny turreted manor house.

IN THE CASTLE BISMARCK, THE BARON IS
PLANNING THE WEDDING OF HIS YOUNGEST
DAUGHTER...

A room at the top – cut-out stars and moon visible through a window. A middle-aged man appears, gesticulating and striding up and down. Sitting stage right is a young woman with her face in her hands.

As the actress takes her hands away I feel – not recognition, because I don't think anybody could see Adèle Roux, the person I know, in this frightened, hungry face.

I WILL NOT MARRY FOR MONEY!

The Baron shakes his finger at her:

THE COUNT IS A MAN OF WEALTH AND
DISTINCTION!

BUT I LOVE ANOTHER!
WE LEAVE FOR THE CHURCH AT DAWN
TOMORROW!

Adèle runs to the door, sobs against it, slithers to the ground; flings herself onto her bed. Cries; then lifts herself on one elbow and, after a moment's thought, leaps from the bed, runs to a bookshelf near the door and pulls a large book from it.

MY LOVE FOR MAURICE WILL NOT BE SULLIED.
I WILL CREATE ANOTHER WHO WILL GO FORTH
AND DO MY BIDDING.

Her hands lift:

WATCH ME AS I CAST MY SPELL—
        ...
        ...

Lightning across the film – but not part of the film – and without warning the scene changes completely.

'That's where the missing bit was,' the technician says.

The castle tower is gone – now an Alpine field, strewn with tiny wild flowers. In the background there is a cardboard-looking church, and hundreds of guests milling about in front. They have the unmistakeable air of amateur extras, over-excited and unsure of themselves: one young man sneaks a glance direct at camera, looks away, then looks back and stands, mouth open, until the woman next to him tugs him away. The film technician chuckles.

A man in a velvet tunic runs to and fro across the screen, his hands clutching at his scalp.

The intertitle reads:

THE NEXT MORNING, BEFORE THE WEDDING,
MAURICE SEARCHES FOR HIS BRIDE...

The technician cuts the motor and smiles apologetically.

'We'll never know,' he says, unspooling the film from the reel. Holds it up to the light. 'Here.'

I hold the silky filmstrip, and together we look at the part where the two scenes meet. One minute mirror; next church.

'Was it found in two halves? Did you stick it back together yourselves?'

'No, it was like this when we got it. That's editing cement. They use it to splice pieces of film together. Whoever cut the scene out must have glued it back together again after they'd removed it.'

I run my thumb over the roughness of the join.

A LITTLE DEATH

10. juillet 1913

'SO,' ANDRÉ SAYS, slipping his shirt back over his head, 'what did you think of my wife?'

There hasn't been time for talking, in the first tumble on my own feather bed. The room is moonlit grey; the ormolu clock on the mantelpiece of my new room ticks quietly. He sits on the edge of the covers, his hand still resting on my thigh, smooth under the rich person's sheets.

I arrange my face into the malicious smile he will expect. He smiles back, reassured; always fastidious, he clears his throat and buttons up his trousers. 'No doubt you thought yourself more attractive and more talented,' he says.

'She's what I expected,' I say airily, and he nods and shrugs, happy with the diplomacy of the answer. 'Same time tomorrow night?'

I plump up the coverlet under my fingers. What he will expect me to do: look triumphant.

Thomas had been the one to show me to my room earlier that evening; up, up and round the great spiral staircase, my valise handle sticking to my palm. The walls were papered in cool silk, embossed with fleur-de-lys. Above us there was a cupola, a disc of indigo: an eye peering through the roof.

Each member of the household had their own floor. Terpsichore's was the first and smelled of nothing: the walls of the corridor were draped in pale yellow silk. André's, the second floor, smelled of the factory: cordite and business sense.

And then, knowing, expecting a reaction, Thomas said: 'This is for you.'

He had opened the first door in the third-floor corridor and stood aside to let me pass. I didn't go to the bed or the wardrobe in chocolate mahogany or the cold china vase on the dressing-table or any one of the hundred other beautiful things the room contained; I didn't exclaim girlishly – I was too proud, in front of Thomas. Instead, I crossed to the window and leant out from the waist, squinting into the sun. Directly below was a flagstoned terrace, with a balustrade, and two mossy stone lions for sentinels; it was lit with lanterns, just starting to show in the fading sun. Beyond it, the lawn stretched away for half a mile or so, until it met the fringe of the Bois de Boulogne.

I said, keeping my voice level: 'This is very nice.' A great wash of happiness: *Look, look where I had got to.*

'The Durands take the evening meal at eight. You will hear the dinner bell chime.'

When the time came, I hovered on the upstairs landing, waiting to hear them go down; not wanting to be the first to arrive. As soon as I heard doors opening and shutting I ran downstairs.

When I entered the dining room, I noticed a change in her straightaway: where in our interview she had been calm, now it was as if she was surrounded by a heat haze of energy. She was taking snails from their shells with a miniature fork, her other cutlery laid out before her like a butcher's implements: knife, scoop, tweezers. Not timid: cheerfully pulling at them until they gave way.

A chandelier hung twinkling from the ceiling; servants stood blending into the walls, waiting to serve food from the sideboard. The polished table gleamed my own ghostly image at me; she was seated near the door and André sat at the far end, his back to the French window. He looked up at me and I felt, as clearly as if he had really done it, his finger trace my cheek: *pretty little devil.*

'Do you find your quarters to your liking?' he asked.

'They are extremely comfortable. Thank you.'

He had risen into a reverential half-bow; now he sat back in his seat, his smile in the corners of his mouth.

I looked down at the finicky morsels of food: *amuse-bouches*, a miniature egg perched on a salad, and the snails and dish of sauce – toy dinner – and hovered over the cutlery until I could be sure what each was for.

'Mlle Roux saved my life today,' Terpsichore said.

André pressed his thumb into his wine glass: miniature pink lines sprang to life along the stem.

'Yes, it happened like this: I was re-reading *Thérèse Raquin* by M. Zola, which as you know,' – she paused to press her napkin to her mouth – 'is a great tragedy of disappointed hopes and loveless loves.' Her eyes were busy on the table as she spoke, and her hands swept the snails' shells fussily back into their silver dish. 'I had come to the final paragraph, so desperately sad, where Laurent and Thérèse take the poison and collapse into each others' arms, unable to bear the weight of their guilt.' She lifted her wine glass; her eyes twinkled over the top of it. 'And I sat on my sofa and thought, nothing can surpass *Thérèse Raquin* – I have known it for some time in my heart of hearts. M. Zola is a towering inferno of genius who will never again pass amongst us, so what use is it, then, to stay alive?'

André smiled indulgently.

'So I thought then: *What will it be? Knife, rope or drowning?* My resolve was fixed; I had only to determine the *modus operandi* – I barely heard the door, nor did I hear Thomas escorting Mlle Roux into the room, but unquestionably she rescued me from certain death by my own hand.'

André snorted and smoothed his cutlery, repositioning it on the tablecloth; then looked up as the fish course was brought.

'How do we know that it was not Mlle Roux, performing voodoo in the back of our automobile, who put such thoughts into your mind in the first place?'

She levelled her knife at him down the table. 'We don't. Mlle Roux is therefore a rescuer or a bird of ill omen, depending on your point of view.' She smiled her bright, interested smile. 'In any case, the great work of saving me from myself begins tomorrow. Mlle Roux must always be on hand with matches, to set alight any book which might distress me; to remove tempting nooses, to whisk sharp objects out of my reach.'

André dipped his eyes to his food, smiling and prodding the fish with his fork. I looked up at her, and found she had absented herself, lifting her wine glass and staring at a point in the dark window past André's head. Her neck drooped slightly, in the way that tall people's sometimes do.

I dissected my sole into smaller and even smaller pieces, irritated by what she'd said. She expected me to be at her shoulder with the matches, always on hand to shelter the corners of furniture. It was as if I was a negative person – someone she would only notice through the things I removed.

The shutters in my bedroom window creak in the night air. At the doorway, André pauses: 'The two of you don't have to be enemies.'

'You'd prefer it if we were.'

He grins, and is gone. His light footsteps patter down the stairs to his rooms one floor below, and there is the sound of his door gently shutting.

11. juillet 1913

THE NEXT MORNING I woke up naturally for the first time in years. It was wonderful: listening to the sounds of other people having to work; scratching at André's leftover papery scales with my thumbnail.

The house was all small sounds: the clatter of pans in the kitchen, the sweep, sweep of the housemaids scrubbing down the terrace outside; the regular tread of Thomas carrying food trays to the different occupants of the house's three floors. What there wasn't: polite conversation between Mathilde and Madame Moreau, comparing last night's prices on the landing; Monsieur Z's whining sea shanties echoing up from the street. I'd write to Camille later.

Finally the footsteps came outside my door, and there was a discreet knock and the rattle of a breakfast tray being set down. 'Madame expects you in her study at nine-thirty,' Thomas whispered, and then his soft pad away down the stairs again.

I hopped out of bed and dragged the tray into the room; examined the meal. They had gone to the other extreme from last night's picky nothings: now there was fried kidneys and coffee thick as oil. I pushed the tray out of the room again with one toe, unable to stomach it; and then, because it was still before nine o'clock, dressed and went to explore my domain.

The corridor was warm and sunlit: to the right of my bedroom, doors ran away along a corridor to a picture window at the end, beyond which a tree moved soundlessly, its leaves quivering in a light wind.

I stepped across the carpet runner to the door almost opposite my room, and tested the handle. By daylight, the paintwork in the hall had a bleached-out, dusty look of disuse; the door knob rattled uselessly in my hand. Pursing my lips, I walked to the next door – another set of weary paintwork – and gently turned the handle. Nothing. The same for the next door, and the next, by the window. The leaves outside ruffled, discontented; I tried the rooms on the other side of the corridor, but they were locked right the way back up the passageway to my own room.

I stood outside my bedroom with my hand on the door frame. *This floor is yours*, Thomas had said, beaming at me. But he had not even given me keys to my own room, let alone to the rest of my miniature empire.

Just then, from inside, the clock on the mantelpiece chimed nine-thirty. I pulled the door shut and crossed to the top of the stairs.

When I reach Terpsichore's floor I don't know which is her study so I listen, and sure enough, there is the rasp of a page being turned, behind the door at the far end of the passage.

I knock at the door and hear her clear her throat. 'Come in!'

She has laid the novel on the sofa beside her and now her hands are clasped together. She isn't the only one posing: the room is long and light, with bookcases lining two walls. It reminds me a little of Père Simon's front room, but these books are all new, and if dust spirals in the shaft of light from the windows, it is only showing off. On her left, propped against a cushion, is her discarded breakfast tray: a brioche bleeding a dab of jam.

'Just in time,' she says, and casts her eyes at the novel splayed on the seat beside her, 'I was almost at the poison scene again.'

I'm confused. 'Didn't you read that last night?'

'I needed to look at it more closely.'

'Why?'

She smiles a wicked-fairy smile. 'I wish to understand the best method of poisoning someone.'

'Who?'

'My husband. I'm running away.'

I don't know the rules of this game, so I go quiet.

'So my routine,' she says, 'until the studio comes to its senses: I read in the morning, scripts or studio business, and the afternoons are for exercise and social calls. Does that sound amenable?'

'Yes.'

'Good.'

She looks at me, eyes slightly narrowed, thinking me over.

'You may begin by answering some of my correspondence,' she says, and gestures to the desk under the window, where a stack of handwritten letters is waiting. 'Just write a brief note of acknowledgement to each.'

I don't need a second invitation to sit to something straightforward, and besides, I want to show her what I can do; I pick up the topmost letter, dip the pen in ink, and bend my head. For a while the only sound is the scratching of my nib on the paper, and the soft turning of the pages of her novel. Sneaking a look, I can see that she has started again at the beginning.

The letters are very mixed. They range from the romantic to the pornographic in tone, but are always fervent in their enthusiasm. Five contain the phrase: *You are the greatest actress of your generation.* Two are semi-religious: *A living star come from our Lord to save us.* Ten or more are fiercely competitive, as if she was an army to be laid bets on: *My brother and I have fifty francs that you will be more famous than Max Linder in half a year.* All of them, without exception, write as if they know her; seven ask for her advice on matters of the heart. *Should I marry the man my parents require, for his farmland? But he bores me to tears. And his fingers are so square, the backs of his hands so wiry-haired, and besides,*

I always wanted tall children. And then answer themselves: *I know you would tell me to marry for love, but where will I find a loveable stranger of reasonable height?*

An hour or so passes and my writing hand starts to get tired. She looks up, though I have not spoken, only begun to massage the knuckles.

'Do you need to stop?'

'No.'

She bends her head to her novel again. Her eyebrows are drawn together in concentration, as if someone has put a stitch through them.

At midday the pile of outgoing letters is much higher than the incoming, neatly stacked instead of the tottering mess I had first found on the desk.

As the clock finishes chiming she closes the novel and looks up, smiling.

'Quite the little worker,' she says. 'The previous—'

She clicks her tongue and looks at her feet; she was going to say, *The previous assistant.* 'Not fair,' she says.

I fuss with the composed letters, for something to do. I like the feeling of almost having been in on a secret.

In the afternoon, she shows me the garden behind the house.

There is a high wind which blows our hats half off our heads, and makes us walk at an angle.

After twenty paces she stops, and with a catch of a laugh says: 'May I take your arm?'

For a moment I go blank, then I realise it is to steady her, and hold it out for her to take. She curls her arm round the crook of my elbow, and rests the palm on my wrist, a steady pressure but not too tight. The backs of her hands are very smooth, but unexpectedly covered in a mass of freckles.

She laughs as she catches me staring. 'My whole arms are like that,' she says, too loud because of the wind. 'When we made *La Dame aux Roses*, the amount of Leichner No. 2 to cover it, you wouldn't believe.'

We walk on in silence for a few moments, and then she pauses, and looks around her, the mistress surveying her terrain, and says: 'Where you're from, is it like this, or something else?'

I pretend to be looking at the green lawn and the white blooms in the rose beds, and manage to think of a longish thing to say. 'Not much like this. It's hotter, and the plants are different. But there isn't much, just a few houses, and occasionally people pass through on their way to somewhere else.'

She laughs. 'Bandits and caravanserai, how exotic.'

'No,' I say, 'just deserted.'

She frowns as she reaches for a white petal, bruising it between forefinger and thumb. 'But you got out.'

I don't say anything.

She pulls the petal off, taking a scattering of others with it, scurrying away on the wind.

We walk on for a while. Suddenly she stops, puts her hand palm up to the sky and tuts. 'Rain,' she says, and turns to direct us towards the house.

'Thank you for your company,' she says, when we are back in the salon. 'See you at dinner.'

Then she bends to pick up *Thérèse Raquin* again.

All round the garden I've been thinking about whether I dare say it, and I do: 'I'd use the poison from *Romeo and Juliet* by William Shakespeare, to put him to sleep, and then make my escape. That way nobody has to die.'

'Very good,' she says. She looks into my face, frowning; then the gaze wavers down my body to my feet, and all the way back up again. She looks down at the book, and turns one page, then another, as I leave the room.

The next day, the silence between us, as she reads, and I work, is peaceable; drowsy, even, as the weather is warming, the chill spring winds having faded away.

Later that morning, I look up from my work and see how she frowns at the book she is reading, as if the text is upside down or in another language: her concentration is extraordinary. Her lips are puckered; occasionally they pull back into a sneer, and then purse again.

She looks up suddenly and smiles, crinkling her eyes and lifting the book to show me the new title. 'I've moved on,' she says. 'No more poisoning.'

'Any good?'

'Yes.'

I want to ask something else, but she has dipped her head to the page again. She looks as abstracted as two nights before, when she stared out of the dining-room window; she lifts her thumbnail to her mouth, chewing on the skin there as she reads.

That night, I am propped on my elbows and André is kissing his way down my stomach. 'Are you learning much to your professional advantage?'

'Yes,' I say, shutting my eyes.

'You don't sound sure.'

'I am.'

'Not just answering her letters?'

'No,' I say, 'why?'

'No reason.'

He draws a line with his tongue and I drop back onto the pillow. 'There's nothing wrong with correspondence,' he says. His tongue reaches its destination and I sit back up to watch.

Five minutes later he says it again: 'Correspondence makes the world go round.' His curls bounce on his forehead, perfectly in place. *One of these days*, I think, *I'll tear one out, just to see the look on his face.*

17. juillet 1913

As I walk into the salon she throws her novel down.

'I thought we might pay a visit to my great friend Robert Peyssac. The studio gossip is that he has a film in the preparatory stages, and I want to talk to him about a role before the news gets out.'

Without waiting for my answer she leans across to pull the bell.

Hubert punches the horn despairingly as we rumble over the Pont-Neuf onto the Ile St Louis: horses and carts bombard the automobile, an omnibus trundles past, two rows of blank-faced passengers crammed in, their hat brims touching. At the end of the bridge a bread delivery-woman steps off the kerb, stops dead in the road and stares in at us, her hands gripping the arms of her cart; she mumbles her lip, and then proceeds slowly across the road, threading between the stopped vehicles. Hubert leans out towards her, tapping the side of his head.

'Leave us here,' Terpsichore says, as we turn onto the little central street of the island, 'his house is just next door.' Hubert rides the car up onto the pavement and hops down from the driver's seat to let us out.

The air is sweet with lunchtime cooking smells from restaurants on the island: cassoulet and crêpes. The river flashes unexpectedly at us down an alleyway next to the block, barges drifting in the sunshine, tethered to the quays.

At the front door she turns to me. 'How do I look?'

She is wearing a blouse and skirt in a cobwebby grey; the sleeves of the blouse taper where the freckles start to emerge at her wrists. In the strong light from the river I can make out the down on her cheeks and the flecks of her irises.

'You look the part,' I say.

Looking down at me from her great height, she smiles.

'Now, Peyssac was used to my old assistant. He likes his women quiet; doesn't like to be interrupted.' She leans in to press the buzzer. Far inside the house there comes an answering ghost ring. 'So let me do the talking. He liked Huguette, she was a paragon, quiet all over; her mouth moved but there was no sound.'

I hesitate, then turn my face casually away and say: 'Is that why you hit her?'

'It was a projectile. Not *mano a mano*. And besides, she recovered, for which we are all extremely grateful.'

'You don't seem grateful.'

Her smile is enormous. 'So sharp, Mlle Roux, I could use you to peel an orange.'

I suddenly find I am hot all over: under my collar and on my cheeks, damp-palmed, and glad, because she is distracted: the door has opened, a retainer bows low. We step inside.

In the central courtyard of the big house there is a cobbled square of sunlight, scattered with pots of geraniums.

'Please wait here,' the retainer whispers, and vanishes through a doorway on the far side. Less than a minute later he reappears: 'M. Peyssac will see you now.'

Terpsichore tosses her head and follows him back through the doorway. She has forgotten me now, sweeping down the corridor. I scurry after her, a solo duckling; up some stairs and into Peyssac's parlour.

A grey stuffed gull glowers down at us from a glass case; in the corner, a column of *immortelles* ascends the striped wallpaper, silhouetted lips parted in expectation of the hereafter. And in an armchair in the corner is a little man past the point of middle age, with an immaculate white goatee. He is framed in the light: I can imagine him adjusting his chair fussily as we were announced.

'My dear!' Peyssac cries, bouncing to his feet, all the while looking over her shoulder, his gaze darting everywhere, sliding off me. 'How wonderful! And you are looking so well!' He reaches up to hold her shoulders and look into her face.

'Robert, it's wonderful to see you again,' she says, bending to put the *bises* on his soft cheek. 'May I present Mlle Roux, my new assistant?'

I bob my head. Of course he is too polite to ask about Huguette.

'Charmed,' he says. 'I am Peyssac.'

I nod mutely; from the corner of my eye, Terpsichore's lips twist into a smile.

'Charmed,' he says again, nodding approval at the straightness of my spine. He snaps his fingers to the butler standing in the doorway: 'Tea? Coffee! Cake!' To us: 'Well – sit,' and waves to two wing chairs. I am careful to perch on the very edge of mine.

Terpsichore: 'It's so nice to see you again, Robert. How are the children?'

Peyssac waves away the question, chortling: 'Manon is so high, every time I see her she's shot up another foot. Micheline does the most astonishing sketches: a real little talent!'

'And Marguerite?'

'The same. Perpetually exasperated with my long hours, but she says she still loves me. What more can one expect?'

Terpsichore nods and laughs, as if charmed by his witticism. The sunlight slants down to a point in the middle of the Turkish rug, and suddenly the conversation has grown strained. She and Peyssac smile at each other, and he says: 'To what do I owe the pleasure of this visit, Luce?'

I flush, and hope nobody notices. Had I thought Terpsichore was her real name?

'They say you are making a new film. A sort of revenge fantasia, featuring a ghost?'

'As to that! We are at the mercy of Charles Pathé for the money. But surely you know all about *Petite Mort* from André? We are relying upon him to work his tricks for the ghost scene. Surely he has mentioned it?'

Shouts from the bargemen float through the open window, filling the thunderstruck silence. I sneak a glance at her: her throat is mottled red, but she laughs, and if her voice is not quite ordinary then maybe it is close enough: 'Robert, if I listened to one-fifth of what my husband tells me—'

Peyssac slaps his thigh. 'Quite so! Oh, very good! I must remember to tell Marguerite.'

Whilst he is wiping his eyes, Terpsichore rises to her feet. 'We must dash.' She crosses the room and bends over him so that he can plant a full Judas kiss on either cheek.

She straightens. 'Our best to Marguerite and the girls, and good luck for the film.'

'*Au revoir*, Mlle Roux,' says Peyssac miserably as I pass.

But she cannot resist. My chest aches; I want to tell her not to – as we reach the door, she turns and points at Peyssac, smiling. 'If there's a role, Robert, think of me?'

He freezes, a child with his fingers in the jam pot. Her face freezes too; she turns and marches away from him down the corridor, with me trailing in her wake.

We do not stop on the pavement; she marches us to where the car is waiting and stands, white-faced, as Hubert fumbles with the handle.

He hums as we pull away from the kerb; I watch the wheel spin in his capable hands. We drive back over the river and along the rue de Rivoli with its crowds of tourists and shoppers.

'You see, Mlle Roux,' she says, smiling but not really, 'one is only as good as one's last good role.' She turns her face to the window.

She is quiet again until we are back on the Left Bank, and then she puts her hand over her mouth; her voice comes through her fingers.

'They are piss-weak. Men! Let themselves be pushed and prodded—'

Her great eyes staring out of the window. She says: 'Even when I was the toast of the Comédie Française, it was always doublespeak! Even when the Crown Prince of Russia waited outside my dressing-room every night – even then, parts came, parts went, and we never knew which of us actresses would be favoured next. I didn't come to Paris to be rotated on a spit, and kept in the dark, and played against my friends. Do you know what he said to me, the Tsarevich, staring down his imperial nose? *In Russia we would never treat our artists so.*'

She's too bright to be looked at, and yet it is impossible not to look at her: the flared nostrils, the flush on her neck.

'Peyssac will have asked Eve Bray,' she says, biting the tip of her thumb, 'or Lily Lemoine, or Vivienne! She couldn't act her way out of a sack—'

I search frantically for something to distract her: 'How did you come to be an actress? How did you come to Paris?'

She stares at me; for a long, awful moment it seems she will reach for something, anything to throw at me; then her outline softens.

Luce, i.

Luce's family were Norman, but Luce is not a Norman name. It has echoes of the Mediterranean, and Luce's parents, minor aristocrats, felt sheepish at the christening. Nothing could be further from the south: the wind howled around the abbey church, and mist swept in from the Channel. A maiden aunt stifled her cackles in the third pew – just outside of those reserved for proper family – and remembered the time she and a young cousin had tried to bottle light in a jam-jar during a seaside trip. It was to this sound – high unrepentant laughter – that Luce was given her name.

She was a tiny baby, with such odd-shaped eyes that the midwife's first thought was of those children one sometimes heard of with the beginnings of second heads sprouting from their necks, or webbed feet, as though they were born for being underwater. The midwife had only once seen something of the kind, amongst a poor country family who had welcomed the baby just the same, whisking it away from her so quickly that she barely had time to believe what her eyes were showing her: the stump of a tail, still translucent in newborn frog-skin. It could be hidden under fashionable dresses, but the midwife wondered what happened to these children, all the same. When she handed Luce to the nursemaid, who handed her to her mother, it was with a downcast look, almost an apology.

There was no need. Luce's mother, who at thirty-five fully intended this to be her last child, thought she had never seen anything so perfect.

'She's the picture of you,' she said, holding up the baby to her husband.

As she grew, Luce was enthroned in her similarity to her parents.

She was younger than her brothers and sisters by six years, the only baby in the house, and visitors quickly understood she was the favourite, and took care to toe the line, exclaiming how like her father, how like her mother, she was. She was set apart from the other children by treats, presents, and time spent dandled on her mother's lap; by kisses dropped on the down of her head. Where the older children had been brought into their parents' company only a couple of times a week, to greet each other solemnly and perhaps recite a morsel of verse, Luce was in the great salon with them almost every afternoon.

The nursemaids pursed their lips, and muttered behind their hands – but the Marquis and Marquise ignored them. It was 1880: in America, Thomas Edison was founding his landmark magazine, *Science*. In Germany, Cologne Cathedral was finished, a mere six hundred years after construction was initiated. In Normandy, the neighbouring Duc de Polignac had married a Canadian steel magnate's daughter for a dowry of seven million dollars – and he was still invited to every social function. The Marquis and Marquise, gazing fondly at their daughter, felt a daring thrill at treating her differently from the others; this warmth and proximity, the way they could brush the fine hairs on the child's fontanelle whenever they chose, and hold her up to the window to see the horses being led out to pasture. Perhaps this was what it felt like, being modern.

What Luce's brother would have said about Luce, aged five: she is an oddity. She won't play games. When we try to trick her into playing hide and seek in a far-flung attic, she ends up back at the beginning, watching us run after her. And then, when she can hear an adult is near, she cries, and when they ask her why she's crying, she points the finger at me.

On Luce's sixth birthday, the Marquis and Marquise organised a party for her, five times as lavish as for any previous child. A juggler and a puppet theatre, a collation for the villagers and servants served on the lawn. The older siblings were offered pony rides, and grew frantic with sugar; the afternoon took on a hazy logic of its own, and Luce, wanting a pony ride too, threw a tantrum.

She ground her fists into her eyes and turned puce: the Marquise held her, but she was inconsolable. As she howled, her brothers and sisters' faces turned stony. Servants' eyes narrowed, too; but her parents were distressed by her distress.

The Marquise snapped her fingers to have her own mare fetched from the stables, and to hoist herself side-saddle and have Luce hoisted up beside her.

The Marquis stepped forward. 'Is she big enough?'

The Marquise smiled, and shrugged, and held the child closer. 'Just a canter,' she said, 'just a run to the boundary and back.'

'Take me riding, Mama,' Luce said, imperious.

The Marquis's instinct to protect vied with the enchanting picture before him – Madonna and child on horseback.

'What harm can it do?' he said.

It was only established afterwards, from a logical regression of the sequence of events, what had happened. The manservant who rode out in search of the Marquise two hours later found the mare, rolled on its side and white-eyed, and the Marquise a few feet away. They were on the other side of a hedge which the horse had failed to clear.

Predictable confusion. The manservant picked up the Marquise's body and rode with it back to the house; the Marquis, who had sat waiting, his hands folded in premonition, came out to meet him and collapsed. A second trip was needed to go out and look for Luce. It was dark by that time; the sweep of the lamps found her lying quietly just ten feet from the dead horse, with an open fracture where her femur protruded through the skin.

The wound healed gradually, leaving a patch of shiny skin where the bone had come through. In her attic room, Luce practised walking with two sticks, then one, then none. She was discouraged from spending time downstairs by the maids who looked after her.

The Marquis had become a person glimpsed, in his dark suit, through half-open doors.

A few months after the accident, he made the trip to Luce's room.

'Pack her things,' he said to the maid, 'she is going to Paris tomorrow, to live with my sister there. It is all arranged. It is high time she went to a real school.'

There was nothing; no hesitation. The maid stayed in her curtsy position until she could be sure that he was really gone.

17. juillet 1913

IT WAS CHILDISH TO IMAGINE I could make it better –
and I wanted to be anything but childish: so I said, 'It's sad.'

Her face was turned away from me, to look out of the
window at the green-gold light dappling through the trees; we
were almost home. 'I suppose it is sad,' she said. 'I suppose it did
happen to me.'

She half-shut her eyes and leant her neck against the back of
the seat. The length of her throat was white against the leath-
erette seats.

The car drove in at the gates and rattled up the gravel drive;
Hubert held the door open for us.

She seemed almost to have forgotten I was there; she set off
up the stairs and I followed. She walked so fast it was difficult
to keep up with her. It was only when we reached the door to
her study that she turned and said: 'I won't have anything for
you this afternoon. You may sit with me and read, or sew, or
you may retire, I don't mind.'

I said quickly: 'I'll sit with you.'

She nodded, neither approving nor disapproving, and we
went into the salon. She picked up a paperback. There were
no letters, so instead I took a copy of *Comoedia* from the side
table, and moved shyly to the sofa opposite her; she did not
protest, and I sat demurely with the book propped upright on
my knees, pretending to read.

My chest felt tight, and my arms and legs too big. But she
had said I could join her; I was not intruding, was I? We sat in

silence for ten minutes, and then I stole a glance at her. She had flattened the novel on her lap; her face was turned to the empty grate. As I watched, her features grew pinched. It was like one of those chemical substances I had heard about at Pathé, which hardens on contact with air.

She looked, I realised with a little jolt, her age. In the light from the window, fine strands of silver led down like electric wires from her parting to her chignon.

It was not hard to guess what she was thinking about. So we sat like that, with just the quiet sounds a house will make around us, and all that time she did not move, just went on staring at the place where the fire should have been.

At seven-thirty I left her to go and change for dinner; stood looking at my own reflection, my cheap dress, for a long time, and when I went downstairs at eight, I found both André and Terpsichore already in position.

Precise sounds of crustaceans being broken into; the crack of the spines of the langoustines. André tore off pieces of bread and popped them into his mouth one by one, staring at a spot on the wall.

She will say, *Today we went to Peyssac's*, I thought – or even, *Do you know, Peyssac is getting up a little film, he says you are involved, and I said, it cannot be true because how would my husband not have told me?* All with a peal of laughter and her fingers pincering the stem of her wine glass. I looked at her, half-expecting because I had thought the words, that she'd say them; but her head was bowed and she ate with her usual elegant movements, not seeming to notice anyone else in the room. André continued to put the food into his mouth apparently without pleasure, and then pushed the plate away, stretched back in his chair, and threw his napkin onto the polished table. It flopped, meeting its own white reflection.

He could say: *I was going to tell you, of course I was.* Or *I thought we should rest you from Pathé, let the dust about Huguette settle.*

The main course came. Now Terpsichore did reach for the stem of her wine glass, and turn it between forefinger and thumb, making a scraping noise on the surface; André attacked his food with knife and fork, and *scrape, scrape*, went her wine glass on the table, the red liquid swirling and splashing inside.

After dinner, I went to my room to wait for him. It was only half past nine; ages until he would come, so I pushed the windows and the shutters open to look across the park. The lawn had faded to grey. I could smell jasmine and, from somewhere above and to my left, came the ruffling sound of wings being folded for the night.

At times like this the house itself seemed to listen; each joist and timber straining to catch the conversation.

I tilted my head, sure I had heard something – but not from the window side, from nearer the door. My first, erratic thought was: it is her, coming up to my room, she wishes to discuss Peyssac and form a strategy. *She will sit cross-legged on my bed with me, and we'll talk* – my chest seemed to tighten in anticipation, staring in a panic at the coverlet as if she was already there; and then I realised the sound was not footsteps. I padded over to the door, easing it open. Then tiptoed across the landing and, seeing as it was fully dark and where was the harm, down the stairs to the landing of the second floor.

But here was her perfume suddenly, floating towards me, a little piece of her; and here too, it was possible to understand the sounds, peering over the banister to the ground floor and the living-room door ajar: their voices.

The gulp of her sobbing – André, low and vehement – and then her, repeating the same two words, over and over: *humiliate me.* I stood, shocked by the sound of her crying, staring into the darkness; and then the door opened – and André stood in the light spilling out into the hall. His fingers were curled in on themselves. After a moment he marched towards the stairs.

I had barely reached my room and jumped into the bed when the door opened and he came straight across to me; in a few seconds I felt the whole weight of him on top of me, straining against the sheets.

His hands were cold and he worked up to his own release quickly.

Afterwards he lay on his back with his arm under my neck, staring at the ceiling.

'Why didn't you?' I asked. 'Tell her about the film?'

His eyes gleamed savagely.

'Because it's your business now?' he said. 'Whose side are you on?'

Juliette and Adèle
1967

I am just about to pack up my things, when Adèle leans across the table and says: 'And the boyfriend? What does he do?'

'I don't have a boyfriend.'

She widens her eyes. 'It's 1967!'

I say: 'I don't have time.'

'No? But there was someone. Recently.'

'How did you know?'

'How could you not have somebody?'

I feel the blush starting. 'It doesn't matter, does it?' I say, shovelling my pens and notepad into my bag.

She watches me, her face alive with interest.

'And the film?' she says. 'You saw *Petite Mort*? Was it illuminating?'

I stand. She looks up at me, the picture of innocence. 'It was,' I say. 'Same time tomorrow?'

Her eyes sparkle. 'We do keep our cards close to our chest, don't we,' she says merrily, to herself, as I leave.

18. juillet 1913

THE NEXT MORNING, when I go to the study, she is sitting at the writing desk in the window; curved over her correspondence like a child, a strip of her hair loose, hanging over the page.

'Shit,' she says, holding up the half-finished letter – ink has smeared a fan across the words – and then, seeing me, 'I'm writing to Linder and Feuillade, the same letter to both, telling each that I've been engaged by the other.'

'Why?'

'Don't you want a thing more, if you're told you can't have it?' She shakes sand from a pot onto the ink stain, and then folds the paper and pours the sand off again. I watch her hands move as she reaches for an envelope, slips the letter in and licks the gummed surface. 'Peyssac's finished, anyway. He hasn't had a new idea since 1905.'

'What about M. Durand?'

She stares at me. 'What about him?'

She seals the envelope, turns away to drop the letters onto a tray on the table, then dusts her skirt down, as if searching for what to say next.

Finally she goes to the window, and studies the view, determined, fists on hips. The sky is a flawless blue. 'Let's go out,' she says.

The Allée des Acacias is a long, wide strip of white-dust road running through the Bois de Boulogne. And today it is full of people: some being driven along slowly in automobiles, some in pony traps, but the majority strolling in twos and threes.

'Let us out here,' Terpsichore says at last, rapping on the glass; and the motor cuts, and Hubert hops out and opens the car doors for us.

The other ladies, strolling with husbands and children, notice her: the way she stands, and extends her parasol. And the men, passing by, jog their hands in their pockets and look brazenly at her face.

We begin to walk down the side of the road, following the slow march of the crowd. She doesn't seem to want to talk; she frowns, as she looks at the people walking past. 'Young love,' she says, at last.

I sneak a glance sidelong at her – the straightness of her profile, the way her lower lip is jutting out in thought – and then quickly away.

'And you?' she says, her voice very light. 'Is there a young man waiting for you at home?'

My thoughts turn inescapably to André; I feel my face go hot. 'No,' I say.

She's frowning. 'Nobody at all?'

I keep my eyes on the hat of the lady walking ahead of us.

She looks away and laughs: quick and bitter, and the silence descends again. After a while she says: 'You are an enigma, Mlle Roux.'

And it is in that moment that someone close by says: 'Luce!'

The woman is dressed in grey, with a ruffle at the throat of her blouse: but underneath her skirt I see the toes of riding boots. Her face is long and lean, like a horse's, brown-grey hair pulled sharply back, but the eyes are twinkling, and the skin of her face is leathery, as if she spends a lot of time outdoors.

Terpsichore is grinning; they lean forward for the *bises*; the woman looks at me over Terpsichore's shoulder. Then she takes my hand and shakes it, like a man.

Terpsichore says: 'Mademoiselle Roux, may I present

Madame Vercors, wife of Louis Vercors, former Minister of the Interior.'

'Aurélie,' says the woman. 'Call me Aurélie.'

'*Enchantée*,' I say.

'In the flesh,' Aurélie says, staring at Terpsichore, 'an actual sighting. The girls will be *so* jealous.'

Terpsichore smiles. 'I'm sorry. It's this business with the studio. I've been distracted—'

'I can see that,' Aurélie says, and then says to me: 'We never see her any more.'

When I don't respond, Aurélie turns her scrutiny back to Terpsichore. 'In a month it will be forgotten.'

Terpsichore lifts her chin, her throat moving; to my horror, she suddenly looks as if she is going to cry.

Aurélie says: 'Come on. It doesn't mean a thing.'

Terpsichore gives her head a little shake.

'That's better,' Aurélie says. 'Now, ask me what I've been doing.'

'What have you been doing?'

'Did you know my husband has been corresponding with the anarchists? Oh yes, the actual remnants of the Bonnot gang. *They have some interesting ideas*, he says, *of course I used my personal letterhead, why shouldn't I?*'

Terpsichore smiles fondly at this someone I don't know. 'Oh Louis,' she says.

Aurélie slaps her gloves on her thigh. 'I must go, he's worse than an infant, who knows if the house will still be standing when I get back?' She narrows her eyes. 'Anyway, he's having a little *soirée*. Next weekend. I'll die of boredom if you don't come.'

Terpsichore lifts her head and smiles.

Aurélie winks at me, leans in and pecks Terpsichore on the cheek. Then she waves, and turns and walks away. She isn't like the other women – drifting aimlessly; she has purpose. She disappears into the crowd.

I turn to find Terpsichore watching me.

'So that was the wife of the Ex-Minister,' she says.

I make a non-committal sound and she arches an eyebrow and laughs at me: a surprised laugh, as if she has found something out about me.

'I liked her,' I say.

She smiles; shakes her head, more at herself than me. 'Your mouth gives you away every time.'

Luce, ii.

Luce's Aunt Berthe sits in the waiting room, seeing the spectre of her past flit across the sunlit wall opposite. She is tense with irritation, holding her gloves and purse taut on her knees, smoothing the fabric into submission. She strains her ears but cannot hear anything but the low murmur of voices from behind the audition room door.

On a chair on the other side of the room, next to the door into the other audition room, a lean woman with a Roman nose sits, watching Berthe, who tosses her head, aware of and disliking the scrutiny. Besides her impertinence, the woman is common-looking and poorly tailored. She looks like she knows all about Berthe, though they have not exchanged a word.

'Your daughter, in there?'

Berthe shakes her head and looks haughtily away. 'My niece.'

'The acting competition?'

'Yes.' Berthe suddenly wishes to confide everything, *How ridiculous it is, because this isn't what our family does, we have tried to dissuade her, but she would not be told. How like her mother she is.* The woman opposite is saying: 'My daughter wants to dance. It's better to try the acting, though, because you have a longer career. Ten years is all you get as a ballerina, and she is already fifteen. Have you been to the Conservatoire before?'

Berthe's nostrils flare. 'Never,' she lies. The waiting room looked exactly the same thirty years before; she recognises it all, down to the peeling paint of the ceiling and the little piece of glass missing from the high window.

The door to the dance room opens and Aurélie exits, high-stepping like a pony at dressage. 'I've been accepted,' she says, and her mother clasps her hands in front of her face. 'My darling,' she says, 'you must work hard, you must strive. I am quite overcome! My daughter, the ballerina!'

She looks, astonished, at Berthe, who forces a smile; at the same time, the door to the acting audition room opens and Luce appears.

Luce says nothing to Berthe, who doesn't ask, but simply thinks, *Lord be praised, now we can get on with making her respectable*, and gathers up the child's scarf, still smiling tightly at Aurélie's mother, who is holding Aurélie's coat up for her to put on.

'Did you get in?' Aurélie asks, her arms held out behind her to find the sleeves. 'You look like you did.'

Luce nods, intimidated by the older girl, and obediently wraps her scarf round her own neck.

In the dormitory, it is thought appropriate to have the younger children shepherded by the elder ones, and to mix disciplines, so that dangerous rivalries are discouraged. Aurélie and Luce start at opposite ends of the dormitory and conspire: swapping their way with hair ribbons and sweets down the rows until they are next to each other.

Aurélie teaches her ballet exercises to help her with her stage movements. 'Pretend you are an oak tree,' she says, pressing down on her shoulder.

Late at night, they confide their secret fears. 'I'll only ever be *corps de ballet*,' Aurélie says, matter-of-fact and too loud, so that other girls in the long line of beds rustle. She whispers: 'I don't have it in me, the way some do.'

She looks speculatively at Luce. 'They say you do.'

Luce thinks for a minute. 'They say a lot of things, about how my aunt only takes me home in the holidays because otherwise I'd be a ward of the State and that's common.'

It is a long speech for her, and has Luce's characteristic way of closing off the subject at the end of the phrase. Aurélie settles the sheets about her ears and does a horizontal shrug; she knows different.

Luce takes her first role as a maid in a Scandinavian tragedy in a little theatre in the Faubourg St Honoré, and Aurélie sits in the front row on the first night. Aurélie's face will always be too long and her expression too knowing, but the gentlemen see her nonetheless: rising from their seats and nodding to let her pass to the middle row seat, noting the ballerina's long legs and her hands – even they are muscular – as they grip the stole about her throat.

The lights go down; the play starts. Luce, taken by a violent attack of nerves, looks out to the audience where possible, and at last spots her friend; she relaxes, and the rest of the first act goes better. Aurélie sits with a smile on her face, knowing that Luce has seen her.

The papers are full of it: '*The newcomer Mlle de Jumièges betrays her noble stock, speaking her part with a zest worthy of a much older actress. Her grace and poise are that of a dancer.*' Those critics who have not yet come to the play flock to see her; the sound of frantic scribbling is all that disturbs the reverential silence. It only takes a couple of days before the stage name – Terpsichore, the muse of dance – is coined, which will follow her wherever she goes. Throughout the next year, Aurélie comes to all Luce's engagements, sitting in the front row where possible, once taking an overnight train back from Marseille, where she is playing Odile, so she can attend a premiere.

Juliette, iii.

'See,' says the editor, lifting the strip of film up to the light – delicately, gingerly, with his long pianist's fingers.

'Hand splice,' he says, indicating the section of *Petite Mort* where the missing scene goes, 'uneven, bad workmanship, almost certainly amateur, and now look at the other splices, done in the course of the assembly.' His fingertip brushes a point further down the print, where a thin line joins two frames. 'These were made with a splicing machine, of course, by the film's editor.'

Then he says: 'And you were right about the cement. It's all the same stuff they used in the 1910s. Acetane and dioxane.'

I say: 'So the person who cut up *Petite Mort* was a different person from the editor who made the rest of the joins? And our person couldn't use a splicing machine? But could lay their hands on cement?'

'Yes.'

'That could be anybody.'

The editor has turned his back to me, storing the film strip in its box. 'No,' he says. 'It would be somebody who had access to the materials, and who was familiar enough with the theory to attempt to cut and repair the film by hand. But who lacked the expertise to do it properly.'

He waits. Then, seeing that I have no further questions, he lifts the *Petite Mort* reel into its canister again.

As he is leaving, he stops, fingers on the door frame. 'You said it was found in somebody's basement.'

'That's right.'

'This isn't the safety film stock we use today – it's the old stuff – nitrate cellulose. Highly flammable. If it's stored above twenty-one degrees centigrade for any length of time, it degrades. If you don't handle it right, it may even catch fire.'

I frown. 'What are you saying?'

'Talk to the person who handed it in.'

21. juillet 1913

WE WAITED FOR AN ANSWER to one of the two letters that Terpsichore had written.

The weather had turned dreary; the window panes were spattered with sudden bursts of rain. Terpsichore set me to classifying household bills at the writing desk while she fidgeted and read; when I looked up, I would often catch her staring out of the window, or picking at the lunch tray that Thomas brought, her face pale and thoughtful.

She rarely asked me what I was doing, or told me what she was reading. She just sat there, neck drooping, saying nothing and chewing her lip, for hours at a time.

Dinner times, since the Day of Peyssac, were strained. André always started the meal confidently, talking about the studio and his plans for the next season's films, but finished by speaking almost exclusively to me, as Terpsichore stared over his head to the garden beyond, making the minimum possible response.

At the end of the week, suddenly, over supper, Terpsichore spoke. 'I don't suppose you want to go to Aurélie's party?'

He looked up. 'To what?'

'The salon.'

The crystal sparkled, holding its breath, and he frowned as if trying to remember having discussed it. 'No, but you go.' He made a long arm for a copy of *Le Temps* that was lying on the sideboard.

'Take Adèle,' he said, sheltering behind the news, 'if you need company.'

I didn't dare to look at her, in case I saw disappointment on her face.

But instead she looked neutral. 'Yes,' she said, 'I might do that.'

He cleared his throat, closing the subject.

'There you are,' she says when she greets me the next morning. The air is different in the room: tinged with anticipation. All around her on the settee are copies of *La Femme Moderne* and *La Mode Parisienne*, flipped through and discarded, as if she were looking for something but the thing she wanted has not come to hand.

'I think,' she says, not looking at me, her voice too light, 'I think what we need is to go shopping. I have a violent urge to spend my husband's money.'

Rue de Rivoli is streaming with people; Hubert drops us on the corner of the place du Louvre, swearing under his breath at the hurrying crowd: 'Madame, it's the closest I can get without murdering somebody.'

'We'll only be an hour,' Terpsichore says, and climbs slowly down from her side of the car; I follow, jostling her through the people standing open-mouthed in front of the window displays. The great sign of the department store, LES GALERIES ST. PAUL, twinkles overhead, gold against the grey colonnaded façade; all around me are *oohs* and *ahhs* at the clockwork soldier in the window beating a wooden drum.

She leads me past the shop, and down a side road, and we come to a halt at a front door halfway down the street, next to which a discreet plaque reads: WALLACE MONGE, MAISON DE COUTURE.

The door opens before we knock. A slender man with brilliantined hair stands in the doorway, and holds out his arms with an expression of goodwill. He embraces Terpsichore silently, and holds out a hand to me. 'Wallace Monge,' he says, and I nod, pretending I know the name; 'Come in, come in,' he says, and leads us inside.

I want to look everywhere at once. The walls of the tiny room are papered with designs – elegant female silhouettes. There are orchids in pots, and a miniature palm tree, and a table, behind which a girl my own age is sewing a hem by hand. A row of silk turbans in ascending sizes march along a shelf above her head.

'I have just the thing,' he is saying to Terpsichore, 'let me find it—' and he disappears behind a screen.

The girl looks up from her sewing and smiles at us. I return the smile as best I can, feeling awkward; but she doesn't seem to mind that I am a customer.

'Here,' says the man, reappearing with a sketchbook, which he flips to the back page and holds up for her, so that only the two of them can see.

'Yes,' she says, critical at first, then convinced. 'But can it be ready for tomorrow night?'

They discuss measurements and delivery times; my eyes wander. Gowns hang from hooks on the wall: steel-grey, water-melon, butterscotch. But the dress which catches me out is on a mannequin at the far end: red silk with a wide skirt, the whole embroidered with tiny flowers.

'And for Mademoiselle?' asks Wallace Monge, smiling at me.

Terpsichore says: 'I think she has decided what she wants.'

Wallace snaps his fingers, and the girl who was sewing jumps up and bustles to unpin the red dress from the mannequin. Then he leans in and pecks Terpsichore on the cheek. 'Can I leave you with Denise?'

She waves him away with a smile, and he squeezes my elbow and turns to go.

Terpsichore is watching me, smiling as if from a long way away.

Wallace Monge's foosteps disappear up the rickety staircase.

'You can't,' I say, mortified.

She is trailing a fingertip along the neckline of another dress on another dummy. 'Why? Don't you deserve it?'

In the corner of the room there is a booth with a curtain on iron rings. The girl ushers me inside. She turns away modestly, pretending to fiddle with her tape measure, and when I am in my underthings, she kneels in front of me and begins to palpate, running the measure from my ankle to my hip. When she stands in front of me to pull the tape round my breasts, she whispers: 'Is it her? Is it Terpsichore?'

'Yes.'

She beams. 'They said she had an account. Isn't she lovely, though. Even more beautiful in the flesh!'

I hold my arms out to the sides, like a martyr in an old painting, and look at my face in the mirror over the girl's bobbing head.

She makes notations in a tiny notebook with a pencil so worn down it is barely a stub, and snaps it shut. 'There!' she says, 'we'll barely have to alter it, now let's just see it on—'

She helps me drop the dress over my head. It whispers past my hips, hanging just so, a sheen catching the light.

'Shall we show Madame?' the girl asks, sitting back on her haunches.

'No, don't,' I say, but it is too late, she is jerking the curtain back, and I turn and there she is.

Behind her, the drawings on the wall replicate her to infinity; each of which could be her, the tall silhouettes in their many dresses. But she doesn't say anything, only stands with a strange, blank expression. Her eyelashes sweep her cheek as she blinks once, twice.

It is awful to have her look at me like this: as if she's a stranger. I bob a self-conscious little curtsy to her, trying to make it all right.

Still she says nothing; she lifts one hand, the palm cupping her cheek.

Eventually she says: 'A little narrow in the shoulders.'

The assistant is putting pins in her mouth one by one like cigarettes, and saying through them: 'Yes, of course. Now, shall we change her back?'

Terpsichore turns away, and the girl sighs happily, and rattles the curtain closed again.

When I emerge, smoothing my damp palms against my old skirt, Terpsichore smiles vaguely at me again and we move towards the till.

'I don't have to have it,' I burst out.

'Yes, you do,' she says, taking the pen from the girl, and signing her name with a flourish. The girl blushes at the contact of their hands.

The dress arrives just after dinner. It is spread out on my bed waiting for me when I come back upstairs, and it is still lying there when André arrives.

'Nice,' he says, fingering the substance. 'How much did it cost me?'

He runs his hands rapidly over the fabric, looking for a tag or a receipt; finding none, he gives up.

'Very nice,' he says, standing back. 'I wonder if I should change my mind about the party?'

I bend low over the dress and start to fold it: 'Perhaps tomorrow night, afterwards, I'll keep it on for you.'

'Why not try it on now?'

I push back my hair. 'I just don't feel like it, that's all.'

I can feel him smiling in the dark room. He puts his cold lips to my neck.

24. juillet 1913

MY REFLECTION IN THE MIRROR in my room is fretful. I have smoothed my hair as best I can, but I'm ashamed of the small hairs that spring up on my temples which look so Mediterranean; of the tan of my skin, when everyone else will be pale. The only good thing is the dress, and when I look at it, I feel confused: it whispers to me as I move.

Walking nervously down the stairs, I am met by Terpsichore's upturned face; but all she says is, 'Very nice,' and then turns to the mirror above the console to smooth her hair.

I thought she would look like a stranger to me in her new clothes – a dress in silvery silk, with wide sleeves, like a kimono – but she only looks more like herself. In the mirror, she stretches her lips into an oval and inspects the colour on her mouth, then bats her eyelids: light moves in bands over her hair.

The car rolls along the Quai d'Orsay; stern government buildings rise into the summer evening. A late starling sings from the shelter of the plane trees on the quais as we turn onto Avenue Bosquet; she leans forward to rap on the glass separating us from Hubert, and the car slows and stops outside a white stone apartment block.

A uniformed footman stands outside the large outer door, hands neatly folded. 'Madame Durand, how nice to see you again,' he says, inclining his head. He doesn't acknowledge me; just holds the door open politely for us, and leads us inside.

We step into the tiny lift, upper arms touching, and as my

stomach drops and we ascend, I turn to find her watching me.
'Nervous?'

'A little.'

The footman is shuttling back the iron grille. She leans in
and whispers: 'I have a tip for you. Picture them in bed.'

She winks and, as I turn back to face forwards, my face
raging red, a door is opening and a roar of voices fills the hall.
Aurélie stands in the doorway, wearing a long blue dress and a
tiny hat that fits close to her head, hiding her hair.

'Look at you!' she shouts over the din, exchanging kisses
with Terpsichore. 'Can that be a Wallace Monge?' she asks,
and pushes Terpsichore in a little twirl, holding her hand
above her head. Then she half turns and calls: 'Louis! It's
Luce! And,' – her eyes find mine, and she smiles thinly – 'is
it Mlle Roux?'

A tall, lugubrious man with a walrus moustache appears
by Aurélie's shoulder, and bends to kiss Terpsichore's hand,
and then mine. 'So charmed,' he says, 'I am Louis Vercors,
ex-Minister of the Interior,' and draws himself up impres-
sively. Behind him, Aurélie rolls her eyes and says: 'Can the
Ex-Minister find Mlle Roux a drink?'

Aware of Terpsichore's eyes on me: 'Adèle,' I say, 'it's
Adèle.'

'So charmed,' Aurélie says, and taking Terpsichore's arm, she
leads her away into the room. Terpsichore looks back at me over
her shoulder: a little shrug and a smile that's like a promise.

The room is full of all kinds of people, flushed red faces,
cigarette smoke and laughter. A chandelier sparkles overhead,
but the rest of the furniture in this wide room is modern, all
clean lines and angular shapes; a baby grand piano gleams in the
corner. The Ex-Minister snaps his fingers and a servant appears,
and pours me a glass of champagne.

'Your apartment is very chic,' I say to Louis Vercors, who is
standing mute at my elbow.

He puffs up again. 'It is our official residence; I am granted it in perpetuity in my capacity as a former Minister. On your right, you can see my portrait, painted during my second year in office—'

I swivel obediently, and my eyes travel the room to see where Terpsichore is, and glimpse her glossy head, and her teeth bared in laughter. Aurélie is huddled next to her, their heads close together, pointing out someone else in the room.

I look away. A few feet from us is a strange object: a camera, but a fifth of the normal size, on a correspondingly miniature tripod. Guests are milling around: one reaches out to touch it, and draws her hand back, laughing.

'What's that?' I ask the Ex-Minister, who pauses, irritated at the interruption. 'That is our Pathé Baby camera, a gift of our dear friend André Durand, a device for recording film in the home, for recreational purposes. Aurélie proposes to make records of our *soirées* for posterity. In fact, we used it only last week, at the ceremony of my investiture into the Collège de France in my capacity as…'

I half-turn, desperate; this time Terpsichore sees me, nudges Aurélie and excuses herself, laughing and trailing a hand away from her. 'Please, I think my mistress need me,' I say to Louis Vercors, who nods, sad-eyed – people must be for ever leaving him like this – and go to meet her in the middle of the room.

'Have you tried my suggestion?' she asks.

'I forgot,' – and she is smiling down at me, and the light seems very bright from above, when there is the sound of someone clapping for silence; we turn; it is Aurélie. 'Guests! Take a seat, or if you can't find one, choose the lap of the neighbour who seems most to your taste,' – she grins, appreciative of the laughter – 'we will now hear a *lied* by Schubert from our most esteemed guest, M. Leydermann.'

A murmur, and the guests begin to mill about, picking their positions next to friends. An elderly woman in black begins to flutter her fan; a slender young man in a velvet waistcoat perches on the edge of his seat and shuts his eyes in anticipation.

'Here is as good as any.' Terpsichore pulls two chairs towards us, and we sit.

A few moments later, the hubbub dies down. Someone has closed the window, and the heat in the room begins to mount; a fair-haired young man gets to his feet and moves to lean on the piano. A burst of applause; he bows, all seriousness, and stands, smiling in a glazed fashion at the audience, gathering himself.

We wait, watching him close his eyes and open them again – he is sweating, beads lining his forehead – suddenly he crosses to Aurélie's seat and whispers something. She leaps to her feet, a marionette, clapping her hands together. 'I quite forgot – M. Leydermann's usual accompanist cannot join us, but I told him that someone here would be glad to play.'

A silence; five or six people are looking fixedly at the floor, but not out of modesty; there is the hot, yearning silence of wanting to be selected.

Aurélie is looking directly at us. 'Will you help?' For a horrible moment I think she means me; then I realise she means Terpsichore. Surprise in the room, but immediately there is a buzz of nodding and encouragement; the wish not to be seen to be ungracious, but also a certain ungenerous interest: *Let us see if her playing matches her acting.*

Terpsichore smiles fixedly. 'I suppose I can try,' she says, and there is muted clapping and laughter.

As she gets to her feet, she flashes me a smile – then she walks over and sits at the piano, hands resting gently on the keys, waiting. Behind the audience, Aurélie stoops to put her eye to the camera.

The tenor laces his hands behind his back. 'The Erlking,' he says.

A silent signal passes between them: how it works I don't understand, but they have decided when to begin, her hands hammering, forcing the notes out; a moment later the singer leans forward and follows her.

Who rides, so late, through night and wind?
It is the father with his child.
He has the boy close in his arms
He holds him safely, he keeps him warm.

Her fingers, so precise, so menacing, branches stinging the face of the riders; the child shrinking away from a pale face hovering, keeping pace with them.

My father, my father, don't you hear
What the Erlking is quietly promising me?
Be calm, stay calm, my child;
The wind is rustling through withered leaves.

It is as if she draws all the light in the room towards her; the notes flowing out, an unceasing stream. The tenor leans forward, his face a gargoyle:

I love you, your beautiful form entices me;
And if you're not willing, I shall use force.

Suddenly, slowing and quiet. The horse stands still, high-stepping, eyes rolling back; a light goes on in the farmhouse ahead.

In his arms, the child was dead.

You can hear the servants clearing away glasses in a room beyond; the elderly woman's fan is motionless before her face.

The tenor gives a tense little bow. Terpsichore closes the piano lid, and everyone is on their feet, clapping.

I expect her to get up from the stool to receive the applause, but instead she is pale and pinched. Just as I am starting to worry, she recovers herself, looks towards the audience, and smiles.

~

A tired-looking young man stands and recites some of his poetry, which has been composed entirely without the use of the letter A; then a thin-voiced woman sings a bawdy boulevard song, hands clasped before her, and everyone murmurs that it's charming: but it can't equal what has gone before; the crowd are restless and thirsty, and soon people begin to slip away to continue the evening elsewhere. The Ex-Minister has snared another victim and is showing her a medal case fixed to the wall. I feel Terpsichore's hand close on my elbow, and she jerks her head towards the door.

Since the music I can barely look at her, so I nod. Aurélie comes across the room and enfolds her in her arms, resting her chin on her shoulder blade: 'It was a fabulous rescue; if I were a poet I'd write you an ode,' she says, and then steps towards me and says crisply: 'We'll see each other again.'

I give a little curtsy. 'I'll look forward to it.'

For a few minutes, driving along with the river oily and shining on our right, we say nothing.

'I didn't know you could play.' My voice sounds odd even to my own ears; I hope the darkness in the car will disguise it.

'What surprises you? That I can play, or that you didn't know?'

'That you could play like that, and that nobody knew.'

'Lots of people play.'

I stare out of the window. I want to say, *But people should only have one great talent, not more. People shouldn't be so—*

'Anyway,' she says, 'Aurélie is far more accomplished than I am. She was just being modest.'

I have made a mean little sound before I can stop myself; she turns her head, and I can hear that she has caught it.

It seems as if she may say something, when suddenly the

statue of St Jeanne slides past, lit up from beneath; at its foot, a pair of tramps swing a bottle and sing to each other; one of them raises the bottle to us as we pass, and Terpsichore's face opens into a smile. She leans forward and cranks the window down: '*Vive la France!*'

'*Vive la France!*' they reply, arms looped around each other's necks, midnight friends for life.

She settles back into the corner, against the swaying wall of the car. In the gloom there is just the lustre of her eyes, gleaming like an animal. I suspect, but cannot prove, that she is looking at me.

The car rolls up outside the house; in the now-familiar routine, Hubert hops out and holds the door open for her first, then me.

The hour being late, there is only one table lamp on in the hallway, turned low. When we reach the door, Thomas looms up in front of us, ready to receive our coats. We shrug them off and he hangs them up, and asks Terpsichore if she requires anything else.

'No, thank you,' she says, and he leaves us, his footsteps padding away down the hall.

She waves towards the staircase. A faint silvery light shows us the swoop of the spiral and the landing up above. 'After you, Adèle.'

There are things to say, but what? I do a little spasm, forward and back at the same time; decide on forward, if it's what she wants: 'Thank you, Madame.'

Her laugh, high and not quite right. 'Now we've been to a party together, I think you should call me Luce.' She pauses; the sound of the sea swells and booms in my ears. 'I think it's time, don't you?'

I turn back to her, wanting to offer her something but not knowing what.

She leans in towards me and kisses my cheek. 'Goodnight.'

She pulls back slowly, keeping her eyes fixed on mine: the pupils large.

I turn and flee up the stairs, taking them two at a time, not stopping till I reach the corridor outside my bedroom, where I pause for breath. On my face, the cool pressure of her lips, now fading, like the touch of a ghost.

Caroline Durand, i.

Two days after Auguste Durand died, Caroline Durand went to Thibodaux-Nouveau to be fitted for her mourning clothes.

As he wound the black crêpe around her, the tailor pushed his pins firmly into her flesh. The pins did not hurt much but she was surprised: only two days, and already the gossip must have begun.

As she stepped out of the tailor's, she felt the townspeople watching from doorways without speaking.

Caroline lifted her chin and turned in at the lawyer's offices.

'Mme Durand,' – the attorney pressed her palm between both his – 'so sad – but if you'll follow me—'

In the inner office, she sat motionless as the lawyer opened the envelope and drew out the précis of Auguste's will.

'M. Durand left his estate to your adopted son,' he said. There was no way to disguise the bald truth of it; he passed an embarrassed hand over his forehead. But Caroline merely nodded – it was as she had expected – and got up to leave.

'Wait,' the lawyer said, 'there is something else. A painting – a painting of you?'

Caroline nodded.

'Your husband specified that you be allowed to keep it.'

Caroline nodded again.

For three months she kept up appearances, writing letters, answering condolence cards, eating less, snuffing candles out earlier, letting the servants go one by one. Of André there came no news.

One day, a gentleman caller came, professing himself an old friend of Auguste's paying his respects. Caroline guessed the man was one of those itinerant collectors who went from town to town enquiring after the recent widows, but she let him in anyway. The man accepted tea and made polite conversation: and as he did so, his eyes roved over the teak and the mahogany furniture and settled on her portrait.

He looked at it for a moment, then looked away, but too late: Caroline had seen his interest flick its tail.

As he left he passed her his business card.

Another month went by. One day Caroline looked in the mirror and saw the delicate point of her wrist emerging from the sleeve of her black dress.

She wrote a letter. A day later the collector sent his apprentice, a scrawny youth whose hands shook as he worked, to wrap up the portrait, and a banker's draft was made out. It was enough for a passage to Canada, where she could be anyone she chose.

When the picture was packed and tied with string and carried out of the door Caroline went to her room and lay in the dark for several hours.

The following day she caught the train north.

She loaded her small valise onto the rack herself, sat slowly blinking in her seat. Outside, green turned into distant blue: mountains unrolled, whose tops she couldn't even see, forests of trees that weren't gummy-leaved or trailing. The gradually lowering temperature left goose pimples along her arm.

Juliette and Adèle
1967

'The painting meant that much to her? That she'd starve herself to keep it?'

Adèle leans forward. 'But it wasn't just a portrait.'

'How do you mean?'

'It was herself, at her best, in a time where everything seemed possible.'

Her eyes sparkle. She says: 'Oh yes, Juliette. An object can be a soul.'

Luce and André, i.

A gallery opening in Montmartre, six years later. The low-ceilinged room is crammed with the rich and the modish, making it difficult to see the pictures on display: but nobody is there for that. The artists huddle resentfully in the corners, smoking; and in another corner, with a private table and a private bottle of champagne, two young women sit, their heads bent close in conversation.

Aurélie has brought Luce to the opening to cheer her up. Success has come at the price of exhaustion; a matinée and an evening show to perform every day for the past three months, leaving Luce wan and on the verge of tears, questioning her career. 'I can't remember the lines,' she will say, distraught in front of the mirror, and Aurélie, never at a loss, has a constant stream of events up her sleeve – shows, galleries, intimate parties – with which to distract her friend.

While Aurélie gets up to fetch more champagne, Luce leans forward in her seat, looking at the room. Without thinking about it, she finds herself studying one picture that is already attracting quite a bit of attention amongst the gallery-goers. Luce feels singled out by the woman subject's gaze, which seems to be directed at her.

It takes her a while to get across the gallery floor, ignoring the curious stares, but eventually she stands directly in front of the picture. The brass plate says *Unknown Woman in Louisiana*, and there is a guide price for the following day's auction, hanging on a little paper tag.

Luce notices the woman's expression: covetous, confident to the point of arrogance, but unfulfilled. There is something missing from the subject, she is certain, and she is so busy wondering what it might be that she does not notice a young man with dark hair cut in a fashionable style entering the gallery, turning the heads of the artists, who know a born model when they see one. He appears to know a few people, but not to want to talk. Then, abruptly, he stops in his tracks, cranes his neck, and heads for the same painting as Luce. The way he elbows his way through the crowd is barely polite. Art lovers edge away from him; a woman whispers to her neighbour that the strange young man looks on the verge of some kind of fit.

André reaches the portrait, and stands next to Luce without appearing to see her, though she notices him; his mouth has opened and his face is grey; he manages to stand for a moment, then teeters.

It is the first time Luce, never a sportswoman, has ever caught anything. To her astonishment the young man is not heavy: his lungs and upper body seem to be made of nothing but the air they hold, and she supports him easily on her forearms, her weight thrown forward over him.

But the pose is too painterly, too perfect, to last, and even as the room's artists are admiring the late romanticism of the tableau, Luce begins to shake. They hold onto each other for dear life, but the collapse is statuesque.

Aurélie comes forward from the back of the room, the stems of two champagne flutes clutched in one hand.

André and Luce bought the painting of Caroline Durand together that very same evening, as soon as André had come round from his faint. They paid half the money that was expected for the portrait – each haggling with all their charm, breaking down the alarmed dealer's resistance – then split the price, paying half each, and signed their names next to each other. They left together, with their first joint purchase held awkwardly between them.

STAGE SIREN ABSCONDS WITH EFFECTS WIZARD: it was all over Paris within the week. Debutantes wept and mothers cursed at André's unexpected removal from the market.

Luce's Aunt Berthe returned home that same evening to a venomous little note about the catastrophe from her closest friend. Rushing upstairs, she verified that Luce's room was indeed empty, and covered her powdered face with her hands.

Towards dawn, Berthe lay staring up at the corniced ceiling of her bedroom; water hissed and boiled overhead, circulating around the pipes of her apartment, and she clenched her fists and boiled too; inside her hair-net, each strand had transformed into an individual snake. There was nothing for it: she rose early and summoned the carriage.

She was forced to admit that the Bois de Boulogne neighbourhood was better than expected. This Durand must have some money. The carriage turned up a long drive and swept to a halt in the turning circle outside the front door. Nevertheless, Berthe tossed her head as she alighted from the carriage, and reached up to knock on the door.

Thirty seconds passed – then a minute. Where were the servants? Berthe had never been ignored on a doorstep before. Then the door opened, and André stood there.

'Yes?' he said.

Berthe was fascinated. The man was in his nightshirt.

'I am Berthe de Jumièges,' she told him in her woman-about-town voice, and smiled. Usually the name was enough.

André shook his head, smiled and shrugged.

The voice had been designed to reassure: *We are people of the world together*, it said unctuously, *if there is an arrangement, we will be sure to arrive at it, you and I*. Now Berthe felt her courage failing; the nightshirt's edge twitched in the breeze. What she had come to tell him seemed far away and improbable now, but she steeled herself and said it anyway: 'Her aunt. I've come to take her home.'

André shrugged again, and smiled.

'I don't think she wants to go,' he said.

A burst of laughter, far back in the shadows of the hallway; and Berthe, peering, saw Luce sitting on the bottom step of the stairs, wrapped only in a sheet.

Berthe tried one final line. 'Her father is unwell. I have done my best to keep the newspapers out of his reach but there are limits to what I can do, and if he finds out, the scandal will be the death of him.'

André's expression cooled. 'It comes to us all in the end.'

Berthe gathered herself. 'Then I think, I know, I can speak for the family, I can honestly say we wash our hands of her.'

Luce's stare said: *You did that a long time ago.*

25. juillet 1913

THE MORNING AFTER THE SOIRÉE, my eyes snap open, recalling what happened. What did happen? We went out for the evening. That's all.

The red dress is hanging on the back of the door, where I tore it off last night: I take it to the cupboard and push it behind the other dresses, so that it can't be seen when I open the door. I get dressed quickly, but go downstairs slowly. I will make some breezy remark: *Quite an evening last night! Does your head ache like mine?*

But when I get to the study, she is sitting at her desk again, holding a letter up to the light. Her fingers are glowing red where the morning sun shines through them, and what I had planned to say, I forget.

She jumps when she sees me and her hand flies to her hair: 'Adèle!' and for a too long, appalling moment I think she is going to say, *About last night…* but she doesn't; she looks away quickly, back at the letter.

'Feuillade wants to see me,' she says. 'It seems he has something in mind for me, and wants me to visit him this morning and read a piece of my choosing.'

She folds the letter thoughtfully; then darts a quick glance and a small smile at me. 'Good news, isn't it?'

'Yes,' I say, and then: 'I could come with you.'

She looks at me for a moment; her hand goes to the back of her neck. 'Oh no, you stay here in the cool. I'll be back before you know it.' She looks around the room hurriedly, and her gaze falls on a stack of correspondence by the sofa. 'Could you send the money to the manicurist? And sort out the order for my hats?'

Then she gets up and begins to bustle, looking for the things she will take with her to the audition, her back turned.

I watch her go from the study window, the top of her head bobbing. Hubert smiles as he holds the car door open. The angle lets me see her sitting in the cab, grey behind the glass, her hands folded in her lap.

She will be going up the steps to Feuillade's office, she will be sitting, he will be steepling his fingers and earnestly outlining the proposal; she will be nodding and smiling, a real smile, like the one last night, over her shoulder, as Aurélie dragged her away.

I close my eyes, tired – last night the Erlking galloped white-faced through my dreams – and when I open them, the sun in the room is so strong that it dazzles me; in the shaft of light and the flutter of the drapes I imagine Agathe standing there.

She smirks: *One would say certain things.*

Nonsense.

You have the signs.

It's nothing.

So last night?

What about last night? It was a soirée between friends.

Agathe studies her bitten nails. *Friends.* The curtain twitches in the hot breeze and she is gone.

The clatter of the front door, and excited laughter; feet on the stairs and she walks into the room, with Thomas carrying her coat. 'Imagine!' she says, 'he has engaged me as a highway-woman in a big film called *Dick Turpin*! And the best thing, the best thing is that if it's successful, I am to tour America with it!'

She looks at me, flushed and beaming. 'America!' she says.

I am thinking of her far away in a city of electric light. 'Wouldn't you have to speak English?' I have said before I can stop myself.

Her face closes. 'They will use an interpreter,' she says. 'Feuillade said it won't matter.'

She moves to the desk in the window and rearranges the corners of the stack of read scripts. She has her back to me.

'What about M. Durand?'

She waves a hand. 'It might be best to keep it under our hat until the contract is signed.'

The booming silence is back between us.

'It'll be our secret,' she says. Then, when I don't say anything, she blushes. 'Why don't you take the car? Go into the city for the afternoon.'

'If you want,' I say.

She doesn't look at me. She has turned away again, back to the desk.

All that week, I presented myself to her in the study, only to find her hand on the nape of her neck; she was distracted, absorbed in paperwork. 'You could visit the Jardin des Plantes, and see the leopard,' she would say, with a smile that seemed wide and flat, like a painting, while she fussed with her hair; or 'You could fetch my novels from the shop in rue des Ecoles.'

At the earliest possible point, she'd look away, as if I was an embarrassment. I'd turn, go down to the automobile and ask Hubert to drive me into Paris.

Faces were just faces, seen through the car window; or they were grotesques, staring at me as if they knew me, then turning away. In the Jardin des Plantes, I walked to the leopard's enclosure and found it asleep in the heat, half concealed by the foliage in its cage. The bookshop owner passed me the packet of new detective novels, and it seemed to me that he wouldn't look at me, and that he withdrew his hand too quickly from the parcel.

The evenings were the worst. André seemed in a high good humour, cracking his knuckles and eating enormous portions; Luce seemed hectic, brittle, keeping up a constant stream of society chatter to which he listened, for once, with keen interest. 'This sun will drive us all mad,' he'd say cheerfully, when she related some idiotic, scandalous tidbit for him.

If I sometimes caught her cool gaze on me, when André was distracted by the butler, I tossed my head, miserable, and would not look at her. *I'll keep your secret*, I thought, *but that is all*, and hated the quickening feeling in my belly, and hated even more the misery when I looked up and she had looked away.

One night, waiting for André in my room, I heard the roiling slam of thunder and the drumming of water on the leads.

I got up and crossed to the window, throwing it and the shutters wide; a gust of warm rain blew in my face. The sky was a sickened yellow; wind chased a stray newspaper across the terrace, and in the far distance, I could just make out the tree line, bending in the rising gale.

The weather seemed all the more savage in the manicured landscape: I had a satisfying vision of rose petals being strewn across the garden.

'What a night!' André was suddenly there, rubbing his hands idiotically as if the weather was his department. 'Shut the window.'

'Not yet.' I wanted to be out in the storm, not in here with him.

'I said close the shutters.'

'No.'

He crossed the room and caught at my arm, pulling me

away from the window, stinging my wrist; he leant out and slammed the shutters.

Immediately the room was watchful; too small and hot. He brushed his hair out of his eyes and turned away, tight-lipped, and began to unbutton his shirt, as he did every other night of the week.

I found I was trembling as I watched him. 'You have got me here under false pretences. You have brought me here as your concubine.'

He turned to face me, smirking, fingers still unbuttoning. 'You talk like a girl in a romance novel.'

'You said there would be professional advancement, opportunities—'

He tried charm, striding towards me. 'And haven't there been chances? Peyssac, he's famous—'

'She barely talks to me, she won't even look at me!'

'Adèle—' He took my shoulders and stroked his thumbs down them; I shrugged him off, and he grabbed me again and this time he shook me: my teeth chattered. 'We've taken you in, we've clothed you—'

I twisted away from him, spitting out the first words that came into my head: 'You're wicked. You're a wicked man.'

His lips tautened: he shook me again, harder this time.

I stared back at him, just wanting him out of my room; he looked at me, scouring my face, and then abruptly gave it up.

'Leave, or do what you want,' he said in disgust, dropping me back onto the bed; he crossed to pick up his shirt and stalked out of the room, slamming the door.

1. août 1913

THE NEXT MORNING I lay in bed, feeling sick.

Finally, at nearly midday, I got dressed and went to stare out of the window of my bedroom. Puddles had formed in the uneven slabs of the terrace, reflecting the blue and gold of the sky. In the far distance, a gardener nipped at the roses with secateurs.

The clock on the mantelpiece ticked the minutes into hours. Several times, I thought I heard Thomas on the stairs, only to find it was just the housemaids sweeping the terrace.

I was suddenly appallingly homesick. I sat on the bed and drew writing paper towards me; even as I dipped the pen to the creamy surface, it quivered with things to say, but as it made contact, the words faded away.

Dear Camille

Dear Camille

The pen hovered. *Dear Camille.*

I tore the paper into thin strips and then across again, so that only little squares were left, and those I dropped into the washstand and watched them turn into pulp.

As I turned away, my eye snagged on the carpet near the window, the spot of the struggle between André and me. There was something there.

I walked over and bent down to pick it up between fore-finger and thumb. A key, finicky and lovely like everything else belonging to the house: cool and slender ceramic body, gold filigree head. It was as long as my little finger; it must have fallen out of André's pocket last night.

I put it to my lips, tasting the metal, wondering. But then Thomas's knock came at the door, startling me: I fumbled to hide the key in my pocket.

'Come to M. Durand's study in five minutes.'

André's corridor was dark, and smelled of his pomade. A cough came from behind the door at the end, directly below Luce's study, so that was the one I chose.

There were two tall windows but the shutters were still closed. André sat behind an enormous desk in the centre of the room, his elbows resting on its green leather top. The surface was strewn with sketches and diagrams.

Over the mantelpiece was a portrait: a woman in a flowing white dress against a green and beige background. It was too dim to see more, but I had the odd impression that she was waiting for me to speak.

André was busy writing. 'I'm going away for a while,' he said, without looking up. Now that my eyes were accustomed, I could see the tower of paper by his right elbow was money: tottering stacks of notes.

'Where?' I couldn't take my eyes off the bills.

'To Marseille. There's an inventor who may have the answer to something I've been looking at. So I wanted to ask what you had decided.'

'About what?'

His eyes clouded with confusion. 'Last night, I asked you if you were staying or going.' He looked down at his blotter again, then his hands moved independently, counting notes. 'Because if you are going, we'll find someone else.'

In another age, you would have said he was simple: his literal-mindedness; his ability to catalogue even things said in anger. I thought of how it had been at Pathé: how I'd loved his curly hair.

I said: 'I'm staying.'

'Fine.' He threw the bigger denominations onto a separate pile. Nothing in his face to show we had ever been intimate at all.

André left the following afternoon at five. Alone in my quarters, I listened to the rap of feet in the hallway below, his cheerful shout *goodbye*, and some muttered conversation with Thomas – doubtless telling him to keep an eye on me. A warm summer rain fell; Hubert dashed through the puddles from the car to the front door, umbrella flaring.

You never know how much noise a person makes, how much their presence counts, until they are gone. Very soon there was absolute quiet – that absence which allows you to hear your blood in your ears. The carpets rustled in the minute air currents crossing the floor. Mice scurried about their secret business in the wainscoting.

I sat, ruminating. At last, the dinner bell rang.

I crossed to the wardrobe and opened it, and looked at the red dress hanging there.

Why not? I thought. It was mine, after all.

I climbed angrily into it, not caring if the material snagged, and then stood at the mirror and patted my cheeks red, licked spit into my eyelashes, smoothed my brow.

She turns to look at me as I come into the dining room, her mouth slightly open. I have a sudden, aching glimpse of her as a child: in the back row of a classroom, suddenly picked on by the teacher for an answer.

André's chair is empty, his place unlaid. Thomas hovers for a moment, out of habit, just to the right of the spot where André's shoulder would have been, then moves on to serve the first course to me.

At first everything seems as I have come to expect it. After asking me how my day was, and after my stiff response, she retreats, becoming a faintly smiling statuette; I stab at my meal.

But it is not quite normal; not quite. She says: 'I was going to ask how you have been filling your time, since I have been so occupied with Feuillade.' Her hand briefly touches her collarbone. 'Was there anything worth reading in my correspondence?'

I think for a moment, then say: 'I found a letter from one of your fans. He wishes to know why you didn't keep to the secret rendezvous you had arranged.'

When I look up at her, she has turned pink, staring at me. 'I know of no secret rendezvous.'

I shrug: 'He seemed very sure.'

She stares, flushes deeper. 'I've never heard of him. Truly, Adèle.'

'He said you communicate via a private telepathy which allows you to signal to him your secret desires.'

Her eyes now clearing as she understands; a strand of her hair free and floating by her cheekbone.

'You are teasing me,' she says.

I smirk. 'Admit it... the telepathy was a good touch.'

She has regained some composure; still smiling, now privately, she has swept the strand of hair back into place. 'And what did you reply?'

'I told him you'd meet him outside his house at midnight tonight, holding a white camellia.'

She snorts with nervous laughter, the most unladylike sound, and brings her napkin to her mouth to cover it.

The silence fills the room, making it warmer. She snaps her fingers for Thomas to open the glass doors to the garden; the evening air rolls in. She has a high red spot on each cheek.

She says suddenly: 'I am sorry to have left you to your own devices so much recently. It was work – unavoidable. But I hope that now things are settled we may spend our days together again.'

She pauses, lips still parted as if there is more to say, then looks at me to see my response.

'Yes,' I say. 'I'd like that.'

'Good.' She beams. The silence descends again, thick and nervous. She fusses, making a play of finishing her dessert, and we don't speak. The red spots have expanded to her throat, which is blotchy.

At last she says: 'Best go up,' hitching her skirt to step free of the chair.

For a moment it seems she hesitates, as if she might say something else; then with a smile, she walks to the door.

I listen to her small, precise steps as she goes upstairs.

In bed that night, I touch myself for the first time. My hand creeps to where André used to press with his tongue, and rubs.

The sheets gather damp around my thighs. I imagine crying out to her, her laying her hands on me. *Is this what my husband does? Or this?*

I clamp my other hand to my mouth, in case I have made a sound.

7. août 1913

THE HEAT GATHERS ITS SKIRTS: the temperature rises hour by hour, wilting flowers, the sun huge in the sky. From Paris, the news comes of young women hurling themselves into the Seine in an attempt to cool off. They say it's a curse, that there is a Jonah in the city – *It's the Russians, the poets, the English, the gypsies, the anarchists, the wickedness of cinema, the vengeful ghost of Josephine Bonaparte, your cousin. Your mother. Not my mother!* – fights break out; the hospitals open their doors to get air: hysterics escape en masse from the Salpêtrière, whooping naked through the streets of the city.

One morning, Luce opens a note from Feuillade, reads it through and pouts. 'His daughter is ill. They are going to Switzerland for a cure.'

She refolds it. 'He won't be back for months. I won't have to spend time at the studio after all.'

She says it lightly, tossing the card back onto the pile of unopened correspondence. 'I'll just have to stay here and annoy you.' She looks directly at me.

I am careful to keep my eyes on my book, but it's too much – I have spoken, been incautious: 'You don't annoy me.'

Her eyes on me, cool and thoughtful. 'What a little gentleman.'

I turn a page, hoping she won't notice how my lip trembles.

Later, when it is too much to bear, being in the same room, I turn my head into that hanged-man posture and pretend to

160

be asleep. Under my eyelids I watch her move to the desk and write a letter: no doubt to Feuillade, sending him condolences on his daughter's illness. I look at every line of her, from the curve of her neck to the straightness of her fingers.

When I wake with a start, she is watching me: motionless at the desk, her pen in her hand.

'You sleep like a child,' she says.

The following morning, I smooth my damp palms on my skirt and go to the salon; push the door inwards, and find it empty.

I am agonised: where has she gone? Then I hear laughter through the open window, cross to it, and lean out to see her sitting in a wicker chair on the terrace below. She shades her eyes and beckons me down.

A package of books and papers has arrived – M. Leroux's *The Yellow Room* and other detective novels. She fidgets, fluttering an Oriental fan; beads of perspiration trickling down her temple, reading fast, scanning the page, occasionally drawing in her breath if something surprises her, and then her eyes lift to meet mine: 'The detective has discovered that the person who was impersonating the duchess is in fact an insane priest on the run from the mad-house,' or 'Apparently the murderer escaped the locked room by means of a special hatch in the ceiling, disguised as a monkey.'

Each time she laughs at the expression on my face. 'The monkey was a good touch.'

I rarely smile back, and I never laugh. She must be able to see it all over my face.

At midday she settles her head back, folds her hands in her lap and shuts her eyes.

Searching for distraction, I pick up the *Revue Satirique* and flip through to the caricatures.

I stare at the page for a good ten seconds.

The caricature is a scene from a tearoom: a person sitting at a table in the foreground – a woman, by the swell of her bosom – dressed in a man's suit and hat. She is leaning across, with her arm looped round the waist of a blushing girl sitting next to her, pulling her closer.

The woman is saying to the girl: *Trousers! Practical, not just for bicycling!* Underneath, there is a legend: *Teatime in Montmartre: unnatural love in its natural habitat…*

I look at the bow ties again, my heart thumping in my chest, the trousers the woman is wearing; at the face of the young girl shying away.

'That's better,' Luce says, opening her eyes and pushing herself up in the chair a little. 'Adèle? Are you all right?'

'Yes.' I put the magazine down hurriedly and try to shoo it underneath my chair.

She shades her eyes. 'Something in the news? Something to do with home?'

'Nothing.' The magazine rustles against my bare feet.

She watches me for a moment longer.

Then she settles back in her chair and closes her eyes, her legs stretched out in front. Her pale skin will burn; I worry about how pink it turns, how quickly.

I practised saying it all last night, till the words sounded like nothing. She twitches, getting comfortable, and for a moment I think I almost have told her it.

But her eyes don't snap open, outraged.

Worse: she'd be kind. *I don't understand*, and then, *you mean, like the ladies in the papers? But you know I am not like that. You know I'm married.*

That night, I imagined what she would look like on the pillow next to me, her hair spread out like a fan. Turning to look at me: the slow blink of her eyes.

As I lay there, I heard a sound. It was like the throb of a bee against the window; I thought the insect must have got into my room during the day, so I hopped out of bed and went to open the shutters, only to find there was nothing there The panes were clear and grey in the light of an enormous moon.

Now the noise had moved, humming away down the corridor outside my room. I went to the door, opened it and listened. Definitely, the sound came from the right-hand end of the passageway – I tiptoed out and stole along, pausing halfway to listen, and laid my ear to the waxy surface of the last door. Very faint now, there was just a trilling sound somewhere beyond.

I knew all the rooms were locked, so it was no surprise when I rattled the handle and pushed to no avail. I leant my cheek on the door – *I wonder* – and then turned and scampered back to my room, to fetch André's ceramic key.

It gleamed cool in the faint light; slipping it into the lock, it turned smoothly and the door swung inward.

A small bird was there, brown and indistinct except for the yellow of its eyes. A trail of broken glass led across the dusty floorboards to where it sat, shuffling and terrified; air rushed through the broken windowpane.

I went to it, cupped my hands around it and shushed it; holding it to my breast I crossed to the window and tried to push the sash up with my other hand. It was locked, the glass grimy with disuse. The bird turned its sharp beak into my skin and beat its wings; at least it meant there was nothing broken. I left the room and went to the corridor window instead, rattled it open and put the bird on the sill outside. It moved to the end of the sill without hesitation: a moment later I saw it swoop away.

Thinking of André, his punctiliousness, I went back to close and lock the door, pausing to peer inside as I did so. The room was in disuse and looked to have been for many years: there was an open fireplace in one corner, and several dust-sheeted items of furniture: a chest of drawers, a standing lamp, an old-fashioned crib. There was nothing that I could see of value; nothing remarkable enough to warrant the locking of the room or the keeping of the key about his person.

On the way back up the corridor I tried the key in the other rooms. It didn't fit any. I tapped it against my teeth, thinking; opened the door to my own room again, and almost shouted out. There was someone in the bed, hunched over on their right-hand side, away from me; it was her.

My agonised squeak died away. There was no one in the bed. It was the sheets, mussed where I had flung them off, that looked like someone's body.

Juliette and Adèle
1967

'My grandmother used to say a bird trapped in a room was an omen.'

Adèle says: 'No, the locked room itself was the omen.'

She leans inwards. Then she says: 'But you still haven't told me about Phantom Boyfriend.'

I feel my lips pursing.

'Let me guess,' she says, 'he was from a rich family, and he wanted you to settle down, and when you said you wanted to carry on working, have your career, he cooled it off.'

I say: 'He wasn't from a rich family. We met at university. We were involved in student politics together.'

'*Politics*,' she says, 'and what was his name?'

'Is this relevant?'

'Oh, because you're the one interviewing me?' She leans back, arms folded.

I tell her how he left my apartment in the middle of my deadline without saying goodbye, took his coat, and never came back. How I'd seen him at the cinema last week with another girl, who was wearing a cashmere sweater.

Adèle listens intently.

When I've finished, I find I'm looking down at my notepad, blinking. Tears of embarrassment, mostly.

She watches me for a moment. Then she leans forward and says: 'Why are you crying? It can't be because you think he is worth crying over.'

I shake my head, my lips pressed together.

She says: 'But there's not a thing wrong with you. Nothing at all.'

Juliette, iv.

The weather clears into bright sunlight. To the north-east, the city is being replaced by another version of itself: gleaming geometric blocks in creams and pinks, instead of grey stone, row upon row of faceless windows; a nest of cranes, their angular necks drooping with the weight of the concrete they carry.

I turn the car down the slip road, and into Vincennes.

Dilapidated and sooty tenement blocks; a café missing several letters from its name. At the end of the street, the Square Jean-Jaurès has been colonised by a couple of cardboard shelters leant up against the wall. The cardboard drips the last of the rain and vibrates in the breeze, but its residents are nowhere to be seen.

Anne Ruillaux's house is a square grey block tacked on to the end of the row of apartment buildings. Once, it might have been genteel: the home of a factory overseer, proud of his second storey. Now, the façade is crumbling off in chunks, and net curtains hang limp in the windows; the house next door has been demolished and lies in a pile of half-cleared rubble.

I lift the door knocker and let it drop.

In the street behind me, a group of small boys has materialised out of nowhere, kicking a lamp-post and staring.

A dog-walker appears at the corner of the street, cap pulled down against the drizzle. The dog whines and strains towards me; its owner pulls at the leash – *Shush, Pitouf, heel* – and walks past, ignoring its yelps.

Something is nagging, something about the timbre of the dog-walker's voice; I look back at the figure walking briskly down the street.

'Anne?' I say. 'Madame Ruillaux? May we speak?'

She turns. The dog watches too, its tongue lolling.

'Can I ask about the film you found?'

She reaches down and unclips the dog's lead – *Go on, Pitouf* – and the dog dashes forward, to stand at the front door, dancing.

A dog-lover's room, not refurbished since the war: ratty wallpaper, an ancient wooden table with chewed legs, a series of black and white photographs on the mantel. In the corner, a wheelchair is folded in on itself, like a stick insect.

Anne has fading red hair, badly cut into a bob, weathered skin, and can't be more than fifty-five: despite the wheelchair, she seems to walk normally. She sits opposite me but says nothing, one hand on Pitouf's neck, scratching his ears.

'You said you found the film in your basement,' I prompt. 'How did you come to discover it?'

When she speaks, it's in a monotone. 'I was having a clear-out. I came across the reel in amongst some other junk. I decided to see if it was worth anything.'

'When was this?'

'A month or so ago.'

'And you didn't recognise it? You don't know how long it had been there?'

She shakes her head to both questions. The same flat gaze.

I ask: 'How long have you owned the house?'

'Twenty years. We bought it when we married.'

'We?'

'My late husband and I.'

'And was the film there when you bought it?'

She thinks about it, shakes her head. 'I'm not sure. I know

there was a lot of junk in the basement.'

'Could the previous owners have left it?'

'My husband was in charge of moving all the furniture in. But he never mentioned the film.'

I say: 'The thing is, Mme Ruillaux, that film seems to have been kept very carefully, somewhere relatively cool. Otherwise it would have degraded much more, or possibly even been destroyed.'

Pitouf whines as she tugs too hard. 'My late husband used to have his workshop in the basement. He ran to hot, so he liked it cool down there. Maybe that's why.'

'Was your husband in films?'

'No. He worked in the supermarket with me.'

'So he never mentioned the Pathé factory, or knew anybody in that industry?'

'No. We met at the supermarket. We always worked there.'

'Did he like the cinema?'

'We used to go once a year, at Christmas. What he really liked was model aeroplanes.'

She shifts her weight in the chair. 'We aren't fancy people. Weren't.'

'When did he die?'

She nods to the wheelchair in the corner. 'A year ago.'

I say: 'Do you have any idea who owned the house before you?'

'No. I don't want any more questions.'

A thin crease has appeared on her forehead, her glance flitting everywhere but my face. It's time to leave.

'Thank you very much for your help.'

She shows me out. The door slams; the small boys across the street stop their game of hoopla to watch me walk to the car.

15. août 1913

THAT DAY, TWO PIECES of post arrive. We have moved back inside; the weather has cooled enough to be tolerable. Thomas brings the salver and deposits it on a footstool in front of the sofa.

She slits the first envelope, pulls out a gold-edged invitation, and frowns. 'Aurélie. She's sent us two tickets to the *Rite of Spring* premiere at the Champs-Elysées. That new ballet.'

I look up from my book.

'Sweet of her,' she says, frowning.

She opens the second letter. Then her hand flattens to her throat, fingers drumming her collarbone.

She clears her throat – 'From my husband. He expects to return on the overnight train and be back with us by eleven o'clock tomorrow morning,' – puts the letter back in the envelope and says brightly: 'That is sooner than expected, isn't it? He must have had some success with his inventions.'

It feels like falling backwards. 'That's good, I suppose.'

'Yes, I suppose so,' she says.

Somewhere in the house, Thomas's voice is low and malevolent; matched by the high chime of a housemaid, being taken to task for bad cleaning; but in the study there is no noise. André coming home early when he could have stayed away. André whistling as he jogs into the house, flinging his hat at the hat stand.

She says: 'It's curious. These past few days, I have had the impression of time standing still, and of the house—' she stops, looking for the right word, 'knowing there was someone missing. As if there was an absence, but not — that it wasn't something to regret. That the house seemed more alive. There was more fun to be had here, within these walls, than anywhere.'

She waits. 'A strange thing, being married. I have woken up each morning, since he went, to the most joyful feeling, the most contentment, since we met. In fact, you could almost say I didn't miss my husband at all.'

Time is a chord trembling. Her skin, too pink anyway from the sun, is pinker still: tender as a newborn baby's.

She says gently: 'Do you understand what I am telling you?'

I sit frozen. *Those women, in their tweeds.*

At long last she drops her gaze to her feet; she seems to gather herself, and says: 'All this talking! Now, will you fetch me my novel? I left it by the doors in from the terrace.'

When I reach the door and look back, she has stiffened, staring at a spot on the rug near my feet, and when she speaks her voice sounds like someone else's: 'We'll still go to the ballet together? We must have a wonderful time, mustn't we?'

I nod, feeling the words recede back down my throat, and close the door softly behind me as I leave.

In the corridor, when I'm safely away from the door, all the crying comes out in a succession of gulping sobs. I run down the corridor, terrified she'll hear.

'There.' She levers my chair round to look at the mirror.

My face: I put two fingers near my mouth, where she has drawn on lipstick, near my eyelashes where she bent, applying kohl, her breath hot on my face.

I am a miserable stranger.

Standing behind me, she says: 'You look like a film star.' Her voice is proud and sad; her eyes meet mine briefly in the mirror, then sheer away.

~

In the dark of the car, I can watch without seeming to. She sits very straight, with her hands folded in her lap, gazing out at the passing houses: lit window after lit window. I enumerate her tiny imperfections: the furrow on her forehead, the patch of dry skin at her throat, scratched red over the weeks, now healing.

'The ballet, Madame?' Hubert says as he opens the cab door for us opposite the shiny concrete block of the Théâtre des Champs-Elysées. 'I don't have to come in, do I?'

She rolls her eyes; he grins. As we cross the street I look back and see him settling into the driver's seat with a cigarette and a newspaper, and wish I could join him. What if I say the wrong thing in front of her? What if she is embarrassed by me, turning away tight-lipped into the crowd?

On the steps ahead is a gaggle of people, all talking loudly to one another; most of them middle-aged and beyond, the men in top hats and the women with their hair piled on top of their heads and ostrich feathers in the set wave. As we make our way up towards the entrance, I catch a glimpse of a familiar figure right in the heart of the throng, his little eyes glinting with amusement, nodding vigorously at someone else's joke. He half turns, sees me, and his face glazes over.

'Adèle?' Luce says, frowning, trying to get my attention; then follows my look to where Peyssac stands. Her eyes narrow but she laughs, and raises one arm.

'Robert!' she calls, loud enough to stop all other conversation. 'Wonderful to see you here!'

Peyssac stares, and the crowd swivels to look at her; and he is caught, he has been seen. 'Yes,' he bleats, 'marvellous!' and like a minnow he turns and slips away.

The crowd murmurs, beginning to piece the gossip together, and conversation starts up again; turning back, she laughs at my expression. 'The old rogue,' she says, to no one in particular, and we carry on into the foyer.

Our seats are in the middle of the stalls. We shuffle past the patrons who have arrived early, two elderly women with haughty, lined faces, and a gentleman with a monocle. 'After you,' she says, all politeness, placing her hand in the small of my back. She levers herself into the seat next to me, her arm lying on the armrest between us.

Her head comes next to mine, too, dizzyingly close. 'There's the Duc de Guise,' she murmurs, 'two rows in front, the one with the weak chin. That's the Duchesse next to him.'

A thoughtful pause. Then she says: 'They say the Duchesse is actually a man, and is frightened to be seen in full light in case her stubble shows.'

'Who says that?' I ask.

'The Duc de Guise's mother, for one. She claims to have come upon her daughter-in-law during her music lesson, singing Berlioz in a pleasing baritone.'

I lift myself in my seat and peer over the tops of the audience's heads till I can see the person: she has half turned to look up into the boxes, and it's true, she is glancing around anxiously, with her shawl pulled up around her ears.

'She does have quite a strong jaw,' I say doubtfully, reporting my findings, and Luce turns back to sit staring at the stage, and laughs.

'What?'

'The Duchesse de Guise is one of my oldest friends. I'll have to tell her she needs a better cosmetician.'

This isn't funny any more. I am blinking back tears, turning my face away so she won't see.

'The Berlioz was a good touch,' she says, and puts her hand on my forearm. The fingers don't retreat.

The lights dim.

A diminutive man struts across the front of the orchestra

pit and, stepping up onto his podium, raises his arms in appreciation of our applause. He turns and raises his baton; I steal a glance at Luce. Her eyes gleam as she waits for it to fall.

A watchful bassoon, swelling to sweep away houses, joined by a clarinet. Dry leaves, lifting and rustling: the audience, whispering behind their hands; two people getting to their feet, threading their way out, with the flushed faces of early leavers. A ripple of laughter courses round the auditorium; the orchestra plays on, frowning with the concentration of sliding up the scales. I glance at Luce: her lips are slightly parted, caught halfway between a smirk and amazement.

When I had asked Luce, in a moment of boldness, *What should I expect, I've never been to a ballet before*, she hadn't even looked up from her magazine. She had flipped the pages and said, *Tulle, expect lots of tulle.*

The curtain rolls back, revealing a stage full of people in costumes of coarse yellow and brown, against a painted backdrop, the swell of a hillside. Immediately behind me, a young rake says loudly: 'It looks like an arse,' and the laughter gets louder. Onstage, the dancers begin to whirl and stomp, throwing themselves into angular shapes: I look at Luce for reassurance – where are the pinks and the ivories, the chiffons and tutus? Someone shouts from a box: 'Nijinsky has found his ballerinas in the asylum!' But it isn't an asylum they make me think of: rather, the animals in the fields at home; rhythmic, undulating, arching their backs. The elderly gentleman at the end of the row has half-risen from his seat, frowning, his tongue running over his gums. He shouts: 'For shame! Filth!' The cry is taken up further forward in the stalls, men and women swaying on their feet; someone else stands up and yells at his neighbour: 'Sit down, imbecile!' and suddenly a fist flies, a white streak, and two men are tussling in the aisle.

A woman next to me stands up, eyes alive with delight at the ruckus. Two more men pile into the fray, and now it seems the whole audience are on their feet, screaming their insults. The orchestra plays on and I clamp my hands to my ears, jostled by the swaying of the crowd on either side. A knot of spectators is leaping the barrier to the orchestra pit and advancing on the conductor: the timpani boom a warning.

Luce's hand touches mine. 'Let's go.' A high sound may be a police whistle or a piccolo. Her glossy head has bobbed away and disappeared; she dips and surfaces, a flash of her frown, her face turned towards me, and she's gone again. I am fighting my way towards the end of the row: there is no way out, just a mass of bodies, and real screams now, blocking my way.

I whip round to escape the other way and see Luce, standing firm against the people pushing against her – her hand extended to me – I reach for her fingertips, catch at them, and she brings her other arm around and hauls me by the waist towards her, until I am pressed up against her, the din whirling in our ears.

I am conscious of my heart hammering, and of how she must feel it; of her right hand in my hair and her left on my waist, their gentle pressure. The noise is all around us; she shifts and her thigh is against mine, and although we are standing in the same way we are not standing in the same way. I look up at her; her eyes are drowsy and speculative; she's saying something.

'What?' I can't hear her over the din.

She keeps looking down at me, lips pursed; then she turns, gripping my hand and pulling me after her as she fights her way towards the exit.

In the foyer, the theatre manager hovers, trying helplessly to staunch the flow of patrons flying out into the street. On the steps, a portly man in a top hat is saying to all who pass: 'An abomination, I will personally bring this to the attention of Monsieur the Minister tomorrow. Assuming tomorrow comes.'

It has been raining; the cobbles are shining wet. Hubert is standing next to the car across the street, looking around in amazement; seeing us, he puts two fingers to his mouth and whistles.

In the car, she leans her head back against the seat and closes her eyes – but she still hasn't let go of my hand.

When we reach the house, Hubert lets us out of the car and says goodnight, and we go inside. It is totally silent. The sky is curiously light: as if it is already anticipating the day ahead.

We walk up the stairs, our fingers laced together, as if it was the most natural thing in the world. At the first landing – her floor – we pause for a moment, the door to her room a hovering outline; she turns to look at me and I look back. Whatever it is she needs to see, she sees it; she turns the door handle, and we walk inside.

A double bed comes clear; thin silvery light through the window. I stand there drinking in all the things that up until now I've never seen: what is private and hers.

Now, as if taken by a sudden shyness, she walks away from me. She crosses to the window and looks out, holding her arms across her body, as if she's cold.

She is standing there, looking out: just her silhouette, the slender, dizzying height of her. She's further away from me than she has been before: and I know – seem to have known for a long time – what I have to do to bring her back.

It will be easier to say it like this, with her facing away.

'There's something I have to tell you,' I say. 'About your husband.'

It feels like a failure; an abomination. There is a humming in my ears.

The clock on the mantelpiece ticks away another second, and another.

She turns to face me. Pale and tall. 'It doesn't matter. Does it?'

I stand rigid where I am.

'It doesn't matter,' she says again.

She walks across the room, slowly and deliberately and stands in front of me; centimetres away. Close enough to see her chest rise and fall in the half-light.

She puts her fingertips to my face and says my name.

Dawn: bruised light. Book spines, arranged on the mantel, came gradually clear; she lay on her side away from me, with her arm flung out.

As I watched her, she opened her eyes – sharply, as if she wasn't sure who she expected to see – and turning, reached for me.

When the first household noises began, we tiptoed up the stairs, her little finger laced in mine, without speaking.

She walked me up to the third floor landing, and there we stopped and looked at each other.

'I can make sure André doesn't come to your room any more,' she says. 'If that's what you want.'

'It's what I want,' I say.

Under her eyes, the shadows were violet. Standing there, she kissed me for a long time, until we heard the servants' voices, very faint, downstairs.

16. août 1913

I SLEPT FOR A FEW HOURS. At half past ten I heard André's cheerful shout hello, and then his footsteps going up to his study; and then nothing, just a long silence and the breeze in the trees.

At half past one I got up and went to her salon. She was sitting upright on the sofa, straight-backed, reading.

Her face softened.

Thomas's footsteps, up and down the corridor.

She bent back over her novel; a high red spot on either cheekbone.

For distraction, I crossed to sit at the desk, arranged myself, picked up a letter. *I have never met you but I love you*, wrote a man from Normandy.

At four o'clock I went to my room. There was nothing to do but wait. I looked out of the window, at the high, white, unreal sky, and wondered how she would dissuade him. What she could be planning, and if it could work. We'd fallen out, André and I, but I was still living in his house: there for the taking.

I went down for dinner at eight. He was there, lounging in his seat, tanned from his trip, but otherwise the same. Looking at him, I wondered how I had ever mistaken his silken waistcoats for sincerity.

He looked up at me, a quick glance under his eyelids. 'You look well.'

'Do I?'

'Very.' He reached casually for bread. I folded my hands in my lap and stared at them. She hadn't said anything yet, or the plan hadn't worked.

Luce said: 'So your trip—'

André tipped his chair back and laced his fingers behind his head, all his teeth on show. 'You should have seen his workshop. He has an automaton so realistic it could be sitting where Adèle is right now. She could *be* the automaton.'

'I think we'd recognise the real one.'

André lifted his wine glass and swirled it. Then he asked: 'Anything exciting happen while I was gone?'

Luce took a sip of wine – the muscles of her throat moved as she swallowed – and shook her head.

At the end of the meal, André sat swilling the dregs in his glass, staring at the wall; she was perfectly composed, opposite him. Eventually she turned her gaze on me.

'Goodnight,' I said, getting to my feet.

As I left the room, she rose too. For a delirious moment I thought she was coming after me. But she followed me to the door and put her hand on the handle.

I stood in the hall, staring back at her.

'Goodnight,' she said. On her face was a fierce look I had not seen before. She pulled the door closed.

I went upstairs to my room and sat in my nightgown, propped up against the pillows, to wait.

I thought about the last time with André. I could hardly remember it: I just had the impression of conserved energies, and no noise, as if noise were an expense he didn't want with me.

After a while I heard the dining-room door open and close.

Her softer steps and his quicker ones going up the stairs: no voices.

I heard him walk up the second flight, clearing his throat. A pause, and his footsteps kept on coming, up the last flight of stairs to my floor.

I pulled my knees up to my chin and shut my eyes; then I reached for the stem of the lamp beside my bed. I lifted it an inch, to test its weight.

The footsteps had stopped; I breathed, and listened harder.

There was a creak of floorboards just outside my door. He was shifting his weight onto his other leg.

We waited, on either side of the door, in silence, for more than a minute.

Abruptly, there was a squeak as he spun on his heel – and then his footsteps jogging back down the stairs.

I waited half an hour, letting the sweat on my body cool, then slipped out of my room and stole down the stairs.

At his floor I paused, but of course there was nobody there.

I continued to Luce's floor. Stood for a moment outside her room; brushed the door with my knuckles.

There was no answer. I pushed it open.

The shutters were faint silvery outlines. I couldn't hear breathing, so she was not asleep; and sure enough, after a few seconds, her shape came clear. She was sitting up in bed.

I walked to the bed. Still no sound.

I climbed onto the bed, knelt over her and kissed her.

Her lips were cold under mine; barely moving.

She let me push back the covers. Her nakedness: a white slender body. The nipples dark circles. I reached out for one—

She held my head in place, and put her hands in my hair.

She pulled my nightgown over my head. The air in the room was summery warm, a gentle draught from somewhere.

As I was bending to kiss her again, she put a hand up to stop me; ran a finger down my jaw. The fingernail dug in.

She pushed me gently onto the bed and rolled towards me; put her hands on my thighs and spread them wide apart.

Looking at her expression, I understood that there was a price, after all.

'He wasn't even—' I tried to tell her. 'He never even—'

She covered my mouth with her hand; then, without checking whether I was ready, she pushed four fingers into me.

'Am I anything like him?'

It hurt: a good pain, but shocking.

'Did he do this? Or this?'

Each movement a separate sound from my mouth. Her eyes, half-shut, watching me.

I took her hand away from my mouth, rolled over and straddled her; took her wrist and pushed her further into me. Bent down and kissed her; told her that if this was how the account would be settled, I'd pay.

Much later, I woke to find her still asleep. Pale light was just beginning to show in the cracks of the shutters.

She slept with one arm curved above her head, protective. I watched her for a long time, then put my hand on her stomach.

Her eyes flew open. She stared at the ceiling; then at me.

'What did you say to him?' I asked. 'To stop him?'

'It doesn't matter,' she said.

I went on watching her. Her nostrils flared.

She said: 'He won't come to your room any more. Isn't that enough?'

She closed her eyes again. Her hand came crabbing over the coverlet and seized mine convulsively: gripping my fingers so tightly they turned red, then white, changing position every thirty seconds or so, finding a new hold.

22. août 1913

IN THE SALON, DURING THE DAY, we did everything we could not to meet each other's eyes.

Sometimes we caught each other out. She straightened her back, arching her neck to release the tension from reading, rubbing the nape with one palm, and in the course of looking at the ceiling, her eyes wandered to mine.

On those occasions time slowed and stopped. Her hand stayed where it was; a smile hovered on her face; the hand rubbed gently, ruefully over her neck, forward and back. The moment would lengthen out until one of the many sounds that made us jump, made us jump: a clatter of pots and pans from the kitchen, or Thomas's step on the stair.

At supper, the sharp pain of watching her speaking to André. In the first days after his return, he had seemed quiet, almost wary of her. But night by night he became more boisterous: drinking more wine than before, making tasteless jokes, watching her with a flushed attention that I could not look at. And at the other end of the table, she laughed where appropriate, exchanging gossip: only a little pallor to show anything was wrong at all. And when he wasn't looking, she would glance at me, warning me to smile, laugh and make conversation: to pretend.

At night, I'd undress for her: a slow tease, the garments falling one by one. She'd lie propped on one elbow, smiling crookedly; and when I was naked, she'd look at me. From ankles to eyelashes. 'You're beautiful,' she'd say. 'Come here.'

Juliette and Adèle
1967

The last of the lunchtime crowd is dissipating; bars of dusty sunlight across our table.

I say: 'Didn't you worry about being discovered?'

Adèle smiles. 'Of course. But then again, not.'

Her fingers hover in front of her mouth: 'I had this fantasy: being caught out. The five short minutes to get dressed; the servants lining the hall. André ejecting us from the house. Our suitcases being flung down the steps behind us. To be alone with her on the drive, with all her ghosts streaming out ahead of us, evaporating on the morning air.'

25. août 1913

IN BED, SHE MADE ME WAIT, trailing a fingertip over me till I almost cried; she turned me into someone I wasn't: I barely recognised the sounds from my own mouth.

But when I tried to return the favour, most often, she'd smile, and shift me gently onto the bed beside her, and turn away from me, onto her other side.

One day, we took a picnic to the Bois de Boulogne.

Hubert dropped us on the side of the main road through to Paris; leaning into the cab, she arranged to have him pick us up at five. She carried the picnic hamper and I took a blanket, and we walked away from the path towards where the trees grew a little thicker. It was a fine afternoon: the leaves and grass buzzed with activity, but as it was a week-day, other visitors were few and far between. We picked our way between the patches of tufty grass and the tree roots, and finally found a spot where there was just one other couple visible in the distance.

We ate in reflective silence, and cleared the plates away into the basket; then she piled her coat behind her head and lay down, shading her eyes with her hand.

I watched her, found myself smiling.

'What?' she said, laughing.

'Nothing,' I said. I'd been thinking how I'd come to the house hoping to take her place. But now there was no longer anything outside her or around her – no films, no future.

She squinted up at me under her fingers, still smiling.

'I'd swear you're taller,' she said.

I looked down at myself.

'Yes, you are. You're only seventeen. You're still growing.'

We smiled at each other again.

'Seventeen,' she said, uncertain. 'An ingénue.'

There was a pause. She laughed, but the laugh faded quickly away.

I suddenly thought I understood. I sat down beside her.

'Is that it?' I asked. 'Is that why? Because I'm young?'

She blinked, lowered her eyes. 'Is what why?'

I bent over and kissed her.

'Adèle,' she said, in her old commanding voice, 'if somebody comes—'

'They won't.'

The sun in her eyelashes; the sound of the birds in the trees, oddly magnified.

When I moved my hand between her legs she caught at my fingers. I took her hand and flattened it on the grass and left it there.

'Do you think I care that you're older? Do you think I'm too young to know my own mind?'

Her face fell.

I slipped my hand under her petticoats. This time she didn't try to stop me.

She turned her head to one side, frowning.

Oh, she said. Turned her head to the other side. I cradled it with the crook of my arm, protecting it each time she turned, again and again, fighting to escape.

And then she was unrecognisable. Laughing and crying together. Her tears slid into my mouth.

Over supper that same evening, André lifted his wine glass and stared at her over the top of it.

'You look healthy,' he said to her. 'Glowing.'

'It must be the fresh air,' she said, cutting demurely into her food.

20. septembre 1913

ONE DAY SHE LOOKED OUT OF the salon window and said: 'I think this is the last fine day. What shall we do with it?'

I shrugged. It was true: the light had that slanted quality that meant autumn. I had no particular needs, now, apart from being with her, so it didn't matter to me if we went out – but I wanted her to have what she wanted.

She turned, clicked her fingers. 'The boating lake,' she said.

In the car, she held my hand loosely, under cover of our coats, and pointed out the fashions of the ladies walking along the Allée des Acacias.

'Do you remember when we met Aurélie by accident here?' she said. 'I thought you were going to knock her out.'

I smiled at the memory, but didn't comment, because it seemed like another person. How small my aims had been then: grasping after fame. I never thought about acting any more.

'My knight in shining armour,' she said contentedly, snuggling down amongst the coats.

Hubert parked the car on a stretch of grassland. She told him to wait, and we walked towards the lake. There was a small boathouse, and a wizened old man hiring rowing boats. Luce picked her way towards him; I saw her flash a smile, and coins changing hands.

When she came back, she was triumphant. 'He wanted five francs,' she said, 'but I beat him down to three.'

I rolled my eyes.

'It was the principle,' she said vaguely, already shading her eyes and pointing at the rowing boats drawn up on the bank. 'That one, don't you think?'

We crossed to the boat and hauled it down to the water. There was the business with setting it upright, and testing its water safety, and finding the oars; all of which I loved.

'What are you thinking?' she said.

I'd been looking at her shoulders: how she pulled the oar handles back, tight, then the release. The shower of tiny droplets scattering back into the water.

The lake was not busy – it was too cold for that. There was just one other couple in a rowing boat: a young girl and her beau. The girl clutched her hat and screamed as it tried to blow away.

'Your shoulders,' I said.

She smiled at me, and shook her head in mock disapproval.

I watched her face. That puckered frown she occasionally had, that I remembered from before, pulling her eyebrows tight.

The girl in the other boat finally lost her hat; it blew away from her, skimming across the lake. She shrieked, and stood up. The young man stood, too, to balance the boat. They teetered, for a moment, and then tipped into the shallows; laughing, they stood, the water running off their faces. Then he held up his hand to her and escorted her to shore. She stepped onto the grass as proud as a queen.

Luce had let the oars drift; her eyes had narrowed with enjoyment at the scene.

She turned her face away. Eventually she said: 'What would happen if we just kept going?'

'Where?'

'If this lake had a tributary, a stream, leading off somewhere.'

The oars creaked in their rowlocks. A breeze made the boat tremble in the water.

'Out to sea?'

'Just as far as one of those dilapidated resorts. Those places people go to die. We could stay there for a while. Take a hotel.'

The idea of being alone in a hotel with her was so painfully beguiling that my mind tied the thought off. An image came to me of her on a pebbled beach, dissecting the fashions of the provincial ladies.

'You'd last about five minutes,' I said.

She smirked – 'Perhaps' – and looked down. Then up again, uncertain, and this time, she held my gaze. Her smile was the shyest, most gorgeous thing I'd ever seen.

7. octobre 1913

ONE NIGHT, OVER DINNER, André announced the party. 'We haven't entertained in months,' he said. 'I'm ready to be seen.'

He struck a pose. I turned my face away. I could barely see him these days without wanting to wind my plait round his neck. Just when it seemed he ought to recede into the distance, he was more present than ever: haunting the corridors of the house, always whistling just out of sight.

Luce said, slowly and to my surprise: 'Yes. It's an idea.'

André looked surprised too. 'Saturday?' he said.

'Yes. Why not?' She pressed her handkerchief to her mouth. 'One condition: no Peyssac.'

André grinned. 'In that case: no Ex-Minister.'

'Then none of your stupid trick-film has-beens.'

'None of your twittering fashion-obsessed friends.'

She took a long sip from her wine glass, enjoying, I could only suppose, this idiotic game of bargaining.

I looked from one to the other, trying to see beyond their faces, and failing.

'Fine,' she said, smirking. 'Then we'll have a party.'

The following morning, seeing my expression, she said: 'Is that why you didn't come last night?'

She looked drawn and tired, but in her hand was a caterer's order book.

'It's just a party, Adèle,' she said.

'I wish you wouldn't plan things with him,' I said. I could hear my own voice and hated it. 'Why are you so excited about it?'

She lifted the order book, flapped it helplessly, and shrugged. 'I'm not. These are the things we have to do.'

'I heard you last night. You were flirting with him.'

She passed her hand across her mouth: for an awful moment I thought she was laughing, but the hand came away grim. She was too clever to say the dangerous thing that hovered between us. Her fingers tightened on the book. 'Have you considered the fact that I am doing this for us? For appearances?'

Her colour was high; the long autumn light slanted through the window.

She sighed – a small, unhappy sound – and picked at the cover of the order book. 'This is what people do, my love. They are seen.'

I hated this vision of myself. Didn't I want her to have whatever she wanted? So instead, I said as bravely as I could. 'Let's be seen.'

Her face cleared – relief – sun moving over a landscape; her face twisted into an uncertain smile.

'Our first argument,' she said, and smiled until at last I smiled back. She put the book away, and did not mention the party for two days.

On the third day, the wife of the Ex-Minister visited. She didn't send up a card and wait, she simply followed Thomas up to the salon and walked straight across to plant a firm kiss on Luce's cheeks. She didn't look at me.

'It's the talk of the town,' she said, eyes sparkling, 'your invitations arrived this morning. By ten o'clock I had a dozen phone calls asking me what you were going to wear.' She sat down on a pouffe, her eyes never leaving Luce's face. 'So what are you going to wear?'

Luce tried to laugh this off. 'I hadn't thought,' she said.

Aurélie crowed, and then turned to me: '*I hadn't thought!*
Whatever are we to do with her, Mlle Roux? My love, all the
young directors are coming. Everyone who has a film in prep
will be there.'

She sat back, for effect. Luce turned white, then red. 'Really?'
she said, as though disbelieving. 'Everyone?'

Aurélie leant forward, took her fingers in her knuckly hands.
'Everyone. So let's make a plan. Let's make you seductive.'

I held my breath until I could be calm again.

Later, I sat flipping through one of the fashion magazines she'd
left; Luce was reading, with every appearance of tranquillity.

Without lifting her head, she said: 'She's only trying to help.'

When I didn't answer, she put her fingertips to her eyes.
'She thinks she's helping me, by inviting all these directors.'

'Isn't she?'

She lifted her head and stared at me. She had flushed bright
red.

'I don't know what you mean,' she said.

'She's always helping you, isn't she?'

She stared at me.

'Adèle,' she said, 'she's my friend.'

I took a deep, shivering breath in; we looked at each other.

'It's just a party. Let's just get it out of the way,' she said,
'please.'

She kissed me there on the sofa without a thought for the
servants. Then she laughed, bent me backwards and pushed up
my skirts. 'You don't have anything to worry about,' she said.

14. octobre 1913

SHE INVITED ME to her room to prepare.

I changed quickly so that I could watch her put her make-up on; sat on the bed and pulled my knees up to my chin, savouring the moment.

She powdered her face with big, aggressive strokes; stared at her own reflection, eyes narrowed.

She smiled at me in the mirror.

'Welcome,' André said, walking forwards to the salon door with his hands wide. Standing next to me, Luce repressed a tremor of laughter; the first guest was the Duchesse de Guise.

As Luce did two kisses, the Duchesse's hawky eyes scanned the room. 'Charming,' she murmured, looking at the sparkling gold of the lights placed on every available surface, the sheen on the silk sofas and the obsidian gloss of the windows.

'You look well,' she said to Luce. 'What are you feeding her, André?'

André bowed his head. 'The finest foie gras.'

The Duchesse sniffed. 'The finest foie gras is from my estate in the Cévennes. Luce, your father never writes to me any more.'

André slugged back his champagne and excused himself. Luce said: 'May I present Mlle Roux?'

The Duchesse looked over my shoulder at the arriving guests. 'Oh! It's Aurélie Vercors.'

Luce looked at me, and dipped her eyes, left me and walked over to Aurélie.

The Duchesse peered at the Ex-Minister. 'Of course, he was in trade—'

I was watching Aurélie and Luce embrace, their torsos entwined from the breast upwards. 'Darling,' Aurélie said, pushing Luce away to search her face, 'you look delicious.' Luce gave her a small, brave smile that turned my stomach; put her hand on Aurélie's arm and led her away into the room.

'—ghastly little *arriviste*,' the Duchesse finished, with a last swallow of her champagne, and turning away from me, vanished into the swelling crowd.

People milled around me, talking. I looked around for André, but he was half in the hallway, welcoming guests.

A laugh made me look up. Aurélie and Luce were sitting on the window seat, facing each other, Aurélie telling a story, using her hands, and Luce had thrown her head back, tears of merriment in her eyes. Wiping them, she turned her head and looked at me, sprinkled her fingers to me – *come over*.

Next to her, Aurélie smiled thinly and without encouragement.

Flushed, I drained my champagne glass and looked at my feet. Luce's face turned blank – *please yourself* – and Aurélie leant forward to begin another anecdote.

Heads around me turned towards the door; there was an anxious murmuring. I craned to see who the new guest was, and saw Peyssac. But he didn't appear to have come unannounced: André was gravely shaking his hand, and Peyssac's eyes were darting around the room, settling on Luce and sliding away. The guests around them put their heads together and whispered behind their hands. André said something into Peyssac's ear; and with a final clap to his shoulder, he propelled Peyssac into the room and stood back, his face showing nothing.

Luce was sitting upright, her expression cold. Aurélie stopped talking and turned, put her fingers to Luce's arms and rested them there. I turned my face away.

A cough by my shoulder. Peyssac was there, his goatee bobbing anxiously. 'Mlle Roux. Might I have a private word?'

Luce's eyes on a point between my shoulder blades.

I said: 'Will the hallway be private enough?'

The noise level in the hall was softened, the light a yellow slit under the door. Peyssac stood, pulling at the rings on his fingers with his other hand. 'Mlle Roux, I have an indelicate request.'

I couldn't think what he meant: what was he doing, making a proposition in the hallway of someone else's house?

Peyssac looked at me, evidently discouraged by my stare, then said: 'I am afraid you will think the worse of me; but it is an idea that has been growing and growing in me since I first saw you at my apartments in the summer.'

I glanced at the light under the door. 'I don't know to what you're referring,' I said coldly, 'but please excuse me. I have to find someone.'

Peyssac stepped forward and took my hands in his, just hard enough to make them impossible to retract. I recoiled and he held on tighter.

'Forgive my clumsiness,' he said. 'You have, Mlle Roux, such an open quality: I cannot now consider anyone else in the role.'

Cold air on the back of my neck.

'You will think me despicable,' he said, rubbing his thumbs into my palms. 'I have you in mind for the heroine of *Petite Mort*. Oh, yes, you are quite right to look at me like that: the same part that your mistress wanted.'

With a last rub he released my hands. He was looking at me with an expression of pained eagerness.

'I haven't got any experience,' I said.

'You have the right look, and a natural elegance.'

Peyssac watched my face. He said: 'My girls go on to such wonderful things. To America, some of them, to Italy. My good friend Lily Lemoine, who started out in my pictures, has me to visit every year in her house on Como. She has other houses, of course, on the coast, in the south, where I believe you're from?'

Somewhere in the house a door opened and closed.

'I can't,' I said.

Peyssac's eyes glittered. 'I understand,' he said. 'But in the service of art, we are all compelled to be unscrupulous, are we not?'

He produced a card from his waistcoat, slipping it into my palm. 'Should you reconsider.'

With a gracious nod he insinuated himself back into the salon.

After a minute I was composed enough to go back to the party. When I opened the door, it seemed to me a hush had fallen. André was engaged in laughing conversation with some studio bosses.

For a good thirty seconds I pushed mindlessly through the crowd, looked anywhere but at her, and then gave in. She slithered off the seat and walked towards me; when she reached me, she took my arm and pulled me towards the door.

She marched me out into the hall and towards the stairs.

At the first landing she paused, but a giggling burst from behind one of the doors – some guests had evidently broken away from the main party. We walked on, up and up, until we were alone and everything around us was quiet.

She threw my wrist away from her and turned away, putting her hands up to cover her cheeks. 'What are you doing? In front of everybody.' Her eyes were huge in her face. 'Everybody was laughing at me! In my own house.'

Anger made me cold. 'I thought you didn't care about directors. So what if I talked to Peyssac? You didn't even notice I was gone!'

She stared at me through her fingers. 'She's my friend!'

'She wants you for herself! And you encourage her...'

She shook her head; I crossed to where she was, but she took me by the shoulders.

'What did Peyssac want?' she said.

'Nothing,' I said. A void had opened in my chest: I felt as if I'd crack in two.

She narrowed her eyes. 'What?' she said, giving me a little shake.

I shouted: 'Whatever he'd asked, I would have said no!'

I reached up and caught hold of her hands and did not let go.

Then she made a small sound, of abandonment and surrender: I pressed her against the wall of the corridor and kissed her.

I reached down and lifted her skirts around her waist. She was wet through the material of her petticoats.

I slipped my fingers inside her.

The sounds of her breathing, higher and higher—

All of her muscles tensed, poised on the brink, eyelids fluttering—

I knew immediately whose the footstep was, coming quietly up the stairs.

The top of André's head was visible on the landing beneath. If he looked up, he would see the hems of our skirts.

Not my room: he would check there, and how would we explain it?

Her eyes were wide; frozen open, fixed pleadingly on mine. I took her by the waist and half-dragged, half-walked her down the corridor. We reached the end of the passageway and I fished in my pocket for the ceramic key, and slotted it into the keyhole of the door by the window.

I pushed Luce through it and closed it as softly as I could

behind us, turned the key in the lock, and pressed my ear to the wood to listen.

André walked up the corridor as far as my room. I heard that door open; then it was closed softly.

There was absolute quiet for thirty seconds – I counted them. Behind me in the darkness, Luce held my fingers.

André's voice calling to her.

I tried not to breathe. Another eternity passed; my fingers convulsed on the door handle.

Eventually, there was the squeak of his hand running down the banister, and his feet jogging downstairs.

I turned to Luce: 'We'll say you needed a pin for your dress—' but stopped at the look on her face.

Through the window, there was a faint light from the lamps in the courtyard outside, and the objects I had seen when I visited the room before glowed grey: the lamp, tall as a wading bird; a couple of half-unpacked cartons, the crib.

This is the direction of her gaze: the wicker, hooded object, with its pale mattress leaking stuffing onto the floor. Her hands are clutching at themselves; she does not seem to really be in the room at all, and when I call to her she turns to look at me as if I were a stranger with bad news.

She falls without warning and without cushioning herself: her elbow hits a chest of drawers behind her with a crack, and she lies, knees bent, at my feet.

Then I am pulling her bodily into the corridor, as far towards the stairs as I can. I am looking at her eyes rolled up under the lids; calling for Thomas and seeing André's shocked face as he comes running up the stairs.

The door to Luce's room closed in my face, so I stood outside and leant on the banister to wait.

It wasn't possible to hear any detail – just low voices. Then a silence followed by a sharp cry. I started forward and hesitated, my knuckles poised to rap on the door – and then more talking.

Another silence. The door opened.

'What is it?'

André held the door open for the doctor. 'We've set her arm,' he said. 'She'll need to rest. But there'll be no lasting damage.'

15. octobre 1913

I TAPPED ON HER BEDROOM DOOR and opened it.

Wintry sunlight. Two pillows were propped behind her head, her hair spread on her shoulders; her arm in a sling.

I crossed to sit beside her; bent to kiss her. She put her arm up around my neck; we didn't speak for a long time.

Then she dried her eyes and said: 'They tell me I ruined the party.'

I pulled back. 'Don't you remember it?'

'No. I just remember waking up and being here, with the doctor. I've always been prone to fainting. And I can never remember what I've missed.'

She talked on and on; the words tumbled out, she lost her thread and found it again, watching for my reaction, all the time clutching my hand.

I stared at her, not recognising her.

I said: 'We were in the room at the end of the corridor. Something happened that startled you, and you fell.'

She looked fixedly at the window. At first I thought she was thinking. Then I saw that she was trying not to cry, the tears spilling out at the corner of each eye anyway.

'Tell me what it was,' I said.

Luce, iii.

For months, nobody saw the newlyweds. Autumn turned to winter; Paris expected its first glimpse of them at the Christmas balls, or skating on the Seine, and was disappointed. The house remained a blank gold façade; André sent his notes and ideas to Pathé by post.

In the spring came the news that took everyone by surprise: Luce was going to star in André's next film.

At first it was not believed. Was she not cheapening herself by dabbling in the fly-by-night art of circuses and fairgrounds?

For a few months everything went quiet. It was said, with a wink, that she had reconsidered. The city settled down again: she would turn her hand to tending roses and breeding horses, as every aristocratic wife did, and that would be the end of it.

Posters of *La Dame aux Roses* began to appear on the city walls and outside cinemas. The critics chewed their nails; but when the film print was finally released, it was clear that the venture was anything but foolish, and so everyone pretended to have known all along. *She dignifies the medium. She brings a finery to the coarseness of cinema. She is a star.*

She began to act, not just for André, but for Peyssac, Feuillade, Blaché. The months ran by, turning into three years of relentless happiness: riches, professional success, plenty. And then Luce found out they were going to have a baby.

It is five months into the pregnancy – June, 1908 – and she

is walking in the gardens behind the house. She is alone and exhausted by the extra weight she carries.

She has given up work because the bump was getting too hard to disguise. André wanted to tell everyone, but she would not allow it. So the journalists report that she is struggling with her childhood injury and has taken a leave of absence to recuperate. Nobody knows she is pregnant: not their friends, not their enemies – not even Aunt Berthe, who is a regular visitor now that Luce is famous.

André thinks she fears a miscarriage. Luce has let it slip that her mother suffered several, and so naturally he assumes she does not want anyone to know until she is almost to term. This is not the real reason for her secrecy.

Though it is still early summer, the day is very hot; the air is filled with the overpowering scent of flowers; she feels lightheaded. So she walks to the fringe of the Bois and ducks under the branches. There is an old path here, blissfully shady; she follows it, pushing the branches aside with her fingers as she goes.

After half an hour the path ends at the last thing she expected: a wide pond, twenty metres across. She has never come this far into the woods before; she had no idea the pond was here.

She almost laughs because the water is dark and glossy; she is looking at the exact twin of a lake on her parents' estate in Normandy, which she had sat beside as a child.

How deep is the water here? She dips her toe; her shoe sinks through the water, to the ankle, to the calf, without touching the bottom.

How can she tell André the real reason she wants to keep the pregnancy a secret? How can she say *I'm worried I won't love the child*? She cannot. She cannot say, *Give me more time, lots more time before it's born, and I will be equal to it*, because she knows she will never be equal to it. It is like a dream from which she can't wake; and with each passing day, she feels the thing inside her grow closer.

She could easily slip here, on the mud of the bank; her belly might bump against the pond floor, or she might swallow enough water to bring about an accident.

She stands, tempted and indecisive. *For shame*, she thinks, but distantly: she could have her career back, her old life; everything will be as it was before. She could crawl back to the house, weed draped in her hair, and nobody need ever know the fall into the water was deliberate.

And the child isn't a child yet, is it?

Protesting, the baby kicks hard against her belly: the first time it has moved.

She pulls back from the lip of the pond and waits, fascinated, counting. Sure enough, ten seconds later, still reproachful but fainter, another kick.

As the baby kicks a third time, she finds herself flooded with the last thing she expects – not guilt, not irritation at this demand for attention, but worry for the child. Is it normal for it to kick so much? She puts her hands to her stomach and curves them around it protectively. The skin between her and the womb feels thin under her fingers. Who can she ask if this is normal?

Sadness and irony make her smile. Most women would ask their mothers. She turns and walks back to the house.

That night, André notices that the sparkle is back in her eyes. She goes to bed earlier than usual, kissing him chastely on the lips. He watches her go, relieved. He loves her, but recently he has not known how to help her; now he sees that whatever personal storm she was weathering has blown out to sea and away.

For the rest of the pregnancy Luce is covetous of each kick and murmur. She spends her days on the chaise longue, reading and resting as avidly as some people exercise, eating everything she is meant to eat; she passes the time imagining the baby. Now it is asleep in its permanent night, thumb jammed into its proto-mouth; now it is rotating, stub-fingers pressing the amniotic sac almost to breaking-point. *What will you be*, she wonders, *a man of money and ambition like your father? Or will you be like me?*

André is in his office when the note comes, in Dr Langlois's precise hand: *Labour commenced an hour ago*. He flings down his pen and whirls his coat round his shoulders. The guards watch him go, astonished: though he has wanted to crow the news from the rooftops since he first heard, André has still not told anybody at Pathé that he is about to be a father.

He feels the change as soon as he sets foot in his house. The servants are keeping downstairs, out of harm's way, and everything is very still. He runs up the stairs three at a time, up, up to the attic floor, where Thomas stands, holding a fresh bowl of water, outside the door of the confinement room.

The door is half open; André steps forward, suddenly unsure of himself, even on his own turf. Being an orphan, he has no map for this event: aren't fathers supposed to stay outside?

When he peeps round the open door, he sees Luce stretched – but really stretched, not just lying, every tendon arching in pain – out on the bed. The room smells of exertion. At the foot of the bed stands grey-haired Dr Langlois, peering into his wife, exhorting her with gentle murmurs, over which she screams and screams.

Dr Langlois sees André standing appalled on the threshold, and Luce's head turns to follow the doctor's look, so he receives both looks at the same time: the doctor smiling his reassurance and Luce baring her teeth. He does not know which to believe, but 'Perhaps you'll wait outside?' the doctor says, still encouraging and kind; so he does. Time passes slowly but at least it passes; the screams become weaker. 'That's a good sign,' he says to Thomas, 'she is in less pain, the baby's coming.'

They hear Dr Langlois' voice slightly raised, as though he is telling Luce off. Then the screams become fainter. André nods vigorously – they are almost there now. He does not care if it is a boy or a girl, doesn't care whether it is tall or small or gifted or plain, as long as it's theirs. The day is not quite gone; a pale streak lines the sky above the horizon but that is all.

The sound of crying, quickly stifled; but not a child's crying. Dr Langlois appears in the doorway, wiping blood into a cloth; not his blood.

'I'm sorry,' he says, still kindly, 'she's conscious, and she'll recover, but she has lost the baby.'

André smiles, polite and uncomprehending.

'Stillborn,' Dr Langlois says, shaking his head. He reaches out and puts one palm on André's shoulder, steadying him; the palm is damp.

André pushes past him and into the room. He won't believe a trick until he sees its outcome.

The thing is laid out on a chair, swaddled in its swaddling clothes up to the neck. Its features are all there – the mouth half open, the eyelids fat and closed – but an object more than a human. He expects it to burst into life and take a breath at any moment, but it persists in its silence and its stillness.

'It may have stopped growing a couple of months ago,' Dr Langlois tells him. André shakes his head to say, *But we were so careful*, thinking of Luce sitting beautifully on her couch; and then shakes his head again. He can't see anything of himself or of her in this tiny half-amphibian.

Luce watches André from the bed. She knows what has happened; tears ooze from under her eyelids. When they try to tell her some things about the baby – sex, size – she lets her face go blank, and doesn't hear them. Two days later André arranges a small funeral in the grounds of the house, which she does not attend.

But it isn't over, not yet. They tie her to the bed in the attic, and she forgets things: she forgets who André is and when he comes to sit beside her, she thinks it is a stranger, unpardonable in his rudeness, gripping her hand. *How dare you*, she hisses, and hearing how much like a stranger she has become herself, she laughs.

To try to make it clear to her, they move the empty crib they had bought for the baby into her room. Every day a doctor comes and asks her: *Do you know what this is? Do you remember what it was meant to be for?* Sometimes she thinks she has become an animal: a cat or a wolf or an owl, staring at her own sleeping form on the bed from the other side of the window. She learns to slip the knots around her wrists, and goes wandering through the attics, chafing the skin of her hands to warm the joints, she walks up and down the corridor, thinking she has heard the baby calling for her. But when Thomas comes to fetch her he tells her it is only an owl hooting, and there it is – bluish and terrifyingly large in the moonlight – perched on the windowsill, looking in at her. *I did hear the baby*, she hears herself insisting. Deferential, with a bob of the head, the owl slips off the sill and takes flight; Thomas smiles – *Madame, take your medicine* – and she watches fascinated: the owl's wings move mechanically, a stage prop flying away.

When they escort her downstairs, she is surprised to see that it is still autumn, or autumn again. André's hand is on her arm, guiding her; at her questioning look, he nods: yes, a year has passed.

Everything looks frail but familiar. The chaise longue is as it was, but wafer thin in the pale afternoon light; the desks, chairs are watery and sly; even the books on the shelves seem to be holding their secrets away from her.

From this she deduces that she is still not quite well.

André is in the room, in another chair, but she doesn't know what to say to him. A year!

She knows the stillbirth was her fault, because she had once thought of killing it, and someone, somehow, knew.

It is time André was made aware; it is carrying this secret which has kept her chained to the bed. She opens her mouth to tell André, but feels his hand laid over her own, a warning to keep quiet.

The silence runs down from their joined hands and over them and spreads out over the carpet, blending with the sunset, which is unexpectedly fiery and distinct. They sit like statuary of a king and a queen, saying nothing to each other. Eventually the silence fills the whole house.

Juliette, v.

The man from public records sighs; it's his lunch hour.

He says: 'The cottage that is currently owned by Mme Ruillaux was built in 1930.'

I scribble 1930 on my pad; prop the telephone in the crook of my shoulder and ask: 'By whom?'

Another sigh. 'A M. Undin. But he never lived there; he was an absentee landlord. According to this, it was occupied on a short-term basis until 1945, when M. Undin was killed. Mme Ruillaux bought it at auction.'

I ask: 'How short-term?'

'The tenants changed every year or two.'

'Can you see anything about their occupations?'

He sounds affronted. 'Of course. This is Public Records.'

'Is there anyone who worked at the Pathé factory?'

I imagine him running his finger down a list of names. 'I'm sorry. There's nothing here that I can see.'

'There's no connection? No wife or husband or other tenants?'

'I'm sorry. No.'

I say: 'Can you send me the list of names anyway?'

16. novembre 1913

WHILE HER ARM HEALED, she stayed in bed, and I went to read to her every afternoon.

But she was not quite herself. I chose passages from Zola, to which she listened with a kind of pained attention, as if she were trying to tether herself to the room.

Sometimes, out of nowhere, her breathing became raucous, as if she was drowning in front of me. 'Is it because of the child?' I'd ask; and she'd nod. She would clutch at my hand; I would scream for Thomas, and he'd come running, bringing wet cloths, and smelling salts.

Afterwards we would sit in silence. If I tried to talk to her, about the baby, she would shake her head, squeeze her eyes tight shut, and the tears would come so quickly that I gave it up; pressed her hand and shushed her.

Once, I climbed into the bed beside her. We made love quickly, and afterwards she slept.

In early November she came downstairs.

She stood in the middle of the salon, held her arms out in front of her and smiled. 'I'm so thin,' she said.

I told her the truth, which was that she looked luminous.

She smiled shyly, as if she didn't know whether or not to believe me.

Visitors came. Aurélie, every couple of days, once with a bouquet of flowers so enormous it obscured her face; the

Duchesse de Guise, to sit poker-straight and bemoan the passing of moral rectitude; other women, actresses and friends, whom I had never met before.

André stayed at home. When I passed him in the corridor, he would blow theatrically on his hands and say 'It's too cold to go to the studio.' Nevertheless, he always seemed to be on the way to his study, so I had no doubt he was working on something; besides which, he too had visitors, workmen holding their caps and looking at the fine plasterwork, and Pathé bosses, clearing their throats and waiting for Thomas to take their umbrellas, almost every day, sometimes spending long hours in the study with him, and often staying for supper with us.

He talked openly about *Petite Mort* at the dinner table – the process of arranging the sets, selecting the actors, finding a reliable cameraman – his guests nodding with rapt attention.

Luce ate quietly, seeming indifferent to everything that was said.

At night, it was like a door opening: she spoke to me more. She told me what she was feeling; told me things from her past without my asking; in bed, she told me what she liked and didn't like, in a constant, hoarse whisper, as if we were not the only ones in the room, and she was rough: not with me, with herself. Intermingled with her words were reckless terms of endearment: *My only one. My right hand.*

One night, she took my fingers and curled them into a fist; I pulled away.

I had promised myself I wouldn't cry as long as she was like this. But suddenly I couldn't help it. 'I can't do this,' I said. 'I don't understand what's wrong with you. It's like you don't even see me.'

She had lain down on her back again; now her head turned towards me. Her breathing slowed; not the panicked whispering I'd grown used to.

'I do see you,' she said.

I reached for her hands. 'We have to go away. You'll be all right if you're not in this house.'

She squeezed my fingers in hers: listening.

'Somewhere nobody would know us,' I said.

She took a breath. 'What would we do for money?'

'Spend yours.'

She said: 'It's in André's name.'

'I'll work. I'll make costumes, or clean. I don't care.'

She looked at me critically. 'You don't care at all?'

'Anything.'

She laughed. 'Then it's easy, isn't it?'

The laugh she gave was wild, but I didn't hear that. I heard her saying yes.

Aurélie visited again, and more often, and spent as much as an hour with Luce, sitting, holding her hand and talking in low voices. I welcomed her warmly and offered to make myself scarce, because I had a secret. Even André's whistling and constant presence could not touch my mood: I smiled at him over supper, and laughed at his jokes – laughed for the two of us.

In bed at night, I closed my eyes and gave myself over to calculation. Nearing Christmas, the house was awash with money: gold brocade hung from the banisters, and boxes of expensive fancies arrived every day in preparation for the Ice Ball which they held every New Year. But none of it was cash. Luce and I spent our afternoons making paper chains, whilst I wondered out loud, turning our problem over and over.

She still had sudden fits of panic. She would clutch my hands and shut her eyes tight; but when I asked her what was wrong, she only pressed her lips into a line and shook her head.

'We will really go away,' she said.

'Of course,' I said. 'Of course,' and smiled back at her, happy to see her face clear. 'Now let me think.'

I closed my eyes and let the winter sunlight play over my eyelids, making shapes like a child's kaleidoscope. And in time the plan unfurled as if it had always been dormant in my mind, only wanting an opportunity to be exercised.

31. décembre 1913

NEW YEAR'S EVE: the coldest in living memory. It was too cold for wind, for clouds; the trees rocked silently in the cradle of their roots. Birds fell from the sky in the icy Paris night and, of course, it was the day Aleksandr Romanov died. The ageing Russian princeling was found frozen to death in a gutter in the Latin Quarter, his fingers curled around a bottle of vodka, wearing nothing but a top hat and a happy grin.

In the house, every lamp was lit from eight o'clock in the morning; for warmth, and because there was the Ice Ball to prepare for. Though the guests were not due to arrive till seven, lanterns must be strung to light the path to the lake; refreshments must be prepared and carried out, tray by painstaking tray. A car arrived from Paris with a hundred pairs of ice skates; servants flew to and fro; I flattened myself against the wall on the stairs as Thomas and André supervised the carrying down of a trestle from the upper floors.

Hoping for a moment alone with Luce, I looked for her, and found her by the French windows leading out onto the lawn. She stood, eyes wide, hands clasped at her front, giving directions to a pack of maids.

There was nothing to be done; the maids looked at me too, pink-cheeked and expectant. 'Carry on,' I said, and she turned gratefully back.

It didn't matter. Today was for biding my time.

At five o'clock the sun fell from the sky. Inky blue on the

horizon, then black; I watched from the window seat of my room. A solitary maid worked her away along the string of lanterns leading out across the lawn, lighting each one.

Just before seven, the slam of carriage doors; shouts of laughter; hail-fellow-well-mets from the front of the house. Then the sounds were sucked down the central corridor and with an *Isn't this charming*, the first guests emerged onto the terrace at the back of the house, underneath my bedroom window.

It *was* charming. The terrace was flooded gold with torch-light. With a surge, the lawn was suddenly filled with people: shadows walking towards the wood. The going was picky: a woman-silhouette leant on her husband's shoulder, cackling, as she struggled along in her delicate shoes.

Then came the knock I had been waiting for.

'M. et Mme Durand are making their way to the lake now,' Thomas said.

'Thank you.' I smiled at him for the first time in months. He shut the door. I turned back to the window, and sure enough, there they were: André, with Luce on his arm.

He was sleek in his black overcoat. She was wearing furs, under which shone a white dress that I had never seen before. The bodice glittered with tiny jewels.

I slipped down from the window seat, crept down the stairs and along the corridor to André's study. A piece of luck: the door was unlocked. I had brought a candle, so that nobody would see the electric light and wonder who was in the room; I crossed to his desk and started pulling at the drawers, looking for the stack of money, or something like it, that I had seen him count out before. The first drawer opened without resistance. It was empty.

Then the second drawer; a spare pen and ink-pot rattled, and a third item. I held it up to the light: tiny and golden.

I stood in the darkness, turning the little key over and over in my fingers, wondering what it could unlock. All I knew about theft came from films, where the burglar would tiptoe into the house, pause to peer greedily at the sleeping demoiselle, then creep into the library and find a safe located behind some exquisite painting.

I moved about the room, thinking; and my eye fell on the portait hanging over the mantelpiece. I raised the candle: green swamp, gold sky – and wondered how I could have missed it the first time. That knowing smirk belonged to Caroline Durand: the portrait was the portrait from the story.

Could it be that simple? I thought how André might like to hollow out Caroline as she had hollowed him out. I slipped my hand behind the frame, looking for a catch or a lock; and with a flick of one finger the painting swung away from the wall. I laughed under my breath as I slotted the little key into the metal locker set into the plaster and opened the safe door.

A sheaf of papers at the front. I pulled out the tottering stack and held the leaves up to the light one by one. Deeds to the house; the purchase of an automobile; a marriage certificate, which I considered burning, then put back in place.

At the back of the safe, my fingers felt wafery paper; I pulled out a tightly bound bundle and found it was not money, but what looked like a will. I scrabbled with my fingers at the back of the safe: there was no cash in there.

I went to slam the locker door shut, piqued, when my fingers brushed another object: cold metal, which I had first thought was part of the inside of the safe.

I drew the revolver out into the light and studied its snub nose, its brutal little tongue. For a moment I considered taking it, for its workmanship, strictly to the purpose and nothing more, struck me as beautiful – but then I reconsidered. It would be better for André not to notice anything was missing. Laying it back in its place, I shut the safe door, blew out the candle and crept from the room.

~

The cold was edged: my breath froze into a cloud before my face as I joined the last of the guests heading for the lake.

I was the only person walking on their own – all the rest were couples, and nobody spoke to or looked at me. After twenty aching minutes, we were suddenly at the fringe of the Bois. The lanterns showed us how the path straggled in under the eaves of the woods; there were giggles and fallings-over, as the ladies of the party grappled with the uneven ground. Then the track broadened out, and suddenly we were on the edge of a white clearing.

From behind me I heard a chorus of well-bred *oohs* and *aahs*. The lake's frozen surface was perfect, violet from the moonlight and streaked gold from the lanterns strung in the branches overhanging the banks; the trees closed in on every side. The ice was already covered in skaters, zipping adroitly here and there, insects to flowers. A long table for refreshments was stationed on the far bank: steam rose from a vat and behind the table I could just make out Thomas standing watching the scene. Set a little further back was a bonfire, just beginning to take; a couple of ladies had already retreated nearby, holding their hands out to warm them.

I looked around for Luce, and saw her standing with André in the very centre of the lake, in a knot of admirers. She was laughing at a joke or an aside; her hand still resting on André's wrist. As I watched, André leant forward to add a bon mot and she, along with the other guests, threw her head back in laughter. She turned to watch André tell the rest of his anecdote, her face shining, her fingers gripping his arm, her lips rouged.

It was strange: like going back in time to before her illness.

As I wondered what to do, how to approach her, a footman tapped me on the shoulder. 'Skates, Mademoiselle?'

I said yes, and stared as he put a pair of white boots in my hands; the blades were clean but hungry-looking. But the only way to Luce was across the lake, so I bent and struggled into them, and placed one tentative foot on the ice.

Immediately the world tilted. *Steady*, laughed a man as he whooshed past me. I put another foot down, and stood, wobbly-legged, on the ice; tried to advance, picking up each boot as though walking. *Careful*, another man said impatiently – I glimpsed his flashing eyes as he whirled away, arms laced behind his back.

Why hadn't I been born rich, so that winter sports were second nature? I gazed at Luce, willing her to turn and see me. *Darling*: but she was talking now, engaged in a story, her gloved hands moving in the air.

The inevitable happened. A lady shrieked as she cannoned into my sprawled body; her skates missed my outstretched fingers by half an inch.

Firm hands gripped me under the arms and hauled me upright; clever eyes staring at me from a lean, weather-lined face.

'All right?' said Aurélie Vercors. 'No bones broken? Back on the horse,' and, her fingers tightening on my forearm, she pulled me after her. 'That's it,' she said, as, despite myself, my ugly-duckling stumble drew out into smooth strokes, 'just let yourself go.'

'I have to speak to Luce,' I said.

'Not until you can put one foot in front of the other,' she said brightly. She was wearing a fur-trimmed grey dress, her hair drawn back into a tight bun.

My skates made a sound like scissors as we moved over the ice.

'Good,' Aurélie said. 'You're a natural.'

She moved with absolute ease. On our second circle, she jerked her chin at Louis, standing alone on the bank, watching us nervously, still wearing shoes. 'He doesn't skate. Too much thin ice in politics as it is.'

I didn't even smile. Luce was still invisible behind the knot of guests.

'What is your plan, Mlle Roux? Are you going to storm over there, and fall as you reach her, and give André the satisfaction?' Bright eyes watched me from above her Roman nose. 'A scene is never worth one's time. We will stay back, like this, and choose your opportunity with caution.'

I could not think of a single intelligent thing to say to this. We skated on.

'Refreshments,' Aurélie said. We had reached the drinks table. She snapped her fingers to Thomas, who passed her two cups of mulled wine. 'Now come and sit with me on the bank.'

She tugged me over to the firm ground and helped me climb a way up the bank. I wrapped my hands gratefully round the mug and peered through the steam.

'Come in under the eaves, the view's better,' she said, and without waiting for an answer she grabbed my hand and led me a little way under the tree line.

There was nobody else about; the trees extended into the darkness behind me. Aurélie was right: we were afforded an excellent vantage point. From here it was possible to see the entire canvas, the way the whirling lights and shadows combined. I had never thought of Aurélie as someone who could appreciate the form of things.

'So,' she said, 'here you are alone, when by rights every person with eyes in their head should be asking you to skate.' She spoke without pity: merely outlining a problem.

'How did you – did she—' I asked.

'She didn't have to tell me. It was obvious, if you know her as well as I.'

There was a little pause. I turned back to the problem at hand.

'She has to be her social self tonight,' I said uncertainly. I wished I could believe that was all it was: just camouflage.

'Oh, no doubt.' Aurélie swirled her wine and looked out

over the frozen lake; laughed as a large woman in furs fell over, arse in the air and her red round face angry, and began shouting at her husband.

'It never ceases to amaze me how people who are born rich carry on,' she said. 'It's as if the world should be perpetually to their liking.'

'I thought—'

She watched me over the rim of her cup, dark eyes twinkling. 'My parents were grocers in Orléans.'

'And now?'

'Now I'm married to a bore. But I have security, my books, my stables and I find that I can watch those people out on the lake and not mind if they hardly see me.'

'She's different,' I said. 'She isn't herself. She hasn't been for a few weeks.'

'And why do you think that is?'

'I don't know. I can't think how to help her.' It was surprisingly easy to talk to her, sitting here away from the rest of the world.

'Here,' she said, taking off her stole and reaching across to wrap it snugly round my shoulder.

'It's been since the faint,' I said. 'I can't seem to get her to listen. Sometimes she's there and sometimes she's not. And then, things like tonight—'

'She seems to pick and choose who she is.'

'Yes.' I blushed. But there was a warm feeling, too, the spice of the disloyalty.

'So what are you going to do about it?'

'I don't know.' I thought unhappily of the empty safe. The plan seemed stupid – out of reach and childish. I turned to look at Luce. She was talking to someone else now: as animated as I had ever seen her.

'In the meantime, what about you?'

The wine had made my cheeks hot; I pressed my palms to them to cool down.

She murmured: 'It seems there are a lot of things you're not sure of.'

She reached for my hands, and folded them in hers, and gave them a squeeze. 'That big house, and André so very present all the time,' she said. 'I suppose you must ask yourself: *How long am I prepared to wait?*'

'I don't know,' I said again. She was still holding my hands loosely in hers. It was more for something to say, than anything else: I felt dull, and tired. It was as if the wine had drawn a curtain between us and the rest of the party, skating in endless loops.

She drew a pattern on the back of my hand with her thumb. 'One must wonder how many other opportunities one may miss along the way?'

Her look was lowered; at first I didn't understand. Then she looked up, and the old Aurélie was clearly visible in the cast of the lips.

I pulled my hands away. She knew then that she had miscalculated; she licked her lips. 'But wouldn't you agree, we only regret the chances we didn't take?'

I stepped back, away from her clutching hands, towards the ice.

She smiled her lemon-slice smile, followed me forward and gripped my wrist, and we stood like that, in tension, running away impossible.

Her voice was a low murmur: 'She'll wring you out and run back to what she knows – it's how she is built.'

'You don't know anything about us. She loves me.'

There was something like tenderness on her face. At the same moment, the crowd parted and I saw Luce, laughing and talking, not ten feet away, a circle of admiring, fashionable women around her.

'Come now,' Aurélie said. 'Did you really think you were her first?'

~

I stepped off the bank and half-skated, half-staggered as fast as I could across the ice. From the corner of my eye, Luce turning, confused, to watch me go.

On the other side of the lake, I took my skates off and started back down the path towards the house.

I had reached the lawn before I heard her footsteps behind me, looked around and found her close enough to touch.

She moved round till we were facing each other; stood watching me, her chest rising and falling. She looked like the person I had thought was mine, the person I had met in the salon all those months ago: her face lovely with exercise, her eyes sparkling from all the fine conversation and clever jokes.

'Why didn't you tell me about Aurélie?'

Her eyes widened. I saw it clearly now, how she darted here and there, looking for the right thing to say.

'It was a long time ago. Nothing.' Her eyes cut downwards. 'Why, what did she say?'

'That you use people up and let them go. Is that what you did to her? Were you in love with her? Are you still together now?'

'No,' she said. 'No, it wasn't like that.'

I shake my head. 'What haven't you told me? What's going on now, that you won't tell me about?'

She closed her eyes, tight: but not before I had seen something flicker in them.

I slapped her. A casual, arcing blow, but hard, because it made the small bones of my hand hum.

Her head snapped sideways; she put her hand to her cheek to test for blood; finding it, she put her fingertip experimentally to her tongue, and was her old self again; all the way back, wiping out everything, to the person I had seen being expelled from Pathé, eyes narrowed and glittering. In the distance, the pop and fizz of New Year fireworks bursting over Paris.

221

Juliette and Adèle
1967

Adèle looks out of the window, watching something else.

At last, she takes a sharp breath in. 'But you said you had something to ask me,' she says.

I slide the list of names the man from Public Records had sent me across the table. She reaches for her handbag, extracts a pair of reading glasses, and perches them on the end of her nose.

'What am I looking at?' she asks.

'These are all the people who lived in Anne Ruillaux's house before her.'

'Anne Ruillaux being the lady who handed in the film canister?'

I say: 'Correct. Can you tell me if you recognise any of them? The man from Public Records said they had no connection with Pathé, but I just thought one of them might be familiar.'

She studies the sheet. Slides it back across the table.

She says: 'No. I'm sorry. I don't recognise anyone.'

She watches me for a few seconds. 'When I have a problem, I turn the telescope around. Look at it from the reverse angle. Start again from the beginning, or recommence at the end. Might that be of some assistance here?'

I put my fingers to my temples and press inwards. 'I'm not sure.'

'What is the beginning of the mystery? When was the last time anyone saw the film?'

'During the fire at the Pathé factory,' I say. And look up at her.

Juliette, vi.

The Pathé archivist beams when she catches sight of me, her pointed face opening.

She walks towards me, carrying a box-file, and puts it on my desk.

'The Pathé fire of 1914,' she says. 'This is everything.'

'Thanks.' I pull the box towards me and lift the lid.

She hovers. 'Is this to do with the missing film?'

I am leafing through the newspaper articles about the fire — *Inferno at Pathé factory — Workers evacuated — No fatalities...*

'They started the fire,' I say. 'The person who stole the print set the factory on fire to cover up the theft. I'm sure of it.'

The archivist frowns. 'But the papers all said the fire was an accident.'

'It's the only way the thief could be sure nobody would know the film had been stolen. This way, everyone would assume it had just been destroyed along with everything else. It wouldn't even be missed, and nobody would come looking for him. And you have the records, don't you?'

The archivist stares. 'But nitrate cellulose is so flammable. The reaction generates its own oxygen, so it just burns and burns. When a film reel caught fire at the Paris Bazaar in 1897, the fire continued for days. A hundred people died.'

I say: 'You mean whoever started the fire couldn't be sure the firemen would be able to put it out? Without loss of life?'

'Yes. Whoever it was must have been really desperate.'

She looks down with distaste at the papers arranged in a fan on my desk.

'He's in there somewhere,' she says. 'Your ruthless person.'

5. janvier 1914

I'D DREAMED OF HOW this would feel; the cosmetician asking me to bend my head a little to the right, and with deferential flicks of her wrist she dusted my right cheek with powder. Then she invited me to offer a pretend kiss to the mirror, and painted my lips, and then put kohl just underneath my eyes, which wavered away from their own reflected gaze.

'All done,' she said, starting to replace her pots and unguents in her make-up case with precision and fastidiousness. Everything in its proper place.

I wanted to ask her to stay with me until it was time to go to the stage, but she kept her back to me. I heard the snap of the clasps fastening her bag, and she left the room without saying anything else.

The dressing room is quiet apart from the ticking of the pipes overhead. I put my palms on my knees and listen to my own breathing.

A knock at the door: the camera assistant. 'It's time.'

It had taken me a few attempts to get through to Peyssac on André's study telephone; a few tries to understand how the dialling worked, and which end one picked up. And then I had to choose my moment, before the household was properly awake and I could be interrupted.

Peyssac's early-morning-peevish voice came through on the crackling line: 'Yes? Who is it, please?'

'It's Adèle Roux.'

I thought: *Perhaps he won't remember me.*

A hush, as he considered. 'How wonderful to hear your voice again.' The delicacy of the pause. 'And do you have good news for me?'

'Yes.'

'Delightful. So pleased.'

Another pause. What do you say to a co-conspirator?

'Can you be free in two days' time, say, at nine in the morning? We will arrange for a car. And – given your situation – yes, I think we can complete your scenes in a single day. Nobody need know until such time as you choose to tell them.'

'Thank you.'

I was about to hang up when I thought of the money; I'd need it if I was going to live independently again. 'I will want to be paid,' I said.

Miles away, Peyssac spluttered. 'Of course! Your wages will be available to be collected at the Pathé offices, the day after filming, as is customary.'

I replaced the receiver without saying goodbye.

The night before the filming, I packed my valise and slid it under the bed. Straightening up, I hesitated, listening.

Then shook my head: of course that sound was not footsteps, coming to my room. It was only the floorboards complaining as the house tacked into the wind.

'That is our final shot. Thank you, everyone.' Peyssac bounces forward, hands clasped. 'Mlle Roux. Words cannot express – it has been an honour. I do most fervently hope we will work together again.'

The cameraman is turning away, collapsing the tripod. Extras mill about, chatting, getting out cigarettes. The light coming through the studio roof is tinged with pink.

In the dressing room, I am left alone to remove my make-up:

the Vaseline in long, greasy smears; the kohl, picking at it with watery cloths to get it out of the creases under my eyes.

At the factory gates I get into the car Peyssac has provided: the latest model, its engine builds to a roar before we purr away.

The streets unribbon. At a greengrocer's, I see Mathilde. Her spidery fingers are engaged in examination of fruit – she holds a plump apple up, inspecting it for bruises, then drops it satisfied into her string bag and looks up, scanning about her for the next thing.

I raise my fingers to wave to her: she sees me, her head turning as the car passes; her face too unlined, her dress too fine – it cannot be her after all. Not-Mathilde: not someone I knew. The woman turns away, crossly, as if I have offended her.

When I get home there is a fluttering sound: looking up into the curve of the stairwell, hundreds of sheets of paper are floating down towards me with a sound like wings.

A silk slipper is discarded on the lowest step; its fellow has been hurled further, and lies on its side under the console table.

Thomas comes hurrying down, his carefully professional face disarranged. 'Come quickly,' he says, loops round and starts to run back up, with me in his wake.

I hop over a pair of silver-backed hairbrushes balancing on the steps. At the visible destruction something in my chest has begun to flutter inconveniently: by the top of the stairwell, the walls are lurching. *Can it be,* they ask, *that with your stubbornness you have finally made her candid?*

'Your valise had gone, so naturally she feared you had gone with it,' Thomas says. He pushes at his brilliantined hair as he stands outside the salon door. 'She will expect you to explain.'

Without waiting for me to tell him that the valise was only pushed out of sight, he opens the door inwards for me to go in.

The twin vases from the mantel have smashed, eggshell on the floor; books have been torn from the shelves and had their spines viciously broken. The writing table where I used to sit is an insect on its back with the legs snapped off. The only intact object in the room is the sofa where I used to sit, and this is where Luce is.

She doesn't hear me come in: she is rubbing her face as though she wants the top layer of skin gone.

When she removes her hands, she forgets to be angry: her eyes fill up with grateful tears, and then she remembers, composing her face.

'I'm so tired of being tired,' she says.

Above her cheekbone there is still a bruise the colour of parchment.

She says: 'With Aurélie, I had something, very briefly, a few years ago. I wasn't myself, and I got better, and then it wasn't important – at least, not to me. We carried on as before, and I tried to make it all right with her; but she's never let me forget it, and now I don't know if we're even friends. I think I knew, unless I was careful, she would bring me trouble in the end. And now she has.' A breath in. 'I should have told you.'

Trees sway silently outside the window. It's my chance to tell her where I have been. I want to say everything. How abandoned I felt when the make-up went on, sitting alone in the dressing room; how I could only think of how she would do this gesture, look in that mirror. Of how in another world she would be proud of me, playing this part.

I will say it. But before I can open my mouth, she says: 'I think it's time, isn't it? I really think we ought to go away.'

Silently, from one fraction of a second to the next, in the great wash of relief, I let the chance of a confession pass. I will tell her when we are right away from here. Sitting on a beach, her knees bent under her, massaging a grey pebble as we look out across the Pas de Calais, she will pre-empt: *Did you think I didn't know you'd been to the studios? It never mattered.*

She is looking up at me. 'Or have I burned my bridges?'

I poke at a shard of smashed vase with my toe. 'You seem to have been burgled.'

She looks at me, dazed and miserable.

I say: 'When we live together, we'll get better locks.'

She looks at her feet and smiles, private at first, then wide open.

Then she says: 'As soon as we can. Tomorrow, if possible. Is it possible?'

The last thing I expect, and the thing I most want: the sooner the better, for the less chance for the gossip to leak out of Pathé. Nevertheless, I'm so surprised by my good luck that I don't quite know what to say. Was Aurélie right? Will she always pull her fingers back at the last minute and run to what she knows?

But look, look at the broken things all around us.

'There is a small sum of money which is due to me,' – this is the best I can do with the Pathé wage office – 'that can be withdrawn tomorrow morning.'

She starts to laugh and cry, wiping impatiently at her eyes.

That night, in her room, we plan.

'We'll get right away at first,' she says, 'until the dust has settled and' – she takes a shivering breath in – 'we can come back to Paris.'

She smiles; turns her face away. 'We need some out-of-the-way, unfashionable place.' She snaps her fingers and spins round. 'England!' she says. 'We can take the boat at Calais.'

'I don't have a passport.'

Her face falls. 'Calais, then.'

'We can't use Hubert to get to the station. Nobody must know where we've gone.'

She bites the ragged skin at the corner of her thumbnail.

'We'll hail a cab from the road.'

　'What about our suitcases? Won't Thomas see us leaving?'

　'I'll ask him to clear out the back bedrooms.'

　We stand facing each other.

　'Don't worry,' she says. 'This will work.'

6. janvier 1914

HOW THE GARDEN LOOKED from my window that morning: silvery mint-coloured, the blades of grass curled over under their coating of frost. I didn't feel it. What I yearned for was for the day to have already gone to plan.

I turned back to my valise and snapped the clasps shut. The sound was encouraging: definite and businesslike. I dusted my damp palms on my skirt and, going to my bedroom door, opened it a crack to listen, nudging my untouched breakfast tray out of the way with my toe.

The squeak of door hinges, the chatter of servants swelling and dimming as the door swung to. Luce and André must still be at breakfast. I waited; a minute, two minutes passed, and my neck began to twinge from the odd position; then I heard the scrape of a chair being pushed back and André's voice, saying something over his shoulder, and his steps up the stairs. I drew back; heard a door open and close – his study – and then footsteps going back down. In the hall, I heard the rustle of cold-weather clothes, him whistling, and the front door clunk open; the buzz of the car engine, the slam of the door, and he was gone.

I heard Luce calling; walked down the stairs to the second landing. She was standing on the landing below; her upturned face was worried.

'A visitor is coming to the house. He'll be here at half-past eleven.'

'But that doesn't matter. We can wait until he's gone.' André

would not be back until the evening. 'We can still catch the two
o'clock train. It doesn't matter, does it?' I said.

'Oh. Not at all.'

'Just don't let him to stay to lunch.'

She nodded.

We had been whispering, but a door closing somewhere
on the ground floor made me suddenly mindful of standing
out in the open. I blew her a kiss to encourage her; she gave
a little shiver of nerves and a smile, turned and walked away
down the stairs.

I waited till she was gone, then walked down the stairs to
the ground floor. I heard Thomas in the salon, crossed the hall
and rapped on the door. Pretend-confidence made my voice
quiver as I asked him to fetch Hubert.

As he reached the door, worry made me add: 'Mme Durand
wants me to fetch her scripts personally from the studio.'

I knew at once it was a misstep, giving so much needless
information. But all he said was, 'Right away, Mademoiselle.'

I sat on one of the salon chairs, staring out of the window
until the car slid past; Hubert's steps outside the door; I ran to
meet him.

I thought at first that he looked surprised to see just me,
and not Luce – and then shook myself down inside – he was
only surprised to be called so early, and those were just toast
crumbs he was wiping from his mouth. 'To Pathé, please,' I said
demurely as he held the car door open.

As the car crunched down the gravel drive I turned and
looked up at the windows, hoping perhaps she would be
watching us go.

'Just you today?' Hubert said, his eyes big in the rear-view
mirror.

'Just me.'

He nodded, and flexed his hands on the steering wheel.

~

It was clocking-in time when we got to the factory. I looked at the sea of workers milling about outside and wondered how I had ever thought they looked happy. They turned thin, unfriendly faces to peer into the car as Hubert fired the horn; I looked at my lap, fearful of seeing someone I knew.

'Here is fine.' I jumped down from the cab and crossed the courtyard to the tiny administrative lodge on the right-hand side.

Knocking and entering, I found four small desks in a cramped room piled high with all kinds of papers. A man in spectacles looked up.

'I have come to collect monies that M. Peyssac left me. Adèle Roux.'

He peered at me. His hand hovered over a stack of ledgers on his overcrowded desk and he finally picked one up and, licking his finger, leafed through it. 'Now, now, let's see—' He looked through; turned the volume the other way up, squinted, and returned it to its original direction. 'When would the entry be for?'

'It was only yesterday.'

'Oh, *yesterday*.' He dropped the ledger; picked up a second, sighed heavily and began to leaf through. 'My colleague was here yesterday, not me. Let's have a look.'

More hemming and hawing. I thought of Hubert, leaning against the car bonnet, smoking; of André, very close perhaps, maybe even on his way to the studio from his office in Building I.

'This is most irregular,' the old man was saying, 'normally we don't release any wages until the filming is completed. Adèle Roux, Adèle Roux, I don't see it here.'

I could have closed my hands around his scrawny throat. Trying to keep my voice calm, I said: 'M. Durand is my employer and he requires it.'

The man looked up under his eyebrows. 'But in that case,

he would have countersigned the request.'

Another worker, a woman, looked up from her desk at me.

I said: 'Find him. Ask him.'

The muscles in my throat tightened: what if he did really find André? What then?

The man pursed his lips. The woman looked down at her correspondence.

'On this occasion,' he said. He remained tight-lipped as he picked his way across the room to a box-safe in the corner. With agonising slowness he unlocked, counted out notes, recounted and fumbled about for an envelope. The clock on the wall read ten past ten; eleven past; twelve past, until at last he passed the envelope to me.

I counted it in front of him. 'Thank you,' I said, as crisp as the notes I held, and left the office.

Coming towards me across the courtyard was a redhead: Paul the security guard. I turned away, but it was too late: he was raising his hand and calling out to me. He broke into a jog and reached me as I reached the car.

'Congratulations!' he said. 'I heard about *Petite Mort*. Does that mean you'll be back more often now? As an actress?'

His face was all eagerness and goodwill.

I got into the car without a word.

I knew something was wrong as soon as we turned into the drive. Parked up in front of the house were two cars: an unfamiliar Daimler – this must belong to Luce's guest – and then André's studio car and his regular chauffeur, standing by the bonnet, squinting up into the winter sun in his dark uniform, the plume of his cigarette streaming skywards; he waved silently to Hubert, who saluted back, and drew our car round in a wide circle to park next to it.

'Why is M. Durand here?' I asked, leaning forward. 'Whose is the other car?'

'How should I know? Perhaps he's come home early.' Hubert walked round to open the door for me.

Silence in the hall. I took the steps two at a time. There was nobody in the first-floor corridor, so I ran lightly down towards the salon door, which was closed. As I approached, I heard voices from the inside of the room: I laid my ear to the panels very gently. A stern, authoritative voice, holding forth about something, the words impossible to make out: then André – I jumped at how close he was, only a few feet from the other side of the door – asking a question, then Luce, irritably countering something; then the first voice again, making peace.

Something about the voice was familiar but I could not place it: and finally, realising the discussion could go on for hours, I drew away from the door and considered what to do next.

It must be almost twelve o'clock; the meeting would be over soon, the visitor would leave and André would go back to the studios.

I exhaled, looking up at the cupola, a startling blue.

Five minutes passed. The voices went on and on, behind the door; downstairs, the grandfather clock chimed twelve.

Ten minutes became fifteen. I ran up to my room, took my valise from the bed and stood with it in my hand, with some idea of being prepared.

Five more minutes ticked by. Could we wait? But the news had already broken from Pathé. By tonight, she would know what I'd done.

As I stood there, indecisive, I heard the opening of the salon door, André saying something hearty but indistinct, and the party moved downstairs.

I waited, holding my breath, for the purr of a car engine – and finally it came. But then also André's voice, cheerful, from the hall.

Why was he still here?

I hovered in my room, paralysed with indecision.

Then I heard footsteps coming up the stairs to my floor. Hers.

She burst into my room, staring, her hair wild. 'I only have a moment,' she said, 'André isn't going back to the studio, he's staying, he wants me to have lunch with him and then he is having meetings here all afternoon. He's invited some people round for supper.'

I stared at her, aghast.

'I have to go,' she said, hovering and agonised.

'We'll go out the back,' I said. 'There's still time. Meet me by the lake. We can go through the woods and get a cab on the Boulogne road.'

She nodded. Put a trembling hand to her temple. Nodded again.

'Who was the visitor?' I asked.

'Nobody,' she said, and shut the door.

When she had gone, I took my suitcase and crept down the stairs.

Through the half-open dining-room door I saw her sitting at the table, doing her best to smile and laugh; the strain showing around her eyes.

I went through the back doors and out onto the terrace, and when it was safe to run, I did so, my feet thudding on the damp earth, the valise banging painfully against my knees.

For too long I seemed to make no progress: each time I turned the house was just as big as before, and then suddenly the woods were there, only fifty metres away; and then with a shiver of rain on cold leaves I was under the canopy.

I pushed onwards until the branches broke free and I was on the pebble path; five minutes' walk and it tapered; the lake appeared up ahead.

It was not frozen any more, but black and studded with tiny

green jewels of algae. I chose a position near the path, and slid down against a tree trunk to watch and wait.

I calculated two o'clock. The meal would be finished; a cold kiss on the cheek for André. She would be collecting her coat, slipping downstairs and out by the French doors.

I calculated five past two. She would be on her way across the lawn, the grass crunching underfoot, her eyes trained on the distant woods.

Twenty past. A willow trailed its fingers in the lake and whispered, *She isn't coming.*

A branch shook, somewhere in my line of vision: the barest quiver, and then another bramble spray was moved out of the way by a slender hand; her sleeve, her grey dress, her arm and brave face.

She was smiling; she had already seen me and was stepping off the path.

I ran to her. She burst into tears and clung to me.

'I see you brought your wardrobe,' I said, nodding at her valise. She held me, and turned her head to look at it. 'Silly of me,' she said. 'I won't need any of it where we're going.'

She wiped her eyes; I tugged her hand. 'Which way?'

'Over there,' she said, indicating a path through the trees; and smiled.

A rustling behind us: the branches moved aside again and André stepped through the gap. In his right hand, he held a revolver – the one from his safe – idly, as one might jingle a set of keys.

'Taking your suitcases for a walk?' he said.

I glanced at Luce, who had turned white and still.

'Am I to understand that, in spite of everything we talked about, you have made promises to this young person?'

What he'd said repeated in my ears, meaningless. I grasped the essential – that somehow he had found out about us

– without grasping any of the implications.

'She has made promises,' I said, 'we're going away.'

André lifted the gun and tapped his chin with it, thoughtful. 'Where exactly were you going to go?'

I looked at Luce. She had opened her mouth but said nothing. She was white and blank with shock.

'A little cottage in Provence?' he asked. 'Somewhere you wouldn't be recognised? The problem with being an actress, darling, is that everybody knows your face.'

He prodded her suitcase with his toe, toppling it; the gesture seemed to wake her out of her daze.

I said: 'She isn't coming back to the house. She's coming with me.'

'Sure about that?' he said.

I didn't understand. She had fixed her eyes on him, pleading. The revolver twirled in his hand.

He said: 'You haven't told her.'

'What haven't you told me?' I said.

Luce started to cry.

'What?' I asked again.

She put one palm to her stomach and rested it there and looked at me, a look of such liquid misery that at first I didn't understand.

Then I remembered the voice in the salon that morning.

'Dr Langlois,' I said.

André nodded, arching an eyebrow, impressed.

I said: 'When?'

'Five months. Just before I went to Marseille.'

My throat made its own sounds, like an old person.

The ideas flew: keys slotting into one lock after another: 'That night, at the party, the faint – you found out when the doctor visited, when he was examining you. That's when he told you. That's why they made you rest up, because of what happened before. You let me think that you were ill. You let me think you were fragile, and dance attendance on you.'

'I was going to tell you—' she said.

'—when? What did you think would happen?'

She looked skywards. André looked at her with an air of vicious interest.

She said: 'I thought you might understand it was an accident. If you loved me, you might love the child.'

'But it would be half him!'

'And half me. And then, in time, maybe half you as well.'

I covered my face with my hands, not because she was wrong, but because she was right. I would love anything that was part of her.

'Don't cry,' she said, 'it isn't broken.'

How would we know if it was broken? Such things needed time to determine. I looked at her eyes, enormous in her face, the lashes softened by tears.

André slapped his free hand against his thigh, mocking applause.

He said: 'Did you know she took your part? When you were putting yourself in a state because you thought she'd left, she was filming *Petite Mort* with Peyssac?'

Luce's throat worked; her eyes swivelled to look at me.

'It isn't the same,' I said, 'I only did it because I was angry with you, I regretted it as soon as I got there. I was going to tell you.'

André said: 'Come back to the house.'

I spoke faster: 'I was going to tell you, once we were away. I want you to listen. I want—'

André lifted the gun.

'Please,' I said.

Luce looked at me.

She took my hands in hers, gave them a gentle squeeze and then dropped them.

'I, I, I,' she said.

She turned her back on me and took a few steps to André;

stood apart from him, very straight, and looked at me.

André smiled, as if at a private joke; he lowered the gun a little, and said: 'You could take an apartment nearby. If it keeps her happy. What do you say?'

I couldn't say anything. Images came to me in a long cascade. Things that hadn't happened yet: her arm linked through mine, the boom of surf on a pebble beach. The child.

She had raised her chin a fraction: its point angled to me.

I looked at her, really looked at her, and understood I had lost.

'I'll ruin you,' I said. 'I can tell it all over Paris.'

'You won't,' André said.

Luce glanced at him. He had lifted the gun again: not levelled it, but raised it in his right hand, hefting it.

I said: 'I will get a lawyer. Who knows what they might find in your past, if they go digging?'

Then I looked for something that might just kill him with words: 'Your child will be taken away from you. It won't know you.'

The gun lifted a notch. The hole at the end of its barrel pointed at my chest. André ground his hand into his eye socket; then, suddenly, he laughed, as if at the situation, and drew back slightly. The trees around us ruffled their feathers: it seemed as though we might, after all, reconcile. Weren't we a household, after all?

The gun was shaking in his hand.

I heard a loud bang, an explosion: my skin and bone were the explosion, and that was how I died my little death.

Luce and Adèle, i.

One day, just after André has left for the south, a note comes to the salon. It says that Feuillade wants her most particularly to rehearse over the next two weeks. If possible she must come into the city and take an hotel, so that they may work intensively.

She folds the note carefully. The clock on the mantel ticks her decision.

'It is Feuillade. His daughter is ill. They are going to Switzerland for a cure. What bad luck.'

Adèle doesn't say anything. She has her studious face bent to the paperback on her knees. One would hardly know she was listening at all.

'I shall just have to hang about here, annoying you.'

Still nothing. A blink, then the crisp sound of a page turning. 'You never annoy me.'

The first time she has said *you* and *I* in the same sentence: so little, it shouldn't be enough, but it is.

Later, when Adèle's head has fallen sideways in a doze, one watchful thumb still marking the page, she scrawls a reply to Feuillade: *…inconvenience you. Sadly no longer able. May I suggest as a replacement my former colleague Nelly Sinclair, an adept horsewoman…*

With love, L. DURAND. She presses the nib into the page and looks at the sleeping girl, whose eyelids flutter and jerk with the violence of her dream.

THE DOPPELGÄNGER, ENRAGED, STEPS OUT OF THE MIRROR

Testimony of Grégoire MOREAU, Sergeant,
Gendarmerie de l'Ile St Louis

Q. *Describe what happened on the morning of 8. janvier.*

A. At about nine o'clock I was on desk duty looking after the waiting room when the doors opened and I looked up, expecting it to be Mme de Courcet again about her poodle, but instead there was a girl.

Q. *Can you describe her?*

A. Her sleeve up to her elbow was dark brown and her dress was torn. The hem was in ribbons; the whole had been cut about and she looked, in short, very badly treated.

Q. *Proceed.*

A. Well, then she got close to the desk and asked 'Can you help me?' and I said 'Your arm, Mademoiselle!' and she looked at it: 'Oh this! I cannot feel it now at all!' Then a man waiting said: 'Stop staring, can't you see she is about to fall?' [...]

6. janvier 1914

SOMEONE LAUGHING became geese crossing an indigo sky.

Some time later I opened my eyes again. A weeping willow, stippling my forehead with insect-thin branches, drifting in the water around me. I began to panic and kick my heels for purchase. They met resistance: a light sucking sound and they touched mud, and the back of my head bumped against it too: I was floating in only a couple of inches of water, my hips resting on the bottom. I looked up and around, spitting out the cold water, and saw that I was only a foot or so from the bank; tried to push myself up but my left arm folded back in on itself.

A minute later I tried again, and this time managed to drag myself over the lip of the lake onto the bank and scramble backwards to lean against a tree.

I sat cradling my left elbow in my right hand, my fingers playing with the torn sleeve of my dress, then exploring higher. When I found the hole I drew my fingers away just as quick as I'd touched it. I was not brave enough to try again for a long time, but when I was, I found a ragged cylinder between my breastbone and my shoulder, into which it was possible to probe with the tip of one finger.

When I woke again, it was dark. I shivered, looking at the placid surface of the lake. There should have been scuttlings, the brittle noise of leaves drifting over each other, but there was no sound apart from my own breathing.

My shoulder flared, and with the pain came the memory. Three figures stood by the lake, one much beloved, another holding a gun, and the third was me. Luce's fingers straying to cover her stomach and then the muffled explosion.

When the pain had subsided enough, I reached up and felt the weeds laced through my still-damp hair. I saw myself, as if I was someone else again, pushed backwards by the force of the shot and falling into the shallows; Luce and André watching me from the bank. André leading her back to the house, concerned above everything else for the baby: who knew what a shock like this would bring about?

The memory played over and over, now forwards, and now backwards: the cold water hitting my face as I fell, the explosion a horse's kick to the arm, sighting down the hole at the end of the gun barrel and André's trigger finger, a pink blur.

I swung my right arm sideways and tested my weight on it; managed to lever myself onto my knees and a second later, found that I could stand. I held my soaking skirts in my hands for a moment, weighing them; stood there, confused.

How could you think I'd let him do that, she will say. *How could you? I was in the house all the time. And look, it is not serious: just a scratch. Come here.*

One step forward – two, more confident now – and I began to walk slowly back towards the path.

In the open, the wind met me, welcome and cold on my hot face; there was the house, black on the horizon, with its ground-floor windows twinkling yellow.

I went slowly in order not to jog my arm, my footsteps crunching across the grey lawn, but it was unavoidable: every few paces the pain would come. Each time it was too much I stretched my lips and showed my teeth, and in time the pain faded.

Now I began to feel serene: even if André were suddenly to leap out at me, there was nothing more that could be done; he would fade helplessly back into the darkness of the garden and I would keep moving on towards her. As I walked, I grasped for understanding of the situation – something was nagging at me – but my thoughts slid over the essential and found her. She would pull back the curtain and see me; her hand would fly to her mouth, her eyes round with shock. *Your poor arm. Bring it here: we'll call for help.*

Ahead of me was the balustrade of the terrace which led onto the lawn, coming clear; beyond it were the French windows of the dining room, the drapes half-drawn. A blur of movement through the gap: the gleam on the mahogany table, the flash of the footman's white shirt as he bent low, placing cutlery, ready for dinner guests.

When I was almost at the lip of the terrace, I heard a noise and froze. The French windows had clicked open, there was a rush of warm air into my face, and neat footsteps came out onto the patio. Thomas' craggy face flared briefly as he lit the lantern on the left-hand side of the dining-room doors. I waited; heard shuffling movements as he fiddled with the taper on the first lantern and moved to the other side of the door.

What had I been thinking? I couldn't be seen by him, or by the staff: I must not be seen by anyone but Luce. I waited for him to glance out into the garden, agonised: but his gloved hands moved deftly, closing the catch on the glass door of the second lantern; he turned away. The doors clicked shut again.

I looked down at myself; I was standing in the half-shadows at the edge of the pool of light thrown by the lamps. Then, inside the dining room, I saw the door open: five dinner guests, men and women smartly done up, were now bustling into the room. Their lips were opened in laughter and the polite, pleasurable confusion over who should sit where; unable to decide, they milled about, cheeks flushed with drink, and their chatter a muted thrum behind the glass.

Before I could decide what to do, a woman in a fuchsia dress broke away from the table and moved towards the window from inside. She was middle-aged and quick-eyed; she carried a fan which she beat very fast against her chest.

I was not five feet away – just the glass between us.

Charming, I saw her mouth say, looking past me at the view.

I gazed, fascinated, at the plump hand with the fluttering fan.

Come over here, Luce, and look at the lamps.

Luce moved slowly towards the window. She was wearing the dress she had worn for Aurélie's soirée, and her hair in a chignon, and everything was just as it had been, except that two tired lines drew down the sides of her mouth.

I raised my hand to spider it against the glass; her eyes widened. I fought an instinct to turn and look over my shoulder to see what had frightened her: she was looking right at me. I saw her mouth open, her hand go to her throat and then heard, very faint behind the glass, a scream.

Panic broke out in the dining room. The scream went on and on. Luce covered her mouth, then her eyes, and then her mouth with her hands; amidst the scrambling guests André came running into the room, his legs very lithe and his murderer's hands poised to grip somebody.

I saw André's clutching fingers, felt the sharp cold on my neck and face, turned and ran away over the terrace and down the steps. I stumbled over the grass to the left; then changed direction and made instead for the side of the house.

Behind, I heard the alarm being given: men's footsteps spilling onto the terrace to search for the prowler, and a woman's well-bred voice – not hers – repeating over and over: *There was nobody there...*

I stumbled onwards, listening to the voices grow faint behind me, my arm jogging helplessly against my ribs as I ran. At last I reached the corner of the house and slid round it; the soft stone crumbled against my back and the fingers of my spread hands.

7. janvier 1914

I KNEW I WAS GOING towards Paris because every half-hour or so, the lights of a car would dazzle me, shining through the trees on either side of the road; and then the car would crawl, low-slung, past me. Sometimes I would catch a glimpse of the driver's speculative eyes – but those in the back, the rich men returning home from their parties and dinners, remained hidden.

Once a car slowed almost to a halt; a man's face peered out from the rear window, assessing, then caught sight of my dress and the state of my arm and hurriedly gave the signal to drive on.

At last I came to an open stretch of parkland. There were tufts of bushes dotted over the turf – a clear plain half a mile long, leading away to trees, and then the trees dropped away, and beyond it was Paris.

The air was stale and cold: a thousand mansard roofs were just turning into slate, a hint of blue on the dawn. The sun was a rim on the horizon: as I watched, the Seine appeared, winking gold as it snaked towards me, and pinpricks of window lights near and far wavered off.

The 16th must be directly ahead; a flash near the horizon might be the rose-tinted windows of Notre-Dame. I thought I had the Boulevard St Michel and tried to follow it down to the 14th but lost the trail before rue Boissonnade came clear. Each time I tried my effort was poorer, and the lines of the streets blurred into one another and petered out in unlikely endings. The closest I could get was the Panthéon: in one of those windows a mile to the south of its white dome – or perhaps those over to the right – Agathe was turning over in bed, mouth sagging open; and in another, Camille would be sleeping, her thin arms stretched out above her head.

Trees becoming roads: a breeze, leaves shaking themselves at me.

A woman on the other side of the road, wheeling a covered barrow from which rose the smell of fresh bread. Her look, quick and suspicious. The smart tap of her footsteps and the squeak of the wheels going away from me.

Exotic birds in greens and purples. One saying, hands on hips: *It's a wonder you get any trade, looking like that.* Then they scattered in a twirling of parasols and a shimmer of laughter.

Then the sun was higher than I had realised, and achingly bright; the streets were narrower, and emptier, but I had no idea which district I was in. Passing faces were blurs, looming in at me and vanishing.

Someone buffeted into me: pain shot up my arm, and he said, 'Look out, can't you?'

I snatched at him. 'I don't recognise anything,' I said, 'where am I?' but it was like catching a phantom: he pulled his sleeve out of my grip.

'The 14th, of course,' he said, frowning, and walked away.

My gaze began to waver again, useless and desperate, over the stone façades of the apartment blocks – and suddenly I saw the fat face of the greengrocer at the bottom of rue Boissonnade, staring back at me. The coffee-and-stew smell from the restaurant next door, the pine-green newspaper kiosk on the corner, with the boy calling the day's news. A dusty slamming sound: overhead there were even the two familiar women whose names I had never learned, gossiping as they beat their rugs over their balconettes.

I hobbled across the street towards him.

'Mademoiselle Roux!' he said. 'How did you escape?'

I knew, even in my feverish state, that this could not be right.

'Was I misinformed?' he said. 'The police said nobody got out.'

I stared back at him.

'This morning,' he said, and then again: 'Was I misinformed?'

His eyes travelled past me, over the street towards number fourteen.

There was a police officer standing at the entrance to the apartment block, arms behind his back, watching the street.

I walked across the street to the policeman and stood a few metres away, looking at a kicked-in hole in the door. The officer shifted on his feet and looked more closely at me.

'Can I help, Mademoiselle?' he asked.

I cleared my throat. The sound was rusty and unreal. 'What happened?'

'There's been an incident. Three people were found shot in one of the apartments.'

'Which one?'

'Top floor. A landlady, one woman of dubious reputation and one other.'

'What happened to the young one? The girl?'

He frowned. 'I told you, nobody got out. How did you know she was young?'

I began to shake. He was staring at me as if he knew me from somewhere; turning, I walked away from him, and did not look back.

Who was it André knew? It didn't matter. He must have nodded and smiled at his guests as they chattered about the prowler over the remains of their supper – all the time playing with his cutlery and thinking: *What if?*

With brandy and cards passed out, he would excuse himself and run up to his study, and lift the telephone receiver from the cradle; give the rue Boissonnade address. He had written to Mathilde, once, and paid my rent up to date for me so that I could go to live with him. He knew that I knew nobody else in the city.

He would give a description – seventeen, thin, dark hair.

Then downstairs again to sit in the salon, listening to the talk. Waved the guests off in due course; watching them shrug their stoles around their shoulders as they got into their cars.

Much later, the shrilling of the telephone would wake him. They'd found a girl in one of the bedrooms who matched the description he'd given, and disposed of the others when they came shouting. And André would have said, *Yes, fine.* He had never known I had a sister.

I wandered away, towards the river, and went down the steps to the *quais*.

Under the bridge was a fire set alight in an old container, and men and women huddled round. I thought I saw Monsieur Z; I thought he waved; but I was too tired to do anything other than shoulder my way in and curl up amongst the other bodies.

When I opened my eyes it was dark. The moon was a full white coin, and Camille was lying next to me. Her face was as cool and smooth as a child's.

She pursed her lips when I put a finger to her face, and pulled back.

I asked: *Did the men leave a sign by which I can find them? I could go to the law.*

She shook her head.

Then how should we get revenge?

Her glance wavered down to fix on my shoulder; then back to my face.

We lay for a while opposite each other, listening to the shouts of a fight breaking out amongst the people further down the row. She shook her arm out as if it had given her pins and needles.

Where you are – what's it like?

She did a mock-shiver, drawing an invisible shawl around her ears.

Juliette, vii.

When I arrive at the archive, my things have been left out on my desk overnight, the papers arranged in exactly the same order.

There are three articles in the press about the fire; *Le Figaro*, *Le Temps* and *Le Petit Parisien*. They all agree that the fire started about seven o'clock in the morning, in Building J, which was used by certain of the editors. The fire spread rapidly to the surrounding buildings; within minutes the factory was evacuated. Apart from that there is nothing of interest. All of them attribute the blaze to an accident.

Then I turn to the folder marked 'Witness Statements' and a set of papers slip out. I scan them for the Préfecture de Police stamp, and don't see it; flip back to the front sheet and see writing in a tiny, crabbed hand: *Property of Internal Security – Pathé Factory. If found, please return to Building I.*

The typewriter ink on the first statement has faded to pale blue.

REY Edouard
Security Guard – Day Shift
At seven o'clock on 8 January, I was alerted to the fire by a member of my patrol and we went straight to Building J where we saw that the fire had only recently taken hold. We immediately gave the order to evacuate the entire factory.

The largest quantity of smoke issued from the south-west corner of the building, which an editor tells me is where he stores his completed masters, ready to be collected and sent off for duplication.

I did not see anyone in the immediate vicinity of the building.

PHILIBERT Marc
Guard – Night Shift
On my rounds at a quarter to seven I saw nothing out of the ordinary. I was unable to check the door because I had lent my key out the previous night to a director, but I observed that it was fastened and there was no evidence of disturbance.

I proceeded on my way, returning to my cabin at five minutes to seven, and was roused from my cabin by shouts, at which point I made my way to Building J to see a sheet of yellow flame.

In summary, I did not see anything unusual that day. I cannot think of anyone who would want to start the fire deliberately.

There are no more witness statements: just a folder marked 'Photographs'. But when I open the folder, only one print slips onto the desk.

Black and white grins: three lines of men formally posed, in front of the wall of a building. The front two rows are young men, lolling about in overalls and caps. Behind them is a row of five starchier looking, older men in dark suits and ties. Underneath is a date: *7. janvier 1914. Pathé directors and juniors enjoying a break at the factory.*

I press my thumbs to my eyelids until the shapes appear.

Testimony of M. le Docteur HARBLEU

Q. *[...] you were the physician called by Sergeant Moreau to the gendarmerie on the afternoon of 8. janvier?*
A. Correct.

Q. *And your findings were?*
A. I saw a young female of between fifteen and twenty years in age. Her records were not on file and she confirmed she came from a small parish near Toulouse where written certification was sparse. She gave her name as Adèle Roux, 17.

Q. *The wound?*
A. Was clean in appearance, from a small-calibre handgun, from a short distance. The victim had been extremely fortunate; the bullet had passed within an inch of the upper left lung, and exited behind the shoulder. The arm hung from its socket – that is to say, the arm's motor function was naturally impaired – but the victim was able to walk and talk. There was no sepsis. I would say the wound was a day or two old, at best. In short, if one had aimed the bullet precisely it would have been hard to do less permanent damage.

Q. *What was your impression of Mlle Roux?*
A. She let me look at her without fuss. If she felt pain on examination she did not show it.

Q. Did she say anything to you?

A. I asked her who had done it and she said 'M. Durand of Pathé; and his wife.' When I asked her what she meant, she became agitated, and asked for someone to fetch the police inspector [...]

André, vi.

Inspector Japy blows smoke at the façade of André Durand's house.

It is a fine morning, with an improbable seasonal change in the air: the turf underfoot feels springy for the first time in months; white strips of cloud hurry across the sky. In front of the house, a chauffeur is playing a hose over the bonnet of a grey Daimler.

Go careful, Japy's superior had begged, sweating in his over-hot office. *Just find out if the girl worked for them, then find out why she ran away, or whatever it was: end of story.* His boss had dusted his hands of an imaginary embarrassment.

Japy had smiled sleepily. He'd reached the door before his boss had cracked: *Japy! Absolutely no mesmerism! Understand?*

The chauffeur looks up at his approach, flat feet crunching over gravel, and frowns: 'Can I help?'

'Is M. Durand at home?'

The chauffeur blinks at Japy's stained grey overcoat. 'Can I help?'

'You could show me in.'

Japy senses some petty infraction in this man's past – his hands tremble as he drops the hosepipe on the ground.

'Of course,' the chauffeur says, overly keen to please, and leads him towards the great front door.

A tapestry which wants to be the Lady and the Unicorn hangs in the hallway, next to an ostentatious hat stand. Japy fingers the tapestry as he passes: cheap Flemish wool, coarse in its modernity.

The chauffeur is sending anxious little glances back at him, hovering a few paces ahead, calling for the butler. Japy looks at the stairway, vast and curled.

A tall man appears at the end of the corridor.

Japy smiles. 'M. Durand, please.'

The man isn't used to being bossed about; all the more reason to do it, so when he starts to say, 'Do you have an appointment?' Japy changes the tenor of his smile, just lowers the temperature fractionally, and says, 'No.'

'I'm afraid it won't be possible for you to see him today.'

No flies on this one: a past whiter than white, in a monastery possibly. The chauffeur is hanging back, on the edge of disappearing to safety.

'Inspector Japy,' Japy says, producing a crumpled visiting card.

The butler takes it; says: 'Your cigarette.'

'What?'

'Is dropping ash on the carpet.'

The butler goes upstairs. A minute passes. Japy grinds his cigarette stub into an imitation High Flemish ashtray and stands back on his heels to wait.

Another minute; then a door closes upstairs, and André Durand is loping down the stairs to meet him.

'Inspector Japy? Follow me,' and leads him into a salon, where he makes sure to pull out the best chair for his guest; sits on the sofa opposite, running his hand through his hair. 'So, what's this about?'

Japy nods to a vase on the mantel. 'Surely that's First Dynasty?'

'I believe so. It's from my wife's family.'

'In my spare time, I am something of an antiques enthusiast.

One always recognises quality.'

'A second string to your bow.'

'Oh, but I don't consider it a secondary pursuit. Are you familiar with the lectures given by Commander Darget on the topic of magnetic effluvia?'

Durand shifts his weight in his chair. 'I'm afraid not.'

'By which all objects emit – if you will – a sacred emanation, an ectoplasm indicating the history of their displacements? Imagine if a detective were able to interpret the secret signs of a gun used in a murder? Trace the path of the bullet, faintly glowing, through the air? Imagine what tales that vase would tell us if it could!' He pauses, hand held dramatically in front of him, for just long enough to see Durand's lip twitch at the corner. 'No, M. Durand, my interest in objects is of the order of the professional.'

Durand's whole body is relaxed, legs lolling apart at the knees; his voice, correspondingly, is a purr. 'And has this effluvia led you to many convictions?'

'Not yet, Monsieur,' Japy says, 'but one lives in hope. What can you tell me about a Mademoiselle Adèle Roux?'

'Mlle Roux was my wife's assistant, until a few days ago,' he says.

'It is only that Mlle Roux has made some allegations against you and your wife.'

'What sort of allegations?'

'She has been very badly hurt, and claims you are responsible.'

'But that's preposterous.' Durand gets to his feet. 'If anything, we are the injured party. Mlle Roux ran away a few days ago, leaving us in a fix for our domestic position. Not to mention the worry we naturally felt for her wellbeing.'

Japy thinks: *You have prepared even this little speech.*

'What has happened to her, then?' Durand asks.

'She has been shot through the arm. You understand the

position. We are bound over to investigate where possible.'

'Shot? Dear me,' Durand says. 'Are you sure? She was such a demure little person.' He pinches his own lip, thinking. 'A boyfriend, perhaps, someone we didn't know about.'

'She will recover.'

'So glad.' He sits on the sofa. 'But I must admit to feeling very poorly used in all this. To accuse us…!' One hand goes to shade his forehead.

Japy reaches inside his coat for a notepad. 'Would you mind telling me how she left?'

'It was two days ago. We simply came back and found her gone.'

'When you say, you found her gone…'

'Suitcase, clothes, everything. Nobody saw her leave.'

Japy raises his hands to heaven. 'My dear sir! A mesmerist's dream!'

'Pardon?'

'You have only to show me to the lady's chamber, and there I will concentrate my mind and observe the trails left by the missing objects. That will certainly give us a clue to the nature of the mystery.'

He stands, flipping the notepad shut, beaming. Durand starts, as if unsure if this is a joke. 'Is this a joke?' he says.

'I assure you it is quite real.'

Durand pushes the bedroom door open. Japy smiles politely, shoulders past him and looks at the second-rate furniture, the old paint on the shutters, which have been flung wide to air the room.

'Yes,' he says, 'oh yes, I can see we are going to have some success here.'

He stands in the centre of the room, pinches middle finger to thumb on each hand and lowers his head.

'Yes, it was this way,' he murmurs to himself, a moment later, walking swiftly to the door. 'The valise went this way. I can see it. And down towards the stairs, yes, like so.'

He crosses to the landing and starts to descend. Durand waits, arms folded, and then follows him.

Japy leads him all the way back to the ground floor, and hovers in the hallway. The butler has appeared at the sound of footsteps and stands disapproving at the back of the hall.

'Almost,' Japy says through clenched teeth. 'Almost…'

With a swift movement he runs to the great front door and yanks it open, and stands, sniffing the morning air.

Behind him, he hears a cough of laughter.

'Almost…' he says again, seems to deflate, then rallies, turning to his audience, which by now includes the chauffeur and a footman he hasn't seen before.

'No?' Durand says.

'I can sense, definitely so, that she came this way carrying her valise. She left the house, as you told us, through the front door. Everything happened just as you said, Monsieur.'

Durand's nostrils flare. 'You will go back to your superiors and they will, they will give your report the credit it deserves?'

Japy: 'They take me very seriously indeed.'

Durand stretches out a hand. 'So pleased to have made your acquaintance, Inspector. I hope we meet again in better circumstances.'

Japy shakes the hand gravely. 'At your service, Monsieur.'

He waits until he is striding down the gravel path, has waved once, twice to Durand and his huddled staff; then turns back. 'One last thing.' He starts to walk back towards the house. 'Might I ask the privilege of seeing round behind, to admire the rear elevation? One never gets to see these fine old houses from the back.'

Durand smiles. There is nothing behind the smile except perhaps another smile, repeating ad infinitum into the distance. 'Of course,' he says.

Japy ducks his head appreciatively. 'And the girl's effects? They were taken with her?'

Confident: 'Yes.'

'You're quite sure she took everything?'

A flicker: 'Yes.'

'Thank you.' Japy turns and starts to walk around to the side of the house. There is the house wall on the left and then a narrow alley about four metres wide, then on the right a stone wall three metres high, which separates the house from the old stables next door. The space is not much used: nettles and high grass. At the end, sunlight, and a glimpse of a manicured lawn.

He must work fast now: he picks his way over the uneven ground, scanning the grass. The bonfire smell he first noted coming through the girl's bedroom window: is it stronger here, or here? Invisible trails hang in the air before him, leading him into the alley.

Halfway down, he destroys a dandelion clock with a single kick and squats to part the long grass. Sure enough, a cloud of little ash ribbons flies up at his face. On the ground in front of him are blackened chunks of suitcase leather; you can make out the remains of a handle, and brass studs, which of course did not ignite, lying in a little heap to one side.

He reaches for the handle, and turns it over. There is the silver back of a hairbrush, the bristles burnt away. And underneath that, a sodden lump of half-burnt paper is nestled in the grass. He picks it up, looks at the faded velvet ribbon tying the bottom half of the letters into their charred bundle. Holds them up to the light.

Only the top half of the page remains, written on with a crabbed, cramped hand, on paper so fine as to be almost transparent.

3. juin 1913. Dear Adèle...

At the other end of the alleyway, the light is suddenly

blocked. It's the butler: white-faced, sent to pre-empt the discovery, but too late.

Japy scoops the burnt offerings of the girl's suitcase into his handkerchief and pockets them.

The butler is still waiting. His lips quivering as if he wants to speak, but in the end there is nothing to say.

Juliette, viii.

PHILIBERT Marc
Guard – Night Shift
On my rounds at a quarter to seven I saw nothing out of
the ordinary. I was unable to check the door because I
had lent my key out the previous night to a director, but I
observed that it was fastened and there was no evidence of
disturbance.

The archivist threads her way between the filing cabinets and
bookshelves towards me. I point to Marc Philibert's statement.
'Would it have been normal for a security guard to lend a key
to a director?'
　She peers. 'I wouldn't have thought so. Security was very
tight. They didn't want anyone stealing their ideas.'
　I say: 'Edouard Rey, the day guard, says that there was no
break-in. So whoever got in must have had access. And Philibert
mentions that a director borrowed his key the night before.'
　She frowns. 'That's interesting.'
　'Something else. Isn't it strange that there are only a few
witness statements, and just this photo – no others? It's as if
someone's looked into the dossier already.'
　We look together at the photograph. 'Do you know who
any of these people are? The directors, I mean? The ones in the
back row?'
　She scans the print. 'No. We do have some material from the
bigger name directors, but I don't recognise any of them.'

She drums her fingers on the desk. 'But there's someone who might know. His name is Rinaldi. I think he was at Pathé back in the day. He's a professor of modern cinema now. He lives just outside Paris.'

4. avril 1914

THE HALL WAS LINED with eager faces in police uniform
– every able-bodied man from colonel to private must have
turned out to see the show – and from beyond the large, closed
double doors to the gendarmerie came a sound like the baying
of fairy-tale wolves.

My lawyer Denis Poperin – a thin, serious youth with a
consumptive death rattle – took my forearms in his hands and
looked at me.

'Ready?' he asked.

I nodded. He reached up and pulled the veil I was wearing
down over my face.

He nodded to the youngest police officer, who removed the
bar and opened the doors.

I saw the street crammed with people, all faces turned
towards me. Half of them had notepads; one enterprising soul
had set up a camera; a blinding flash of light caught me with
my arm half across my face. The crowd surged forward and the
police guard pushed them back. A car purred twenty metres
down the street, surrounded by a ring of policemen.

'Did you invent your story? Did you make it up?' someone
shouted as Denis manhandled me through the crowd. 'You
should be ashamed!' cried a woman, and spat, though her aim
was bad, and the gobbet landed on the man next to her.

Someone threw the first projectile as Denis tore open the
cab door and bundled me in; it slithered down the glass of the
window. 'All right? All in?' said the driver, his big, anxious face

peering back at us through the partition, and Denis nodded, too breathless to speak. The car began to move. Disappointed faces followed us; the crowd howled louder and some began to run alongside. The police driver swore and shaded his eyes, as if trying to see a clear path.

I sat, listening to the crowd call my name. Denis said: 'Are you clear on your lines?' I nodded. 'But are you?' he asked. He looked out of the cab window, white-faced. We were rolling along the rue de Rivoli now, past the Galeries St Paul with gaggles of shoppers queuing outside.

The low walls of the Pont au Change seemed to fall away on either side, exposing the churning water beneath. Then we were on the Ile de la Cité, and the same noise, the baying, rolled towards us. Looking ahead, I saw the Boulevard du Palais blocked with people.

In the cab, the driver hunched over the wheel and slowed down, unable to make any headway; the crowd scattered on either side of the vehicle, their faces changing into sneers of recognition. Pointing, shouting: I watched the news spread. Up ahead, policemen lining the high railings of the Palais' forecourt moved towards the gates, and started to open them; swearing, our driver swung the car round.

'Come on,' muttered Denis, craning his neck to see what the delay was. I turned to my left and saw that it was another car, inching forward, arriving at the same time from the opposite direction. It was black and official-looking, with two figures sitting in the back seat.

The car swung round and drew level, competing with us for the front spot. The person looking back at me from the cab window, not three metres away, was Luce.

She was very changed; lines in the corners of her eyes and reaching down from her mouth had not been there a month before. I also saw that she was frightened, the muscles in her throat moving. The wide, dark eyes snapped shut and open, then stayed open, staring at me. I looked at her waist, just visible above the level of the window; it was as flat as when I had first met her.

She gave the ghost of a smile and shifted her shoulders sadly. I remembered her in the house last summer, inspecting a new dress that had been sent to her in the wrong size. *My, Adèle. What a pretty pass we are in!*

I felt myself want to smile back. Just then, our cab driver swore again, and the car lurched forward and gathered speed.

Juliette and Adèle
1967

'What happened to the baby?'

Adèle says: 'She'd given birth prematurely.'

'What happened to it?'

'She was in custody. Her family took it away with them.'

She looks at me and shrugs: a bitter smile. 'Rich people closing ranks.'

I say: 'What did you feel?'

Adèle looks at the back of her hands. 'The papers said that André took it hardest. He broke his cell, threatened guards, and made wild predictions about the end of the world.'

4. avril 1914

'GIVE ME YOUR HAND,' Denis said as we stepped out of the car. The noise hit us: from the line of people queuing for seats in the public gallery, which snaked round the courtyard, to the crowd stuck outside, gripping the bars. Some were screaming my name; some were screaming Luce's name, or André's. Denis's fingers closed round mine and he drew me onwards; a tight ring of policemen formed around us and ushered us through the tall doors and into the Vestibule d'Harlay.

'Wait here,' said the officer.

I stood looking up at the decorated ceiling, high overhead, and down at the red marble swirls of the floor, and I didn't feel anything very much.

'All right?' Denis asked. He gave me a sickly smile, pale to the gills, the hair plastered to his forehead. 'All right?' he said again. I nodded.

The officer reappeared. 'Please,' he said, 'we are to seat you before the crowd is let in, the judge says, to save a riot.' He ducked his head to invite us to follow him, and led us towards the doors at the end of the vestibule.

They opened onto an audience room seating about two hundred. At first it seemed a mass of fluted oak, but then the different levels asserted themselves: the judges' raised bench at the front, and the jury's to the left-hand side. Denis led us to a bench in front of the judges', and fussed about organising his papers. He shot me a look: 'You'll want to look nervous,' he said, as I folded my arms across my chest. 'Like we discussed.' He fiddled with the collar on his red prosecutor's gown.

Just then there was the creak of a small door opening in the panelling on the right-hand side of the room; a police officer appeared, followed by André, then Luce; then by a walrus-moustached man dressed in the defending lawyer's black. Denis met his level stare, then cleared his throat and began to shuffle papers again.

The defendants were led straight to the dock and sat. Luce looked down at her hands. André looked up at me, his face blank. He stared, as if searching for something; from my eyes down to my hands and back up; he frowned. I looked back at him, until he too folded his arms and looked away.

A clatter at the back of the hall; the policeman had crossed to the main doors to open them, and a moment later the hall was flooding with people fighting past each other to secure the best seats in the gallery. They were all men, women not being allowed as spectators, and they were consequently unafraid to be seen staring. The front row of the seats came up to five feet behind my chair; I heard the whispering assessments of my dress, my shoulders and my waist. For the first time, I felt my stomach squirm, and looked to Denis; he saw my face and said: 'Not bad. If you could just be a little paler.'

The courtroom filled with people, moving crab-wise along the fixed wooden benches. Men were all but in each other's laps: a fight almost broke out near the door when one of the workers who had been saving a seat to sell changed his mind and wanted to keep it for himself. The policemen ran around the seats and back – sheepdogs penning in a flock – but still it took five minutes to calm the crowd enough to let in the judges.

I studied the presiding judge's face carefully as he walked in, flanked by his juniors, and made his way up to his lofty seat. He was a man of a certain age, bearded like the rest, but his beard was speckled with white. He moved with difficulty, lifting one leg after the other to mount the steps; and when he was there, he looked around the courtroom with infinite weariness, his gaze settling on me for a mere fraction of an instant before he said: 'Call the members of the jury.'

Had they a daughter? How old? Had their families ever been the victims of any violence? The jury members turned caps in hands, a soft rub-rub of cloth on skin, as they submitted to Denis's questioning. And then Maître Lazard's rich voice: *What were their opinions about the cinema? A fine profession? Had they any special feelings about people not born on these shores?* The audience behind me shuffled their feet and whistled, bored: the judge hammered on the bench for silence every five minutes. Denis returned to our seat to cough into his handkerchief in between bouts of questioning. A man at the back stood up, cupped his hands around his mouth and yelled: 'Pick me! I don't have any prejudices about women!' before a policeman put a hand to his collar and hauled him out. His laughter echoed from the marble walls of the Vestibule; his footsteps squeaked away across the floor.

'If I am correct,' the judge said, at the end of two temple-massaging hours, 'we have a jury now. Am I right?'

'Correct, Your Honour,' Maître Lazard smiled unctuously beneath his moustache. The jury members who had been selected stood up a little straighter, and looked around the courtroom with evident pride.

'Then I will call M. Durand to submit to my preliminary questions.'

André stood, head lowered, hands folded in front of him, and made his sober way to the witness stand. Catcalls from the gallery: he didn't react, just kept the same grave demeanour, the model of the earnest, caring boss. I cursed, inwardly, his face – that lying phsyiognomy which could appear to be anything it wanted.

Le Temps, *4. avril 1914*

NEWS FROM THE COURT
THE SENSATIONAL DURAND TRIAL'S FIRST DAY

[...] took the stand, dressed in a sober but elegant suit, and answered the presiding judge's questions with a countenance which, far from being nonchalant, showed how keenly he felt the seriousness of the charge.

M. le Juge: M. Durand, you and your wife stand accused of attempted murder and actual bodily harm. What do you have to say in the first instance?

M. Durand: That I regret it.

M. le Juge: Do you mean to say you admit wrongdoing?

M. Durand: On the contrary, I regret whatever circumstances have led our former employee to make such an accusation. She must have felt some slight or injury, unnoticed by myself and my wife; whatever we can have done to provoke such a response, I regret it wholeheartedly.

M. le Juge: Are you saying you provoked Mlle Roux's accusation?

M. Durand: Who knows what goes on in the mind of another? A refusal to furnish her a new wardrobe; to increase pay or prospects? Who knows which small slight may have become magnified, over time?

M. Durand, a self-made man, spoke at length about his upbringing in the Americas, and the path he had trodden rising to the heights of the film trade; a role which, he admitted, had sometimes led him to neglect his home life in the pursuit of excellence. He refuted utterly the imputation of any improper romance between himself and Mlle Roux, saying:

M. Durand: I am a man of simple habits, Monsieur. Cinema and my wife are my only pleasures.

M. le Juge: And you refuse Mlle Roux's claims of relations within the household and that when she threatened to disclose them you took action?

M. Durand: I do not dispute that Mlle Roux had romantic interests. But not with us.

M. le Juge: Your meaning being?

M. Durand: It is not for me to comment on what attachments she had. I believe M. le Docteur Harbleu will advise on this in due course.

The judge then called Mme Durand to the stand. Unlike her husband, Mme Durand, who wore an elegant black gown, gave only short answers.

M. le Juge: What do you respond to Mlle Roux's claim that you made advances on her?

Mme Durand: What did you call it?

M. le Juge: Advances, Madame.

Mme Durand: 'Advances'?

M. le Juge: Mme Durand, are you quite well?

At this point M. Durand stood and requested that his wife be allowed to rest, her recent troubles having left her under a strain, and this request was granted under special dispensation.

After the lunchtime recess, the judge chose to call Mlle Roux to answer his preliminary questions.

Mlle Roux, of small appearance, took the stand and looked

the judge directly in the eye as she told of her early youth in the Languedoc. She then answered questions on her time in the Durands' employ.

M. le Juge: At what point do you say you started relations with M. Durand?

Mlle Roux: Almost immediately. It was his suggestion that I come to the house.

M. le Juge: Rather than set you up in your own apartment like most men?

Mlle Roux: He wanted it to be convenient.

M. le Juge: And how did you plan to keep this a secret from Mme Durand?

Mlle Roux: He didn't care about that.

This elicited some laughter from the men in the gallery, who were doubtless imagining the reactions of their wives were they openly to install a concubine in the marital domicile. M. le Juge then asked about Mme Durand.

M. le Juge: In your statements you allege that there were relations between yourself and Mme Durand.

Mlle Roux: That is correct.

M. le Juge: Can you tell us about these relations?

Mlle Roux: There were various encounters.

M. le Juge: Encounters?

Mlle Roux: Various relations between us.

M. le Juge: But Mme Durand being a married woman…

Mlle Roux: M. Durand was a married man, but it didn't stop him.

At this point uproar broke out in the court so that M. le Juge was forced to eject certain members of the audience in the name of public order. Shouts of 'Liar!' and 'Perfidy!' rang out from every corner […]

4. avril 1914

'THIS IS VERY BAD,' Denis Poperin said, lifting his wine glass to his lips. His Adam's apple worked; he wiped the dregs from his mouth and looked at me. 'What were you thinking?'

We had retired to the gloomiest corner of a worker's café near Montparnasse, where we hoped nobody would recognise us. It was not far from Denis's home and my temporary, police-funded apartment; it was far enough away from the Palais de Justice. I looked away from him, at the accordionist playing to the assembled crowd. She was about the same age as me, but utterly lost to what she was doing: swaying on her feet, framed in the window, her fingers melting together on the keys and stops. Occasionally her eyelids would flutter, as if she were scanning the crowd for someone: then they would shut firmly again, blocking out the world.

'To admit to relations with Mme Durand. We agreed — didn't we — you were to play it down; imply she had made an unwelcome pass. Not that you went along with it without putting up the least resistance.' He sighed. 'I should fire you.'

The accordionist's tune lifted to its conclusion: she bowed and smiled, and her assistant, a small boy, produced a hat for coins. The customers raised their hands in applause and called '*Encore!*'

'Why didn't you? Dissemble? You could have said she tried to force it. Nobody could have proved a thing. You could have said anything...'

Luce, her skirts in her hands, stumbling from room to attic

room. I shook my head at the boy, who had appeared at our table, jingling the hat. 'What will happen next?'

'It speaks!' said Denis, looking around the room with wide-eyed amazement. 'The judge has made up his mind already, but he will call other witnesses, though what use it'll do us, I have no idea...'

'But they found the gun. And the valise...'

The boy waited patiently, the hat held out in front of him.

'There are a thousand others like it! And no bullet! And the valise – the valise got us as far as a trial, I grant you, but it's not enough. I will make a brave attempt at a closing speech which will be minced by Maître Lazard's eloquence, and then you will tell me you can't pay me because you have not, have never had, a bean.'

He slumped further in his seat, fished about in his waistcoat pocket for his matches and attempted to light a cigarette.

'Please, Mademoiselle,' said the boy, 'my mistress says are you Adèle Roux of the Durand trial? Because if you are, she would like to sing a special song for you.'

Denis drew himself up in his seat, suddenly self-important: 'It is she,' he said, 'and I am her lawyer.'

A man by the bar had swivelled in his seat to scrutinise us, and now turned back to his comrades, head low between his shoulder blades; the news spread to the head waiter, polishing glasses, who moved along the bar to a cluster of men hunched over their drinks.

Amused glances, and caps being pushed back on foreheads; the beginnings of a leer.

'Let's go,' I said.

'I'll defend you,' Denis slurred.

I pulled on his sleeve, hauling him to his feet. Masculine laughter rang out from the walls as we staggered crab-wise to the door.

The red lights of Boulevard Raspail, advertising rooms by

the hour and basement-level nightclubs; a street cat yowled for cover as Denis lurched away, spinning across the pavement, finger raised for a last put-down.

'You think you can have it all your own way,' he began; tumbled over his own feet and folded up; teetered sideways into the foetal position, and was suddenly asleep.

His snores, after his voice, were gently wheezing and childlike.

I looked up at the sky and gritted my teeth.

The sound of the café door opening and closing behind me, and a musical exhalation: the accordionist was standing next to me, her instrument slung over her shoulders. It made whimpering sounds as she moved.

She, too, tottered; then, leaning her hand on my shoulder, she bent down to remove one shoe, and lifted the broken heel to the flickering café light.

She sighed, and threw the heel across the street; it rebounded off the night shutter of a shop and clattered away. Then she patted her pockets and a cigarette was suddenly between her lips, and a match flaring.

She had a shrewish, carefully made-up face; the crookedness of the smile, which I had dismissed before as uneven, now seemed her best asset. Her hair was dark, like mine, lifting in wisps away from her face.

'You look,' – she shook the match out and squinted through the smoke – 'just like I imagined. Not everybody does. Your lawyer, for example, cut quite a dash on the front page of the *Revue Moderne*, whereas—' She prodded Denis with her shoeless foot; the stockinged toes rasped on the material of his jacket, but he did not wake up. 'Whereas you look just like I thought.'

She held her elbow with her other hand, the cigarette aloft, threatening to set light to her curls.

'Difficult evening,' she said.

I nodded. She blew out smoke.

Neither of us said anything. The café door swung open and disgorged a group of three burly men, who called goodnight to each other and each set off in a different direction. The street grew quiet again.

A big smile inched across her face, crinkling her eyes and revealing a set of small white teeth. She stuck her foot out in front of her and wiggled the toes, then said: 'Chaperone me home.'

Later, I walked back to my rented apartment from gas lamp to gas lamp. It was that point of the night when everything had shut down. Cafés had been closed for hours, their signs extinguished, the revellers long since gone to bed.

As I walked past the wide, tree-lined junction of Raspail, I thought I heard a footstep in the street behind me, and turned, my mouth opening as if I was going to scream for help.

But it was only an old paper bag, which rose in front of me, crackled and wafted away across the cobbles and sank out of sight.

Juliette, ix.

It is late afternoon by the time I reach the address, fifty miles into the wooded country south of Paris. I miss the turn-off the first time; reverse perilously in the 2CV to make the turn. Sunlight dapples through the leaves of the plane trees that line the private drive. Beyond that a field of cows lift their heads to watch me pass; the car bounces from pothole to pothole.

Holding the door open is a small, elderly man in a tweed jacket. He smiles and beckons, beams as I shake his hand. Then he turns away into the hallway: 'Follow me.'

The corridor is lined with burgundy candy-stripe paper: after a few metres the space widens suddenly into a light and airy room, with open French windows leading out onto a lawn.

Rinaldi moves towards a sagging armchair next to the French windows and lowers himself, wincing, into its cushions. I choose the seat opposite.

'You've come all this way,' he says. 'It must be important.'

'I wanted to ask you about the Pathé fire.'

'Oh,' he says. 'That. Such a long time ago. I'd almost forgotten.'

'Were you there?'

'Not exactly,' he says, waving a hand. 'I was in the complex, working in accounts, as usual. A sad day. All those things destroyed, all that equipment. You could feel the heat of it right across the other side of the factory.'

I take the photograph from my bag and hold it out to him.

'I found this in the Pathé archive. Can you identify any of the back row?'

He smiles, reaches for spectacles on a thin chain and, levering himself forward, takes the picture. 'Oh, now, that is a thing,' he says. 'What memories. Thank you for bringing me this.'

He points to a figure on the far left: wrinkled forehead, receding hair. 'There I am,' he says. 'In my Sunday best.'

I say: 'I'm wondering whether one of these people might have started the fire. The witness statements imply that a director borrowed a key to get into the post-production building. And there was nothing in the dossier apart from this photo. It's as if it was left there for me to find.'

Outside, the sun is at its lowest point before vanishing: the light has thickened to burnt orange through the French windows.

M. Rinaldi places the photograph on the table.

'Well,' he says, 'aren't you thorough.'

He traces the photo with his fingertip. 'You're correct. There is someone in that photo who wishes they weren't there,' he says. 'The factory was always full of gossip. That's Basile, the Basque — dreadful accent. This was my friend Paul Leclerc, who went mad over a girl from the factory and tried to hang himself.'

'Adèle Roux knew him.'

Rinaldi nods briefly, uninterested. 'And this was the keeper of the menagerie they used for dramatic tableaux — Otto, from Bavaria.'

He hesitates, then his finger moves over the back row, skating over the smiling faces and coming to rest on a man a head shorter than the others; a pointed white goatee, a round face and blackcurrant eyes. Unlike the others, whose broad grins are full of lazy confidence, his smile is tentative.

'This is my friend Robert Peyssac.'

'Peyssac who made *Petite Mort*?'

Rinaldi puts his palms on his knees and sighs. 'The story

was that he used to meet young people, young workers, in empty buildings of an evening. He was fond of borrowing the keys from different security men each time, so as to cover his tracks.'

In the photograph, Peyssac's hand is resting lightly on the young Rinaldi's shoulder.

I ask: 'And what happened to him after the fire?'

Rinaldi sighs. 'He died.'

'How?'

'In the war. Like everyone else.'

'Wasn't he too old to fight?'

He says: 'Almost. For all the other directors, Charles Pathé obtained a dispensation to save them from the Front: he got permission for them to make patriotic films. But not for Peyssac.'

Somewhere on a floor overhead, a clock chimes softly, over and over again.

'That would explain why they didn't involve the police,' I say. 'They knew who it was and dealt with it on their own. And why the dossier is so slim. They only kept the pieces of evidence that proved the case.'

He nods.

I say: 'I don't understand. He was so excited about it. Why would Peyssac steal his own film?'

Rinaldi lifts his shoulders. 'Something that happened all the time: espionage. If he was in the pay of a rival studio, destroying the film could have earned him a substantial bonus.'

'But why? He was an artist…'

He says: 'But he liked money, too.'

I think about Peyssac's apartment on the Ile St Louis, the silk chairs that Adèle was not allowed to do more than perch on.

'But why would he cut out one of the scenes?'

Rinaldi shrugs. His finger brushes the photograph where Peyssac's hand falls on his younger shoulders. 'A memento?' he says.

Testimony of M. le Docteur HARBLEU, ii.
8. avril 1914

Q: Dr Harbleu, I understand you also work on psychological cases for the Hôpital Pitié-Salpétrière.
A: That is correct. I am considered an expert in the assessment of the psychological state of patients, specialising in hysteria.

Q: But you have said that Mlle Roux appeared quite calm when you met her.
A: That is true.

Q: And since? Have you had much contact?
A: I have been to visit her once or twice, at the behest of the Police Chief, in my role as attendant medical officer. It has been my business to check on Mlle Roux's wellbeing and fitness to give evidence.

Q: So you would say you have a fair grasp of her, how shall I put it, mentality?
A: I would.

Q: And what is your opinion?
A: At no point from the shooting onwards has she displayed any of the redeeming female emotions – no crying, or remorse, or agitation.

Q: And your thesis?
A: I can only go on a similar case some years back.

Q: To whit?

A: The case of Bertrande Iliot, chambermaid to a prominent civil servant, Aristide Perrin and his family, of Nîmes. Note the similarities instantly: a woman of the servant class, young, relatively attractive, living in the same house as a rich and powerful man.

Q: Go on.

A: Obsessed by Perrin to the point of illness, Bertrande Iliot took a kitchen knife and slashed at her forearms, then presented herself with these injuries to the local gendarmerie. She claimed that Perrin had inflicted the injuries. A classic obsessional fantasy of the ill-educated female mind.

Q: How does that relate to the gunshot wounds in the case of Mlle Roux? Surely not self-inflicted?

A: No, in that case, an accomplice. As M. Durand hinted previously, he suspected that Mlle Roux had a romantic liaison outside the house – some youth whom she persuaded to carry out her shooting.

Q: But that is grotesque!

A: True psychopathics are, when challenged, extremely frightening. They do not understand that you are telling them 'no'. I would not like to have to set my will against Mlle Roux's on any point at all.

Testimony of M. DURAND
8. avril 1914

Q: M. Durand, you have agreed to take the stand again to clear up
some small points pertaining to the alleged valise discovered by
M. l'Inspecteur Japy on your property.

A: Quite so.

Q: In his statement, M. l'Inspecteur says he found burnt pieces of
Mlle Roux's suitcase in a side-passage by your house – Exhibit A,
thank you, clerk. Now, in his statement he also says you were quite
specific that Mlle Roux took the suitcase with her?

A: I was.

Q: And yet, here was the suitcase, burned!

A: Permit me to elucidate. Inspector Japy arrived unan-
nounced, catching me quite unawares, and still perturbed by
Mlle Roux's disappearance. He introduced himself, sir, as a
Mesmerist.

Q: A Mesmerist!

A: He proceeded to sniff the air of Mlle Roux's room, and say
with confidence that she had gone, I don't know, to the East
or something.

Q: Really!

A: Your Honour, I ask you: which is the most preposterous?
A grown man claiming to smell out the spectres of objects-
gone-before, or a busy and preoccupied husband, forgetting

a small fact about someone else's suitcase? I realised later that Mlle Roux must not have taken her valise, and that it, along with the other sundry items she had abandoned, had been burned by my manservant.

8. avril 1914

AS ANDRÉ STEPPED DOWN from the witness stand he winked at me.

It was not the subtle half-droop of an eyelid you might expect from a man on trial. The audience laughed and nudged one another, liking to have caught the little dumb show.

Denis laid a hand on my forearm. I looked to my right, to where Luce sat; there was just the habitual stare straight ahead. If looks were gunshots, that one mahogany panel next to the high window would be bored right through. André reached the seat next to her, fluffed his coattails out behind him, sat and whispered something to her with a smirk; she nodded vaguely, her eyes never leaving that spot on the wall.

The judge pinched the bridge of his nose thoughtfully and said: 'Maître Poperin, have you any more witnesses to propose for the prosecution?'

'No, Your Honour.'

'Maître Lazard? For the defence?'

Lazard, reptilian eyes half-closed, shook his head.

'Then I cannot see how we can drag this out further. We'll proceed straight to the closing speech for the prosecution. Maître Poperin, are you prepared?'

'I am.'

'Then I suggest you gather your notes.'

These last words were said in a raised voice; I was vaguely aware of the sound of a door opening at the back of the courtroom; hushed voices; heads turning. The judge glanced up over his half-moons. 'And then, Maître Lazard, we shall proceed to your closing speech, if there's enough time in today's session.'

I turned to see what the commotion could be: it seemed someone had broken into the courtroom. The guards were holding onto the woman's dark coat by the elbows; a small boy, not more than five, hung from her hand.

'No women in court. You must come back later, Madame, if you wish to admire the frescoes.'

There was a current of laughter; the woman tugged herself free of the court officials and took a few steps down the central aisle, dragging the child with her.

At first I was not sure it was her. All the fight had gone out of her face, and the plump cheeks had sunken in. I could not fathom what she might be doing there, in her best hat and good coat and kid gloves.

'I must speak to the court,' she said. Now I knew it was really her: that you-and-your-fine-ways voice, hard and clear. 'I have new information about the case.'

Denis reacted first. 'Your Honour: for the defence or for the prosecution?'

The judge had taken off his half-moon glasses; he folded them away under his robe, frowning. 'Well, Madame?'

Her voice hardly wobbled. 'The prosecution.'

Out of the corner of my eye I saw André lean forward suddenly, his head close to Maître Lazard's; the judge frowned.

'What new information, Madame?'

Her voice turned belligerent. 'Swear me in, and I'll tell it before the court in the proper fashion. I know how these things ought to go.'

Maître Lazard was shaking his head; in André's fierce whisper it was not quite possible to make out the words. At last André sat back, but not fully – his hands gripped his knees.

The judge looked towards the window for inspiration, and

then said: 'Come up to the stand, Madame, and we will ask you to say your piece. Come now, you can leave your boy in the back there.'

While she was sworn in, André turned to look at Luce. She was looking at me, head tilted back, her eyes half-closed.

Testimony of Elodie KERNUAC
8. avril 1914

Q: What do you have to tell us that's so important? What is your connection to the case?

A: I work at the Pathé costumery, I'm the chief costumière there. Where Mlle Roux worked – we knew each other. Before she moved to the Durands'.

Q: So?

A: So I also knew M. Durand. He was our boss.

Q: Come to the point, Madame.

A: Please will someone stop up the ears of my boy, Charles-Edouard? I don't want him to understand what I am about to tell you.

Q: Very well, Madame. See. Your son is outside.

A: While I was there – when I had first started at Pathé, some five years ago – this is difficult for me to say, as a respectable woman – M. Durand made certain advances on me, which I did not repel.

Q: To clarify: you were his lover?

A: I would not call it love. We often used to meet in the basement where the costumières worked, after hours. I was flattered by his attentions. He was very dashing and handsome and attentive, and I was very young.

Q: We are not disputing his charms, Madame. But where is the relevance?

A: We had – relations – for some months. At the end of that time, he proposed that I should come to live with him and his wife, and serve as her assistant. He made me promises of things – with my career – that he would see I had advancement, and all I had to do was tolerate his wife.

Q: So effectively, he made the same offer to you as he made to Mlle Roux?

A: It seems so.

Q: And you say that you were his mistress?

A: I was.

Q: You are aware that M. Durand has sworn before a court of law that he is a faithful husband? You know what a crime it is to give false testimony in the sight of the Law?

A: What I am saying is, he is not an honest man, like you all think.

Q: And did you agree? To the offer of a job?

A: I had heard of Terpsichore's – pardon me, Mme Durand's – reputation around the studio as a hard task-mistress, and I didn't fancy it one bit.

So I told him that it was a 'no', and from then on we met less frequently. In time the visits stopped altogether, and I understood that he had – shall we say, he had moved on to pastures new.

Q: But all this is in the past? Five years ago, you say?

A: Four.

Q: So you allege an affair with M. Durand in 1910. What does this have to do with the possible attack on Mlle Roux?

A: It was about a year after M. Durand left off coming to see
me. I was working late one night, on some costumes for a big
film with complicated ornaments – the last people had left the
building hours ago. I remember because it was the start of the
summer and you could just hear, if you strained your ears, the
birds on the roof of the building, cooing like they do on warm
evenings. I was hurrying to finish so I could get outside.

Then I heard footsteps, the costumery door opened and
M. Durand was there. I could see straight away that he was
not himself. His shirt was unbuttoned down to three buttons
and he smelled of alcohol and something else, something
sharper.

He came into the room and stood in front of my sewing
machine. 'Whatever is the matter?' I asked. He half-fell into
the chair I offered to him.

He sat there and he just stared at me. 'Whatever is it?' I
asked. I suppose I was fussing because he frightened me, just
looking and looking like that.

He tried to say something then, but it was too garbled
for me to make out. His breath reeked of wine; I thought
he might be sick, and moved the costumes out of the way of
him; he laughed to see me taking such care of my work.

'You are a good employee, Elodie,' he said. He reached out
to touch my cheek but he missed, and his hand fell away.

'I don't know what you mean, sir,' I told him; he was
already looking around the room as if he wanted to speak, but
had forgotten what he wanted to say.

'Terrible things happen in the world every day,' he said.

'Yes, sir,' I said. I started to pack up my desk. I thought I
had the measure of him then: an argument with his wife, and
he wanted a listening ear and a woman to tell him he was
worth something. Well, I wasn't employed for that; I wanted
to go home.

He mumbled some other things then which I couldn't hear,

and went suddenly to sleep, or seemed to, his chin on his chest.

So I packed up my belongings and put my coat on, wondering whether to leave him there. Finally there was nothing for it but to go to the door and stand by the light switch ready to extinguish it.

'Are you going to be all right?' I asked him, trying to get him awake. On the one hand, I didn't like to leave him; but the rest of me wanted to get clear.

He half-woke up. He said, quite distinctly: 'Unless the summer is a dry one.'

I thought I'd misheard. 'Whatever can you mean, sir?' I asked him.

At that he seemed to come to. He looked just like his old self: that brazen stare, undressing you, if I may be bold. Then he laughed at me and said, 'You're a good girl, Elodie.'

I gave up trying to understand it. I shook my head at him and smiled back, and then I left. When I got to the courtyard I took a deep breath. I remember thinking how good it was to be there, in the fresh weather, with the evening ahead of me.

Q: And then?

A: Shortly after, the gifts began to arrive. A bunch of flowers, first, from him; but there was nothing between us any more – at work we avoided each other.

I then came home to find a fine necklace in a box pushed under my door, and his signature on the card. After that, a box of exotic fruit; a hat from Mme Chanel in the wrong size.

The kind of gifts men think women like. And never anything written on the card apart from his capital A.

You don't want a powerful man to feel he owes you something.

I began to think back to that evening in the costumery. And I started to wonder, what was it they would find, if the summer was a dry one?

Juliette and Adèle
1967

'And then?'

'And then. Inspector Japy got up from the front row of the gallery, where he had sat throughout the trial, and made a case that the trial should be halted whilst an investigation was made of the lake at the rear of the Durand property.'

She sips her coffee. 'The courtroom was cleared, the police marshalled, the Durand house emptied of servants, and the special department set up camp in the grounds.'

'What did you do in the meantime? Were you free to go?'

'Denis and I waited in his apartment, in cafés, in the Jardin du Luxembourg. We enjoyed the sun.

'On the eighth day we were sitting on a bench in the Jardin des Plantes, admiring the panthers prowling round and round their cage. A sergeant came running to where we were, and asked whether I could follow him please.

'We were taken in a police cab. We arrived at the woods just as it was starting to be twilight: pale air, fluttering things in the bushes. The police experts were still working all around the lake. They had arranged on the ground all the objects they had found: coins, old strips of fabric, a couple of wedge-shaped pieces of blue-and-white china. Relics of picnics past.

'They led me to a shelter by the far bank and drew back the curtain and showed me a set of bones, laid out on a soggy tartan blanket, with dead leaves still underneath. They had not cleaned the whole skeleton yet, only the femurs – bleached yellow, like a museum exhibit. I remember how long they seemed in comparison to the rest of her body.

'I told them to cover her up. The policeman was surprised. He said: "We are not the malefactors." I told him I didn't care, and I pulled the blanket over her.'

She holds her hands out on the table in front of us.

'How did you feel?'

She considers this. 'The policemen took me out onto the bank and asked me, *Is this where what happened to you, happened?* I said yes and showed them where it was I woke up after the attack, on the west side, by the trailing willow. They wouldn't look at me; they kept their eyes on their work.'

She smiles faintly. 'I was glad to see that they had to look down.'

Luce and André, ii.

And suddenly there is just this girl, standing in the hallway with enormous eyes taking in all the things she can't be used to seeing. And André standing behind her, watching her look; and she, Luce, says nothing because she doesn't want to break up the tableau.

André says: 'I want you to meet Mlle Doulay, from the costumery, who is here to look through your wardrobe and alter the things that need altering.'

Luce says: 'How nice to meet you, Mlle Doulay,' and the girl positively gapes, then a smile breaks out all over her pretty face. She has extremely good teeth but doesn't smile as if she knows it.

André says:'I've had the spare room made up for an overnight stay, since your wardrobe is extensive.'

They all laugh, and go their separate ways – the girl escorted upstairs by Thomas, and André, over his shoulder, gives Luce a white-toothed challenge of a grin.

That night, over dinner, the girl doesn't know what cutlery she should use; she plunges in, and then waits, confusion puckering her brow, looking to her hosts for help.

She is breathlessly enthusiastic; answers questions about Pathé ('It is the finest, most splendid place in the entire world, probably, so vast and so rich') and the costumery ('We are a sort of band of sisters, all working to help each other, and the materials are so fine'), wide-eyed and serious, so that Luce has to try not to catch André's eye. But after every answer there is a pause where it is impossible not to just look at her: at the cream of her skin and the freckles on the backs of her hands.

Towards the end of the meal, emboldened by the wine, which she can't be used to, Mlle Doulay starts to ask questions. *Have they enjoyed the state of wedded bliss long?* She talks like an etiquette manual from the 1890s. André says, frowning to hide his smirk, *just under six years*, pretending not to remember the precise date.

And has your union been blessed with fruit?

Even the girl senses it was not the right question, and colours, but does not know how to get back. André does well: he says, a little coyly, *Not yet: but we hope*, and snaps his fingers for Thomas to bring the wine.

As the last plates are cleared away Mlle Doulay does not realise she is supposed to excuse herself before the hosts; her face reddens as the silence grows, and she finally palms-up from the table and says goodnight. Luce listens to her light footsteps ascending the stairs.

They are left alone together in the dining room; things unsaid flutter around the candlelight.

The following morning, Mlle Doulay sits on the salon floor surrounded by taffeta, tulle and organdy, scissors snip-snipping gently along a seam. Always the frown of concentration: everything is to be taken seriously, but not just in a general sense – each thing she comes across, Luce thinks, is a new thing.

The girl holds aloft a gown whose bodice has been ruffled to hide the fact that it has been let out and let out again around the waist, and says: 'Are you sure this must be altered? The silk ruching is very fine and we won't be able to save it.'

'Yes,' Luce says. 'Put it on the mending pile. I have lost so much weight recently.'

Mlle Doulay lifts the dress and looks past it to Luce's thin waist, and nods, understandingly but without understanding. Anyone else would have arched an eyebrow, asked the question: but facts roll off Mlle Doulay like water, and she bends her head obediently and goes on snipping.

'I have been unwell,' Luce tells her, 'and have only been back on my feet a few months. Flat on my back for almost a year!'

Nothing.

Later, Mlle Doulay spreads the dressmakers' thin paper onto the parquet and draws arcs in pencil on it; her hair snakes loose and falls over her eyes but she doesn't notice this, either. Luce watches one tendril fall, then the next, until more hair is out of the chignon than in it; then watches as the girl sighs and sweeps it off her face and behind her ears.

That evening, the girl drinks more than is good for her. Perhaps she isn't sure what is the polite formula to refuse wine; or perhaps she doesn't want to. What she wants is to hang on André's every word, nodding rapidly, and making little observations not to the point, just for the sake of saying something to him.

At the end of the meal she excuses herself – placing a hand on the table to steady herself – and bobs a curtsy to Luce as she leaves. Her steps scurry up the stairs.

A moment later, hurriedly, André pushes back his chair, mopping his lips with his napkin.

At the door he says: 'You only have to tell me not to.'

Luce thinks about it, shrugs, and smiles. He hovers, momentarily uncertain, wanting something more from her, and then ducks his head and exits the room; his footsteps jog up the stairs after the girl's.

Luce lets a few minutes pass and then she follows, her hand crabbing up the banister into the darkness of the stairwell.

She reaches the third–floor landing and listens, unsure which room has been given to the girl; aware, in her tingling hands and feet, of the attic and what the doctors said she must try not to remember. But there is no need to be anxious: it is very obvious which room contains Mlle Doulay, from the breathy, rhythmic 'oh' coming from behind the door closest to the stairs.

Luce shuffles closer and lays her ear to the cold wood panels, and now it is possible to hear André's grunts, the creaking of the bed; even the rustling movement of the sheets tangled around their legs.

She always wondered what she would feel if this were to happen and now she knows.

Jealousy and distress, it turns out, are born of surprise; therefore she isn't jealous or distressed. She only feels – and this is not a surprise either – a hollowing-out of the loneliness that has become habit over the short time she has been well again, making it deeper.

She tries to understand why it should be so, and realises that by this act of being with Mlle Doulay, André has taken action where she has not. He has chosen to cast out his solitude behind him, like a medieval devil. Sure enough, there it is, coming out: a hoarse, protracted cry from him, overlaid by the girl's fluting moans.

The next morning, the girl sits on her salon floor, cutting out paper patterns, and they have a pleasant conversation. Luce recounts amusing stories of her friend Aurélie's exploits being married to the Minister of the Interior; the girl listens, wide-eyed.

Even over dinner the conversation flows between the three of them. She watches the not-so-subtle glances Mlle Doulay shoots André over the top of her wine glass quite calmly, and when André hesitates at the door, she waves him away.

She doesn't mean to go upstairs after them; she intends to turn off at her own floor, but finds that she has climbed the next two flights almost without thinking.

This time there is more noise: André is being rougher. The girl sounds almost distressed, her breathing reduced to thin wisps and then a strangled whimper.

Luce hesitates, her palm flat on the door. Then she turns and walks down the stairs to her own room and gets undressed for bed as usual. Her hand, when she reaches up to unhook her necklace, has a fine tremor in it. She looks at the tremor in the mirror, holding her hand level and watching it vibrate against thin air.

The next morning, the girl says: 'You look pale, Madame,' and Luce is so surprised that she answers, 'I am always pale.'

'I suppose that must be an advantage, in your career,' the girl says. She is sitting on the salon floor with her patterns arranged around her: a child at play. 'They say that Madame Sarah Bernhardt envies you your complexion, I read that in a magazine, is it true?'

Her neck droops as she leans to pick up a far-flung fragment of chiffon.

'Yes,' Luce says, 'it's true.'

The girl looks up, her mouth a perfect oval. Then she does another unexpected thing: she blushes. The colour creeps up her neck and over her cheeks until she is the colour of a radish. 'Imagine,' she says, 'having Sarah Bernhardt be envious of you.'

Imagine that.

Luce asks the girl questions, not vague conversational ones without issue, but listening to the answers with a kind of hunger in herself that she did not anticipate.

Mlle Doulay vouchsafes she has two brothers, both of whom are a little rough, and that she wanted to better herself. She considers working in the costumery to have bettered herself; she will be quite happy one day to become chief costumière, if she works hard enough.

Luce finds herself saying: 'You could aspire to more.'

The girl bends her head. 'I could never be like you,' she says, and bites her lip. 'The things you've done, the people you have met. And living in a house like this!' She looks up and around, her face shining with happiness. Then she blows the hair out of her eyes and continues her work.

It has been months, it may have been years, since anyone has told Luce they wanted to be like her. She looks down at her hands: the tremor is still there, but the skin on the backs is flushed and healthy-looking. Come to think of it, she is warm, not uncomfortably so, but in the pit of her stomach, a slight fluttering. Something tethered about to take flight.

That night, she puts her cheek to the cold door as well as both hands.

You! André shouts inside the room, then says over and over, *you, you.*

The girl moans. She sounds nothing like herself. She sounds older.

Luce shuts her eyes.

Days grow into weeks. Luce's clothes are cut to pieces and reassembled under her fascinated gaze: the cloth supple and refined in Mlle Doulay's hands. Nobody speaks of her leaving. The household seems better. André laughs like he used to laugh when they were first married: full-throated, teeth on show.

They talk about everything. Mlle Doulay seems to like to listen to her talk. Luce tells her anecdotes of her time at the studio; which directors are pleasant to work with, which less so; tittle-tattle about the other stars in the Pathé portfolio. The girl frowns as she stitches, sitting with Luce's dresses draped across her lap, listening and asking the odd question.

Occasionally she sighs. 'It must be wonderful,' she says, 'it must be just wonderful.'

Luce says: 'You could act, if you chose to. I could get you a role.'

'Oh, not me, Madame,' the girl says, holding a needle to the light to thread it.

One night, Luce lays her cheek to the door as usual. She hears Mlle Doulay's breathing become rapid; the jerking of the bedstead, and André's heaving groans.

Faster, closer. Then Mlle Doulay's voice. Louder than normal, saying an intelligible word for the first time, not her usual vixen sounds: the word she is saying is a name, which is André's.

She sighs it out, familiarly. Luce imagines her smoothing the curly hair from André's brow, looking at him with tenderness.

She listens, to hear if perhaps she was mistaken. Then André says, low, as if giving in to something, another name: the girl's, it must be. *Victoire*, he says, over and over. *Victoire.*

Luce turns and makes for the banister, and goes down the stairs as fast as she can. Undresses, tearing at the newly mended nightgown, and lies in the dark, her chest heaving but unable to get in enough breath.

In the morning she does not remember going to sleep. She remembers the dream she has had: the girl bending over her, smoothing the hair from her brow. In the dream Luce has mumbled something, and pulled the girl down beside her. Startled eyes clouding over; they reach for each other. When she wakes up she thinks for a moment the dream was real: perhaps it was.

She goes to the salon to wait for Mlle Doulay. The clock strikes nine; then ten past. At a quarter past the door opens. The girl comes in with head held low, and says: 'I am very sorry. I overslept.'

She does look sorry. She looks strained.

'You are pale,' Luce says.

'No more than usual, Madame.'

'Yes, you are very pale.'

There is a pause. The girl sits in her accustomed chair, face down, reaching for her sewing. 'You are kind to look out for me, Madame.' Then she blushes, holding up a dress, and says: 'This is ready to try on.'

Luce looks at the girl. Then she goes to her, takes the dress and makes a play of rubbing the fabric between her fingers. 'Very good,' she says, 'very fine.'

Then she starts to change in front of her, slipping out of her day-gown.

The girl looks away, in a panic.

'Let us see it with the petticoat you fixed the other day instead of this one,' Luce says, and removes her under-things.

The girl won't look at her. The autumn light slants through the window panes and illuminates her feet, which are the object of her special focus. She goes to fetch the petticoat without turning to face Luce, and when she hands it over, her fingers tremble.

'Now help me into the dress,' Luce says gently.

Where the girl puts her hands on her waist to help her, Luce feels how hot is the contact of their skin: it takes two attempts to fasten each button.

When it is over, Luce crosses to look at herself in the full-length mirror. As if she has been given a licence, Mlle Doulay's face hovers over one shoulder, now looking and looking and blushing and blushing.

'It fits,' Luce says, smoothing the material over her hips.

The girl turns quickly away and busies herself collecting up Luce's clothes.

'What is your name?' Luce asks. 'I mean, your given name?'

'I thought you knew. Victoire,' she says. 'It's Victoire. I thought you knew.'

She straightens. She holds an armful of garments, flushed from the effort.

Luce smiles.

~

The girl spends all her days in the salon now. When she runs out of mending, she comes to sit on the floor by Luce's feet, and reads.

One day, Luce reaches down and twirls a tendril of her hair around her finger. The girl says nothing. After a moment she inclines her head forward to give Luce better access to the nape of her neck. Her neck, her shoulders and cheeks are a warm pink. Neither of them speak. After a while the girl forgets to turn pages.

The dinner bell makes them both start. The girl gets to her feet hurriedly, smoothes her skirts and almost runs from the room.

Luce sits thinking, her eyes gleaming in the firelight.

The following night, September 25th, is a wild one: trees rock outside the windows, and the light goes quickly, leached from the sky in a single swoop.

'We'll sleep well tonight,' André says over supper, rubbing his hands idiotically. Mlle Doulay looks down at her plate. Luce wants to reach for her hand: can it be the girl is afraid of storms?

They finish the meal in silence; just the rain bursting across the dining-room windows in great spatters. André gets to his feet, mopping his mouth and smiling at them.

The girl still won't look at Luce until the last moment; and then it seems she cannot tear her eyes away.

'Goodnight,' she says.

'Goodnight,' Luce replies, and, as an afterthought: 'Sleep well.'

'Yes,' the girl says, distracted.

Luce doesn't go to listen that night. Nor does she undress.

Instead she waits in her bedroom, reading *Thérèse Raquin,* for half an hour; then shuts the book and pads to the door, opens it and goes to the stairs.

She has guessed correctly. From the floor above comes the soft closing of André's door; his footsteps across his bedroom floor.

She mounts the stairs; one flight; two; until she is standing outside Victoire's door.

She lays her cheek to the panels. No human noise: just the wind that is everything, going through the house.

Softly she turns the handle and pushes the door inwards, waiting at the threshold until her eyes have adjusted.

Blackness turns to grey; then the soft shape of Victoire's bare shoulders. She is turned on her side away from the door, but there's no sound of breathing, just a sound of listening. In the room is the sharp smell of sex.

Luce crosses to the bed and stands there, with her arms folded.

The waiting is terrible, but also pleasurable.

Victoire doesn't move.

Luce puts a hand on the girl's shoulder to half-turn her – no resistance. So she stoops, her hair trailing over the girl's face and exposed collarbone, and presses their lips together.

Nothing. Then the girl makes an indeterminate sound; after a moment her mouth starts to move under Luce's.

Luce can smell André's cologne on her.

The girl's eyes half open – shining slits in the grey light – she reaches her arms up and loops them around Luce's neck.

Lower in the bed there is an indeterminate shifting and straining under the covers; Luce reaches a hand down and begins to rub over the sheets, at the fork of the girl's legs.

'Victoire,' Luce says. The girl sighs Luce's name. Sighs again. But then jerks: starts to struggle and push the hand off, and sit upright.

Now she looks startled, half–mad, her breath heaving.

'No,' she says.

Luce bends closer to calm her, placing a cool palm on the girl's forehead: this time the girl shrieks in alarm, tries to bat the hands away, and when it doesn't work, shouts out, a loud, inarticulate sound. Luce releases her; the girl pulls the covers close up under her chin.

'What is this?' André says, standing on the threshold in his nightgown, hunting rifle in one hand, lamp in the other. 'I thought we were being broken into.'

'I was asleep!' Victoire says.

'You were not asleep,' Luce says.

André puts the lamp on the bedside table, takes in Victoire's expression, and looks at Luce. He is looking hard at her now, trying to see under her skin.

'What is this?' he says again.

Victoire says, clutching at the sheets, colouring: 'She is a madwoman, she tried to kiss me, and come to me in my bed.'

'Hypocrite,' Luce says.

André looks at her as if he is seeing someone new.

'Why should you always have what you want, and I never?' Luce says.

'I will go to the police,' Victoire says. 'I will go to the police and tell them Luce Durand is a monster!' She hops down from the bed, all white-eyed, and runs across the room to the door.

André catches her in mid-flight and holds her firm; now he has her by the waist, turns his face to whisper calming words in her ear; she stands transfixed, listening to him.

André places the point of his chin on the girl's head: over the top he looks at Luce, and his lips curl upwards.

It is very simple for Luce to cross and close her hands around the stock of the hunting rifle in his hand, without really knowing what the gun is for and what she would do with it, and silently André's hand tightens on the barrel, and they struggle, while Victoire buries her head in his neck and sobs and does not see.

Then plaster is flaking from the wall by the door and her ears are ringing, and the girl is no longer standing but lying on the parquet, dark red spreading over the sheet still wrapped round her. André is looking down at the gun in his hands, at his finger still wrapped around the trigger. He drops it. It clatters to the floor and falls next to the girl.

André is the faster thinker. He ushers Luce out – closes the door and when the servants come running, tells them it was just the sound of the storm, a tree falling, a natural occurrence.

When the sun comes up he goes to the servants' quarters and gives them an unexpected day off.

They walk out to the lake, sure of being unobserved, with the bundle slung over André's shoulder in a fireman's lift, Luce walking behind.

At the lake he wraps Victoire in the canvas covering. Luce has a last glimpse of the girl's face. She looks very young, almost a child; but the beauty makes Luce feel nothing; or rather, it only makes her feel cold.

André slips stones inside the canvas wrapper and heaves her off from the bank at the point where he knows the water is deepest.

He goes to Luce and slaps her twice; once across each cheek.

Back at the house, with the servants starting to return, cheer and cooking smells, Luce shakes and begins to vomit. She makes no move to get to the commode.

'I can't stay here tonight,' André tells her, but she doesn't answer. The servants have come to hover in the doorway, afraid; André considers what is best and telephones Aurélie Vercors, who arrives just as he is leaving.

Aurélie crosses to where Luce is and puts her hands to her face. 'Tell me everything,' she says.

After that, she and André will not have anyone in the house but themselves and their long-term domestic staff. They never host a dinner or a salon; they make excuses not to invite guests in. There is no need, anyway: they are more in demand than ever, every night a new party to attend in Paris, arm on arm, smile on smile.

Luce is enraged by the stupidity of the ordinary maids, but neither of them suggests an alternative.

One evening, at the very start of 1913, the front door opens and another girl stands there, and André behind her.

'This is Huguette,' he says, 'from Pathé. She has agreed to be your new helper.'

After the shock, Luce sees that Huguette is very plain – almost comically so. Her hair hangs like spaniels' ears down her neck; her face has a sharp quality, as if she is inclined to be pettish.

André says to Luce, in the flat voice he uses when he does not want to show emotion: 'I can't watch you in difficulties over simple things.'

The girl watches the two of them, a private tennis match. Inside herself, Luce hunts for alarm, for some sort of echo, and feels nothing.

Perhaps she was right: perhaps all that really did happen to someone else.

'Yes,' she says, 'Why not? Yes.'

Juliette, x.

The archivist snaps the switch for the fluorescent tubes and they click on, one by one, keeping pace with us down the narrow aisle between the shelves, finger to her lips as she counts her way along.

'P for Peyssac,' she says, lifting down a large cardboard box. 'This is everything that was left to the archive in his estate.'

We lift the lid.

A mushroom cloud of dust clears. The box is only a third full, its paper cargo yellowed and crumbling.

The archivist lifts the topmost layer of paper away. 'Do you want me to read through these?' she asks.

I shake my head, scanning the contents of the box. 'We're looking for a container. Something airtight, ideally – where he could put a strip of film.'

The first object to surface is a slim metal case, its hinges rusted.

The archivist looks at me; I snap it open. Inside the case is frayed blue velvet, in which a slender medal is nesting.

'Croix de Guerre,' the archivist says, turning the silver cross over. 'From 1915. It must have been awarded to him just before he died.'

There is nothing behind the velvet and the back of the case.

The next thing is a set of fountain pens, their barrels dark with age; the archivist crouches, her elbows tucked into her body, and unscrews the barrels one by one.

The only other thing left in the box, aside from the letters, is a photo-frame, which I take out. I unclip the frame and lift off the wooden back; take out the photograph and check between the picture and the frame. Gently shake the ensemble.

There is nothing. I hold the photo for a minute, staring at the space between the frame and the back of the picture, then put it back on the desk.

We look at the empty box.

'I'm sorry,' says the archivist. 'There's nothing else.' She smiles. 'I suppose it's lost for ever,' she says.

'I suppose,' I say.

'Maybe he destroyed it.'

'Maybe,' I say. 'But why go to the trouble of cutting it out in the first place? If it meant so much to him. If he wanted his work to be preserved for all time. This was the place to do it, wasn't it? Temperature-controlled, safe. It doesn't make sense.'

Something is fighting for attention: a tune I cannot identify. Something Rinaldi said.

I reach for the photograph again. Turning it over, I see Peyssac paterfamilias. His worried face set in a stern frown, he stands with one hand on the shoulders of each of his daughters; his wife hovering behind and to the left, her face a pale smudge. The little girls stare solemnly at the camera, their expressions blank. The taller is wearing a white dress, shoes and veil, posed in an attitude of piety. Just some spidery writing on the reverse of the picture. *On the occasion of Micheline's first communion; to my dear wife. Your Robert.*

I'm still for so long that the archivist's hand reaches out, and she gives my shoulder a gentle squeeze; I jump; we stand, confused, looking at each other.

'Are you all right?' she says.

'It's nothing,' I say. Then: 'People keep mementos of people, don't they? Not of things. Images of loved ones. Like this photograph.'

The archivist shrugs. 'I suppose so. Why?'

Juliette and Adèle
1967

'And then?'

Adèle spreads her hands. 'The trial, in the form it was, ceased. The charge against Luce and André was now murder on top of the attempt on my life, and as it was a capital charge, they were tried for it first. Victoire Doulay's parents were the pursuers-in-justice, and it was their lawyers who led, not Denis. The police took a month to assemble the burden of proof. The Doulay family hired an office for them to prepare the case. Although, as it turned out, there was no need.'

'Why not?'

'The judge asked her if it was she who had shot the girl, or whether it was her husband who had done it. He was giving her a chance to claim her innocence. I remember she waited, and she looked all over the courtroom, up to the ceiling and over to the windows as if someone passing outside would tell her what to say; and then she came to where I was sitting, at the table next to Denis.

' "Yes," she said, "I decided to shoot her." '

I say: 'Just like that?'

Adèle sighs. 'Just like that. The easiest thing in the world.'

'But why? Why did she confess?'

Adèle smiles. 'Why? Because she was guilty.'

'And then they questioned André?'

'Yes. He did his best to pretend that she had implicated him maliciously, but her account of the shooting had been so clear that it was believed. Besides which, there were practicalities: it

313

would have been difficult for her to have carried Victoire to the lake without help.'

'They were shipped out to Guyana on the morning of the ninth of June.'

'And what did you feel when you knew she had been transported?'

'Some parts of me felt heavier, others lighter.'

'And when you heard about André?'

'I was surprised. I had not thought he would become involved in petty squabbles; certainly not before the prison transport even touched land. I had thought he would demonstrate more *nous*. The article said he was thrown overboard with the shank still in his guts.'

'Then?'

'I worked hard, and got promoted. I moved to Vincennes, to my apartment, and have been here ever since.'

'Have you been happy?'

She takes a moment to think about this.

Then she says: 'It has always been surprising. Aurélie Vercors came to visit me, after her divorce. She was with a woman about my age, who looked at her as though she was the beginning of everything.'

'And Luce?'

Adèle says: 'I read about it in the newspaper. There was a little article to say that she'd been released after five years at the work camp and lived in anonymity nearby for five more years. That it was only discovered who she really was when she died.'

'And how did you feel when you heard?'

'I had the impression that the walls of my apartment were made of a thick, viscous liquid: that I could put my hand through them if I wanted. Everything was fragile and surrounded by a radiant glow: if I tried to go to the door, the door would bend away from me. I thought I was in another room: the salon at the house. The quiet of the silk sofa and the spirals of mica in the sunlight from the window. *I am a speck of dust. I am dancing for you.* Except she was not in any room any more.'

The door to the café opens; someone comes in, orders coffee. The waiters' voices laughing with the new customer.

Adèle is looking at me with a wide, blank smile.

I say: 'And in that time, the time she was free, she never tried to get in touch with you? And you never tried to look for her?'

A shrug. 'Everything we had to say had been said.'

Seeing my face, the smile twitches down at one corner. 'What is it, Juliette?'

'Nothing,' I say. 'Just cold.'

Juliette, xi.

Rinaldi opens the door on the second ring, his face showing perfect surprise, then awkwardness.

'What can I do for you?' he asks. 'Is everything all right?'

'I need to ask you about the photograph of the Pathé workers.'

He smiles warily. Then he relents. 'Very well,' he says, and turns to shuffle away down the corridor towards the salon.

'I'm not sure how I can help you, really,' he says.

'I don't think Peyssac took the film,' I say. 'I think it was someone else. Someone who had the opportunity, who was there on that day, but with a different motive.' I take out the photograph. 'I think it might have been this man.'

Rinaldi sighs. 'Paul Leclerc?'

I run my fingernail over Paul's eager eyes and hairless chin. 'The security guard. The one Adèle Roux told me about. You said he tried to kill himself over a girl who worked at the factory.'

'That's right. In late 1914, I think. He almost hanged himself in the Bois de Vincennes. Very sad.'

'Who was she? This love of his life?'

'He never told me her name.'

I drum my fingers on the photo.

'What happened to him?'

Rinaldi says: 'He left the factory. He'd hurt his back; he wasn't able to work afterwards. He did marry someone else eventually; he ended up living with his daughter on the outskirts of Paris.

She and her husband looked after him. I had a card from her when he died.'

I lean forward. 'What was the daughter's name?'

'Anne something. Something beginning with R.'

It is dark by the time I arrive at the house in Vincennes.

I hammer on the door for a full minute until there is the shuffle of footsteps coming down the hall corridor and stopping just on the other side.

'Your father was a security guard at Pathé. He was the one who stole the film.'

The door stays shut. Inside the house, the dog begins to bark frantically.

'Let me in. I could call the police.'

Silence.

One. Two. Three. Four. Five. Six. Seven. Eight—

Anne Ruillaux opens the door.

She crosses her arms across her chest and suddenly begins to cry: child-like, her fists in her eyes. 'He made me do it,' she says. 'He said, *When I'm gone, take this to the archive, and say you don't know how you got it. Don't tell them I worked at the studio.* We never had much because of looking after him. He said I was due some money. He said it wasn't wrong because the real wrong had been done by the man who made the film. He said we were helping to make everything right.'

In the back, the dog howls its distress, flinging itself at the inside of the closed door in a scrabble of nails.

'Why couldn't you leave me in peace?' she asks.

I say: 'Was it because of the girl that he stole it? The one he was in love with and tried to kill himself over? Was it so he could have something to remember her by?'

She watches me.

'It's because she died, isn't it?' I say. 'He wanted a memento?'

Silence. She shakes her head.

I stare at her, thrown. 'What do you mean?'

Anne says: 'She asked him to destroy the film completely. It would be dangerous to her if anyone saw it.'

'Dangerous?'

'Yes. She could get in trouble with the law.'

Somewhere in the distance an express train passes, on its way south; and when the sound is over, I find everything is clear.

The enormity of it: bile rising into my mouth.

'But he didn't destroy all the film,' I say. 'Your father cut out a scene and kept it separately. That part really was a memento, wasn't it? It was the only scene she was in. That's why he bothered to cut it out, instead of just keeping the whole film.'

A nod.

Silence. Then I say: 'Do you know where he kept it?'

She says grudgingly, as if it's of no consequence: 'He asked to be buried with a cigarette case I hadn't seen before.'

Juliette, xii.

You're walking along the *quais*, between the Pont-Neuf and
the Ile St Louis. Long, slanted light; breeze in your hair like
someone running their fingers through it. The trees beside
Notre Dame are shaking themselves free of their leaves.

You've come here because it's where you go to make
decisions, with the city around you like a blanket. The late-
lunch cooking smells. Near here a girl walked and bought a
postcard of Max Linder; over there, a car rattled home from
a party at the Ex-Minister's apartment; the statue of St Jeanne
d'Arc was lit up underneath the moon.

Of course there is a bruise: the burning sensation of being
tricked, because she has been lying to you since you met. But
underneath, what you feel is surprise. Surprise, because now
that you're here, there isn't a decision to make.

To come to the end, and find you are not the person you
thought you were.

Wind on the surface of the river. On the parapet above a
tourist points his camera at you: *click.*

You lift your hand and wave.

Juliette and Adèle
1967

She frowns as if she hasn't understood. 'You're leaving Paris?' she says. 'A holiday? Where will you go?'

'I haven't decided,' I say. 'Somewhere new.'

She smiles at me. 'Then this is our last meeting,' she says. 'And you've brought some chapters of the book for me?'

'No. That's not what it is.'

'What, then?'

'It's a silent filmscript, of a kind. I think you'll find it interesting reading.'

The café door opens and closes – and that's when she guesses, now, before I have even spoken.

She folds her hands over each other. 'Tell me it instead,' she says.

'We open on the silhouette of a man, hanging from the branches of a skeletal tree. He rotates, as if on a thread; we think he's gone, but then three men rush into the frame and support his legs. One climbs up to cut him down and we see that the man is alive, after all. He clutches his throat and gasps for air. His friends gather round.

'The intertitle: WHAT COULD DRIVE YOU TO THIS HATEFUL CRIME OF SELF-DESTRUCTION?

'Then I think we cut to a close-up of Paul Leclerc's face as he begins to tell his story.'

She doesn't flinch when I say his name. 'Continue,' she says.

'Then we have another intertitle. YOUNG LOVE IN SUMMER.

'We watch a younger, happier-looking Paul walking in the same woods with a pretty girl. She has long, dark hair, she's in her late teens. They exit the woods, holding hands, and go through the Pathé factory gates, where with much blowing of kisses, they part ways, each to their separate section.

'A montage follows. Paul and the girl in a café, flirting; Paul and the girl strolling on the riverside. Paul walking her back to her apartment. He stands mooning in the street while she leans out of the window and waves to him. Next to her, at the window, a fat woman with eyes like currants smokes a cigarette.'

She puts her hand to her mouth: as if she's suppressing a smile.

'Then we cut back to Paul's mournful face. He says *I would have done anything for her. But nothing stays the same for ever...* and we fade to the next scene, in a Pathé studio, empty apart from a few people. A cameraman is filming a young girl, Adèle, who looks startlingly like Paul's girlfriend. She is standing on a stage with various mirrors arranged on it. A director walks around and around the set, agitated, waving his arms and shaking his head. Suddenly he stops. Points. Paul's girlfriend is sitting beside the set, holding a make-up box on her lap. She lifts her head, places her palm on her chest – *Me?* – and allows herself to be beckoned forward. The director snaps his fingers – *You, Camille!* – and someone brings an empty mirror-frame forward and places it on the set. Paul's girlfriend goes to stand on one side and the girl stands on the other side. The director claps his hands in joy and tells the cameraman to start filming. Paul watches from the doorway to the room, a dreamy expression of pride on his face.

'Cut back to the group of friends surrounding Paul by the tree. One of them has a knowing expression on his face. *So her head was turned by the chance of fame?* he says. Paul shakes his head. *No. This was different.*

'Now we go to a dark and stormy night. An exterior of

Camille's apartment, rain spattering its windows. Camille's sister, Adèle, runs to the front door and opens it. She vanishes inside.

'Cut to Camille asleep in her room. The door bursts open and Adèle rushes in. An older, stringy woman hovers in the doorway, her hand over her mouth; behind her the fat woman we saw at the window before. We now see that Adèle is bleeding and clutching her arm.

'Camille says: *Who has done this to you? Why? Is it your employers?*

'Adèle nods. *They have killed me.*

'Camille rushes Adèle towards the bed and leans tenderly over her.

'Adèle's lips move as she tells Camille the story; Camille nods, listening. She gets up. *I'll fetch the doctor.*

'Adèle says, *Don't leave me…*

'Then we see Camille exiting the block and hurrying down the street. As she leaves, a pair of men carrying a gun creep down the street to the apartment block's front door. With exaggerated caution, they sneak inside. Lights go on in the hallway of each floor as they ascend. We see, in silhouette, the thin woman, Camille's landlady, throw up her arms in panic and fall down; in the next window, the fat woman is felled; in the final, Adèle too crumples to the floor.

'The criminals make their escape into the night. A second later, Camille hurries back. We see her ascend the staircase, silhouetted in the windows of the apartment. She stands for a moment and then turns and walks away. She exits the apartment block, just before the police arrive, in a pantomime of whistle-blowing and truncheon-waving. Nobody notices Camille slip away.

'Now we're getting close to the end. In the next scene, Camille stands opposite Paul Leclerc in a different apartment.

'Close-up of Paul's agonised face. He shouts *There must be another way.*

'Camille says: *If you love me, help me avenge my sister.*

'She is holding a gun. She passes it to him and spreads her arms.

'Covering his face with his hands, he shoots her. She clutches her shoulder but remains standing.

'She says: *And now you must see to the other thing.*

'Paul nods, weeping, and exits.

'In the next scene, he arrives at the factory. He removes a set of keys from his pocket and unlocks a shed. He goes to a cupboard in the corner and picks out a film canister. The title says *PETITE MORT. A DRAMA OF A HAUNTING. WITH DOPPELGÄNGER SCENE.*

'He shoulders the canister and produces a matchbook from his pocket; strikes a match and, coughing as the first smoke starts to show, exits the shed.

'He appears, triumphant, back at his apartment, with the canister. The room is empty. His face falls. He searches frantically for Camille but she has disappeared.

'Cut to a police station. Camille, clutching her arm, walks towards the entrance and disappears inside.

'Now we cut back to the present-day scene in the woods. Paul's friends' faces are now alive with interest, whereas Paul's face is written on with misery. She is gone. *The only fragment of her I have is kept here.* He fishes a cigarette case from his pocket.

'His friends look at each other and shrug, thinking he may have lost his reason. They pick up Paul and carry him off-screen, leaving just the solitary tree with the noose hanging from it.'

Camille Roux and I look at each other for a long time.

She says: 'Why, according to your theory, did Paul Leclerc steal the film?'

I say: 'Imagine if it had been distributed. People would have flocked to see it. Looked closely at the person in the mirror. Perhaps they would have realised the substitution that had been made.'

She purses her lips. 'Wouldn't the murderous employers immediately recognise that the girl on the witness stand was an impostor?'

'How could they reveal that the real Adèle was dead without telling the Court how they knew it for sure?'

'And what happens to the girl? The impostor?'

I say: 'Oh, she lives on into old age. At first she wears a veil around the city; and then, when she feels safer, and when she ages, she takes it off. She congratulates herself on getting away with it. Until, one day, it turns out her lover disobeyed her: he kept the stolen film in her memory. It's a lucky escape – he's excised the only scene with her in it. But what if the missing scene comes to light? She decides the time is right to impose her version of events on the world.'

A pause.

'You hired me because I was inexperienced,' I say. 'It suited you to have someone young, who wouldn't ask awkward questions.'

There is a glint in her smile. I think for a moment it's anger: then I realise it's pride.

'But you did,' she says.

We sit together, not speaking, for another minute.

Then she says: 'I made a misstep. With Luce, not contacting me after she was released. You suspected something.'

I say: 'She knew you weren't Adèle, didn't she? She knew that day in the car, outside the courtroom. That was why she never came back. I knew it felt wrong.'

Camille nods.

'In hindsight, there were other things,' I say. 'The way you described the Durands' house. It didn't feel like you'd lived there. And of course, you didn't. You only knew about it from reading Adèle's letters.'

Another nod.

'You must have loved her very much,' I say. 'To give up everything to avenge her. To live as someone else for fifty years. Did loving make-up make it easier? Did you see it as a kind of film trick to end all film tricks?'

A final nod. The point of the chin lifting. Water trembling in her eyes.

The waiter brings us another coffee. She smiles up at him and says thank you.

When he's gone she says: 'What happens now?'

I say: 'The past is another country. Peyssac stole the film. Your memoirs will end with me failing to find the missing scene in his archive box.'

She digests this. Her hands, linked together on the table, are perfectly still.

I say: 'There is just one thing I want to know. Was it worth it?'

She laughs. In the laugh is the laugh of a much younger woman.

Camille, i.

I often go to the cinema.

Tonight, the film is an antique, and the audience is made up of older people, like me, and earnest young ones: boys with their arms slung round girls; girls with long hair and intelligent faces.

Velvet drapes open, and behind this curtain, a screen; and behind its façade are things we cannot see – the toe of the black-clad stagehand whisking out of frame, the tick of the camera, the tension in the director's face – an army of ghosts. So we sit numbly in our seats and soak up the tricks and the story, and on the edge of the frame it takes immeasurable work to create it: ropes hauled, hands chafed, a spark in the writer which becomes a germ which becomes a script. We have paid for our tickets, and we think we own this. And the film humours us, because it's an illusion that is created with love.

I turn my head – certain, from the brush of air, that someone has just taken the seat next to me. The light from the screen flickers over her face.

It took me years to find you, she says sadly. *I don't know how long I can stay.*

It doesn't matter, I tell her. *Flesh of my flesh*. Does anyone ever have enough time?